Artificial Light

James Greer

AKASHIC BOOKS
NEW YORK

Published by Akashic Books
©2006 James Greer

ISBN-13: 978-1-933354-00-2
ISBN-10: 1-933354-00-3
Library of Congress Control Number: 2005934826

First printing
Printed in Canada

Little House on the Bowery
c/o Akashic Books
PO Box 1456
New York, NY 10009
Akashic7@aol.com
www.akashicbooks.com

Elle se plaignait d'amour, elle demandait des ailes.

—Flaubert, *Madame Bovary*

To S.A.

Artificial Light: Editor's Note

The book you are about to read has had an unusual, though by now familiar, genesis. Even those who do not as a rule follow developments in the literary world will have been acquainted with the circumstances surrounding its discovery and subsequent celebrity, and doubtless will be drawn to the work by the sensational allure of those circumstances rather than by the prospect of wading through its author's complexly immature prose. Fiat Lux has, since the events circumscribed herein, become a cause, or at least an incident, rather than a writer, a shrewd foreknowledge of which development may be what caused her to instruct, in a postscript appended to the final notebook, that the manuscript be turned over to this university, which, after due consideration, has decided to publish Artificial Light through its own press.

Its contents are here reproduced for the most part in their original form. I have chosen to respectfully disagree with those who argued that judicious pruning of the manuscript would have produced a more readable, coherent work, in the belief that Ms. Lux, under whatever conditions she undertook to compose her book, assembled her words with some care, and that an underlying structural consistency will reveal itself to the patient reader. A more thoroughly edited version may well prove useful at some point, but in the opinion of this editor the first public manifestation of Artificial Light, which will inevitably color and shape both the immediate perception of the book and all future editions, should—must—be as faithful as possible, especially with regard to the four-part structure of its narrative. It is my hope that the mass of Fiat's text will generate a gravitational field of serious scholarship and in so doing begin the slow, ineluctable process of drawing attention away from the lurid aspects of her case and toward the close study of what she has written.

I grant it's not likely anytime soon that objectivity will be restored to the matter. Too many issues remain unresolved, including many connected to the book itself. Certainly, the way the manuscript was found—in twenty-one small spiral-bound notebooks hand-written in a tiny, tidy hand, with a remarkable absence of erasures or corrections, the notebooks stacked in sequential order at Kurt C—'s residence, underneath an enormous window, the panes of which had been punctiliously and thoroughly smashed—retains an aura of mystery, years after the fact. Crime scene investigators determined that the window had been broken from within, according to their report, publicly available to any interested party. I'm not sure any of the details that report contains are telling. The panes of the window were smashed, the notebooks were found, confiscated by authorities, brushed for prints and tested for DNA, and when none of these forensic tools proved fruitful, the manuscript itself was scoured for cryptographic clues. Eventually the people assigned to investigate gave up, the notebooks were turned over to W— University, and the file was closed—officially, The Disappearance of Fiat Lux remains an open case, an unsolved mystery, but no one in a position to care does, any longer—and so What Happened has passed from a criminal matter to a cultural matter, and as with all cultural matter, has dispersed over time to such a degree that what few facts were ever known with any certainty have mushroomed into folklore.

My interest is both more and less specialized. I am not a sociologist, I am not a student of folklore, and I'm not much of a textual analyst. I'm interested in the girl, Fiat Lux, and in what she wrote—not why, or how, or for whom, but what (and not what "what" means, either; that's not the job of this edition—it is the job of this edition to allow others to figure that out, though). Because I think too little attention has been paid to the content of her writing, I have assigned myself the task, or at any rate lobbied to have the task assigned to me (the politics of the academic world are of little interest to the general reader), of editing and presenting this writing in as straightforward (i.e., un-annotated, un-indexed, un-cross-referenced) a manner as possible.

The curriculum vitae of the woman who calls herself Fiat Lux in these pages, when purged of the accumulation of legend that surrounds her disappearance, is ludicrously brief: She was born sometime in the early 1970s, in Dayton, O—, claims to have graduated from A— College in Yellow Springs, O—, claims to have worked as a librarian for the Dayton Public Library, and claims to have saved the world. None of these claims have been or can be verified—especially without identifying the woman behind the pseudonym, which has proved impossible, to date, in part because she's done an excellent job of disguising herself. Ms. Lux disappeared from the object of her salvatory labors sometime in the spring of 1994, and no further details have been uncovered, despite the best efforts of a troop of journalists and academics fascinated by the various aspects of her putative existence.

Some questions of fact are easier to resolve: a) it is true that Orville Wright lived in a mansion on Hawthorn Hill until his death in 1948. There is no way of knowing whether he was, in fact, an opium addict, although certainly no other source survives that could or would corroborate such a claim, and the diaries Fiat purports to have consulted have not been discovered; b) it is true that Kurt C— also lived at Hawthorn Hill, and that his body was discovered there in early spring of 1994. His death was ruled by the coroner a suicide by self-inflicted gunshot, and a substantial quantity of narcotics was found in his blood, according to the toxicological report obtained by us. As with any infamous public figure, rumors have abounded concerning the ways and means of his passing; there are those who insist, rather pathetically, that his death was a ruse and he still lives, fat and balding, on a paradisal island far from the rigors of fame; c) the sections attributed to "Trip Ryvvers" are probably fiction, as no book or manuscript of the title cited by Fiat seems to exist; having said that, many of the specific historical facts cited in these sections are ironically the easiest to validate; and most of them have proved accurate in their smallest detail; d) the "Mary Valentine" sections would also appear to be fiction, though we have identified an incident which in its broad outline corresponds to the accidental death of Michael Goodlife; but despite the repeated efforts of my research staff, no one who knew the person we have tentatively identified as Michael Goodlife will speak to us; e) Sean O'Hanlon was of course very much a real writer, and his long sad slide into insanity has been well-documented in the two biographies that have appeared in the past three years, prompted, possibly, by the renewed interest in O'Hanlon's work as a result of Fiat Lux's passionate advocacy herein.

At the risk of appearing flippant, I'm not sure that any of even this scant information is important. Certainly the question of what's "real" and what's "fake" in Fiat's manuscript is unhelpful at best. Her list of Sources Consulted, appended here at the end of the text proper, contains a few books that do not appear to exist, or ever to have existed, a few that were inexplicably published years after this manuscript was discovered, and a few that, while undeniably extant, have eluded our efforts to pinpoint the results of their consultation in the text. Perhaps Ms. Lux meant to say that their influence was of a general nature, but we simply have no way of knowing. In other instances, she has imported whole paragraphs without attribution, sometimes from books not listed in the Sources Consulted, which can be rather annoying, from a purely editorial point of view. Treat the book as fiction (as a vocal minority of scholars would bid you do), and you will, I think, find much to enjoy and even admire, though you will sadly miss the essential point. That said, the fact—undeniable and yet indemonstrable— that Artificial Light is no more fiction than you or I, gets neither you or I anywhere we want to go.

One not insignificant structural note: While, as noted above, the manuscript here represents every word contained in the notebooks, formatted exactly as found, I have moved the Beekeeper fragment to an appendix, rather than trying (as more than one scholar has advocated) to incorporate the material into the text. Despite the fact that the Beekeeper material is in fact interspersed with the book proper throughout the notebooks, I believe there's enough evidence to suggest that Lux intended her fragmental "translation" as an entirely separate textural entity to treat it as such. My two main arguments can be summarized as follows: 1) Every Beekeeper entry was written on a verso page, whereas the rest of the book was written on recto pages only. 2) A nearly illegible note scribbled on a separate (verso) leaf two pages after the end of the section appears to read, "Move to end?" Admittedly these are rather shifty grounds in which to plant a flag of intent, but it's part of my job as editor to infer thought processes in situations where the author is unavailable for consultation. In addition, I think little is gained by intermingling the Beekeeper material with the recto text, although the reader is free to take scissors in hand and snip the pages in question from the back of the book and interleave them with the rest—those interested in structural integrity should begin the insertion process on page 37.

Especially considering the question of whether the Beekeeper section is a translation of an actual work (no record of such a book has been found, although Lux tells us that her copy was "privately printed"; the Dayton Public Library holds no record of such a book ever having existed in its collection, but that record is incomplete, as books that were sold or destroyed before the card catalog was transferred onto computers were not recorded; you begin to see how thoroughly Fiat plotted her reality) or wholly an invention, I argue, finally, that it makes sense to leave the section discrete, so that the reader may perform his or her own appen- dectomy, or not, as he or she wishes.

Pamela Taylor, M.A., Ph.D.
October 2005

Notebook One

You would be too: lonely and cold and scared. But the *circumstances* are new. Out the window, below whose sill I'm crouched, cross-legged, so that only the top of my head's visible to anyone approaching up the hill, the first few crocus blooms have pierced a blue skin of snow. Spring cannot be far off. But in this room—more a hall than a room, with a twenty-foot-tall ceiling, walls covered in faded red fabric, floor with threadbare Arab rugs and silk-sheathed tasseled pillows—winter reigns. Dead of winter, literal, present. In the corner where I try not to look, in every other corner too. A narrow stripe of colored lozenges, stained glass, runs the length of my high window, which faces west. When the sun sets, the light filters through the red, blue, yellow of the glass and falls in rows of blurry ellipses on the blond wood of the floor: violet, tangerine, sea-green.

Before hunkering at the window, I found a pile of empty notebooks in a desk drawer, and a few pencils. I found three large cans of tuna fish in the kitchen, and a box of crackers. I dragged an iron candleholder with six fat candles next to me, out of sight of the window but close enough to provide light to see, and scrounged from the pantry two cartons of cigarettes and a box of fireplace matches. Also a case of good red wine and a corkscrew and the coffee mug that Kurt found funny. The wine should not be kept so cold, but I have no choice.

I have assembled these supplies, in this place, because I intend to write, for as long as I'm physically capable, until I come to the end of the story. I'm hoping I will not be interrupted before I finish, but that threat is constant, and one reason for the cold and the candles.

If all goes to plan, you will come to know the full extent of my faults: that I am self-absorbed, melodramatic, vain, deceitful, petty, manipulative, superficial, sentimental, moody, dim: the usual human gamut: but I don't mind. I write not to tell you about myself but to explode, by exploring, the labyrinth of self, yours and mine. If my goal were to make you like me—and that has often been my goal, in the past—I might choose a different tack, or, and I don't say this as warning but simply as plain fact, I might choose exactly this way. But please keep in mind that I am a twenty-two-year-old girl from a town in the exact middle of America, if not geographically then spiritually, and you are therefore required by law to cut me some slack. Sometimes I don't know myself whether I am telling the truth or constructing the truth, or whether there's a difference, or why.

The story I intend to tell—that I'm compelled to tell—is not my story, but it does encompass my story. I would not have elected me to write this particular story, or any story, particularly, but as things happen everyone who should have told the story—everyone who was better placed, so to speak, or better able for one reason or another—has died. Even the second-best heads, or hearts, have been incapacitated by circumstance or caprice or simple twist of fate. So there's just me to tell the story, which certainly must extend much longer than the period to which I have been privy. Despite clear evidence of the story's longevity, I will not discuss its origins or guess how long in the even longer course of things the chief players gamboled and japed and plotted their own ends. I only know what happened recently—the months to which I bore personal witness—which you'll agree, when you hear its constituent sum, is bad enough, and sad enough, and probably far too long anyway.

We first noticed Kurt C— a few weeks after he returned to Dayton, his hometown, after a period of accruing apparently world-class fame and fortune playing in a rock band (please forgive my ignorance in these matters—I love music generally, but know nothing about it specifically). He had grown up in a rough part of East Dayton, the product of an abusive and divided household, like most of us, but—unlike most of us— had shown evidence of genuine talent, upon discovering which, he lit out for the hinterlands in search of greater glory. Having found more than he wanted, he retreated to his hometown to live as much like a recluse as possible. It's a familiar story: riches bring only problems, celebrity isolates. It's also a wearisome story, and this is not a biography, after all.

My theory, or what will now become my theory, is

that Dayton attracts as much as it repels its natives. There's something about this city, a kind of centrifugal force deriving from its literally central nature, its beating heartland, that creates a vacuum in the hearts of anyone who leaves, and binds those who stay with unbreakable chains. Though Kurt would have no reason to hold his hometown dear—his childhood friends, such as they were, had long left town or died or ballooned into unrecognizable mesomorphs with mesomorphic broods and Not One Thought in their heads—he nevertheless came back. He could have settled anywhere, in any country, and lived like a Mongolian warlord, but without the need for a standing army. Instead, he came here. He came home.

Sometime in the fall it was rumored he had bought the big mansion on Hawthorn Hill that formerly belonged to Orville Wright. The house, purpose-built to Wright's own crazy specifications, had stood unoccupied for as long as anyone could remember, which was not long, as we were not old. The rumor, as sometimes happens, was correct, and not long afterwards Kurt moved into Albion, as he always called the place. A surprisingly small moving van pulled up in the long circular drive (it was reported, by one of us who decided to watch, I don't remember who, not me), and a couple of movers under Kurt's supervision unloaded a few boxes and several flight cases containing musical instruments stenciled in the way these cases generally are with the name of Kurt's rock band. Most of the musical-looking equipment was loaded around the back and placed in a small room that I saw only once. Kurt may have spent a lot of time there but not when we were around.

We were surprised that anyone would want the place, which was a hulking wreck, and even more surprised that Kurt did not seem inclined to perform many improvements. The mansion's colonnaded portico and massive lawn had fallen into disrepair. There were peeling patches of paint on the white columns and the parts that weren't peeling were blistered and dingy. The bulk of the place was brick, formerly white but aged by weather to a dusty yellow and chipped and cracked like bad teeth, as you see in movies featuring British people. My own teeth are crooked and yellowy and one incisor, victim of an adolescent root canal, has turned paralytic brown.

Before Kurt's arrival, Albion's interior was mostly bare, echoey, dark. When we were teenagers, and probably before that, a ground-floor window in the back had been broken, affording easy access, and we discovered that the empty mansion was a good place to get drunk or take drugs or have sex, back when we needed a place to do these things. Now we all had apartments, or rooms of our own in houses shared with many others, who did not care if we drank or did drugs or had sex.

After Kurt's arrival, not much changed. He'd arrived with very little furniture of his own, preferring to make use of the tattered remnants of Albion's former splendor. With the exception of a small suitcase in which was heaped a tangled pile of monochrome clothes and an exceptionally large, heavy-looking chest which I never saw him open, he had very few possessions. When we started spending time with Kurt at

Albion, we noticed that he liked to keep things sparse. No gold records lined the walls, no posters or artworks of any kind, even though I knew that Kurt himself spent a good deal of time painting in a room upstairs (another room I saw only once). This was something you rarely encountered even among people my own age, who often seemed not so much defined as advertised by their possessions. I would have expected that an older man would have even more stuff, not even less, and at first I found Kurt's asceticism romantic, like in an existentialist novel.

He had no car, not even a bike. Many of us used bikes to move around, but not Kurt. Kurt walked everywhere. To the bars, to the restaurants, to the coffee shop, to the record store. He most often walked north, downhill from Albion, to the quarter-mile stretch of Brown Street from Stewart to Wyoming, the central artery of the artier element in Dayton. Every once in a while someone'd see Kurt struggling uphill, south, on Far Hills Avenue, to the grocery store in Oakwood, which was almost a mile away, or even further up the road in Kettering toward some undiscovered place. In fine weather and rain or snow, he wore the same brown overcoat.

A few weeks after he moved in we started to see Kurt in our locals, the Snafu Hive and The Pearl. These were the two poles around which our social lives revolved. The Snafu Hive was on the corner of Brown and Wyoming. Approaching across the short expanse of grass between the Quikburger and the fire station—the route I usually took from my apartment nearby, on Hickory—you could see the orange border of light around the bar, just above the rust-colored awning, and the sign, which was a blood-orange-fading-to-mustard sun set in a deep blue sky, the sun grazing the tips of some dark leafy trees, and the words *Snafu Hive* below in the same orange-yellow shading. The sign was rimmed also in orange neon hanging from the unused second story of the windowless building. Even in the dark you could see the pale blue-green paint of the second story's aluminum siding peeling, in the streetlight and the neon glow and the floodlights mounted near the angled eaves of the roof. The rough gray-and-white bricks of the ground floor reflected amber from the streetlight and orange from the neon border and the green-yellow-red of the stoplight at the corner and the red taillights of braking cars, too. Inside, black vinyl booths were set against tourmaline walls. Parallel lines of blue and green neon light lined the walls near their top. The stripes of neon from the walls were reflected in the curved glass of the jukebox front. When you tried to see what songs to play you had to hold your hand in front to block the reflection. Candelabras with coarse imitation Tiffany shades hung from the ceiling over each of the booths along the wall, and fake old-fashioned streetlamps were posted halfway up. The ceiling in the front room, where the bar itself was located, was tiled with the playing surfaces of every possible board game.

The Pearl was about half a mile away, located in a remote nook of the Oregon District, but linked more or less directly from the Hive by a concrete pedestrian bridge that transversed the highway. Approaching The Pearl, which was a low red-brick building fronted by twin maples—both still young and lovely gold-and-red in the fall—you were alerted to the purpose of the place only by the muted blue-and-yellow neon beerlight in the transom. We went to The Pearl, which was darker and grimmer than the Snafu Hive, only when the collegiate presence at the Hive became overbearing, which often happened on weekend nights when the University of Dayton was in session.

Kurt came first to the Hive. He sat by himself, for hours, turning pages in a notebook, occasionally drawing or scribbling something. He generally ordered a pitcher of beer and nursed that through the night, sitting in a corner table or an otherwise empty booth. Sometimes he would go over to the jukebox, flipping through the hundred or so albums on offer, and very occasionally he'd feed a dollar or two into the slot and ask anyone standing nearby to pick some songs, explaining that he had no taste in music, but liked the idea of it, which depending on whether they recognized him or not was either a good joke or the truth. At peak hours the jukebox was nearly inaudible over the buzz of the crowd, anyway.

I found the secret struggle between words and music, with its shifting front lines, sudden incursions of bright sound—a singer's yelp, a guitar's howl—followed by equally sudden retreat, as the sea of talk drowned the plaintive whine of some flowery folk-songstress (for instance), one of the more entertaining aspects of bar-going. That and the talk itself, which, whenever I slipped into the bad habit of listening without paying attention, struck up a rhythm & blues of its own. When I was younger I had ambitions to chart the ebb and flow of the conversation among my friends, cross-referenced by personality type and amount of alcohol consumed, but I'm older now and my ambitions have consequently matured.

Nothing about Kurt except the natural force field of fame seemed unapproachable, but for some reason we did not approach him for a while. Not even Mary Valentine or Amanda Early, who approached everyone male, regularly, in the hope that he would buy them a drink. Amanda and Mary were very charming, and silly, and manipulative, and pretended to hate each other. Both were pretty but in different ways. Mary was small and blond, had a face constructed of oblique angles, and wore very tight clothes to accentuate the camber of her shapely nates. Amanda was taller, moon-faced, dark-haired, with heavy, soft breasts that she hid (to the extent possible) under oversized shirts or sweaters. She was both proud and embarrassed of her breasts, which I can understand even though I've never had that problem myself. Mary was smarter, and Amanda neurotic to the point where she'd been prescribed lithium for what her doctor told her was a manic-depressive disorder, but she sold the lithium in order to keep drinking. She was also nicer than Mary, as slightly stupid people are apt to be nicer than slightly smart people.

Boys loved Mary and Amanda, not least because for all their insincere flirting, they were both kind of slutty. I've determined after much research that boys like sluts. The kind of boys that hung out with us, anyway. I'm not really a slut but sometimes I feel like one. Usually when I feel slutty I'm just pretending, though.

For fun. But sometimes you back yourself into a corner. Then you have to fuck your way out, which isn't always fun or a good idea.

Eventually, though, curiosity got the better of Mary, who was more outgoing than Amanda, sometime around October of last year, not more than a month after Kurt first showed up. There were about ten of us grouped around two adjacent booths at the Hive. I saw Mary stop at Kurt's table on the way back from the ladies' room. She leaned over him, her hands resting on the table, fingers restlessly tapping as she talked.

Kurt nodded slightly and she slid into a chair next to him and laughed her frilly, girlish laugh, which was the thing I liked least about Mary.

"What are they talking about? What's he saying?" asked Amanda, sucking intently through a plastic straw at the half-melted ice cubes in her empty drink.

After two minutes or so Mary rose and flitted back to our group. We quizzed her eagerly.

"He says to please leave him alone," she reported, flush with drink and the excitement of something new.

"Everybody's got a gimmick," muttered Joe Smallman into his vodka and grapefruit, sitting next to Amanda.

"What else did he say?" I asked.

"He muttered something under his breath. I asked him to repeat but he wouldn't. So I told him it didn't matter anyway, because I only speak French. So then he said something in maybe French and I said . . ." Mary drew a breath before continuing, ". . . not *that* kind of French."

Amanda looked at Mary, puzzled. "What kind?"

Mary giggled.

"He didn't buy you a drink?" I asked.

"No. Bastard."

I raised an eyebrow.

"Cute, huh?" said Mary, still giggling.

Once Mary had made contact, others followed suit over the ensuing days and weeks. We grew used to Kurt's presence, and he grew used to ours, and more tolerant of our occasional incursions on his table's turf. He was never what you'd call convivial, and certainly not forthcoming (he would never talk, for instance, about what he was writing or drawing in his notebook), but he was never less than kind. As he came to know more about us, he would ask polite questions about our personal lives, without ever seeming intrusive or unduly interested, but at the same time without seeming as if the questions were pro forma or mere conversation. Something about his manner encouraged us to reveal more than we would reveal, or consider wise to reveal, to each other. Had he been so inclined, Kurt would have made an excellent psychologist, so realistic was his engagement with the listener, so attentive and appropriate his questions, so benign and non-judgmental his expression. He could coax startling revelations from the most reticent people, though to be honest none of us were particularly reticent, and the greater part were glad of an audience that had not heard their particular tales of conquest and betrayal repeated over a half-drained glass of weak beer.

Not so much me: I too preferred to listen, especially when Amanda gave an explication of the ways and means of her obsession with Druids, with sloppily drawn diagrams on a series of sodden bar napkins, later taken by Kurt and shoved into the jacket pocket of his pea coat, which was chocolate-brown in color, almost ginger-dark, so that when you first looked you thought maybe suede, but no, the material while soft and texturally similar to suede—like moleskin—was a wool blend. Kurt tried to put the napkins into his pocket surreptitiously, balling them in one quick movement, but I saw. I see more things than I want to see, sometimes.

It's okay, though. I was part of the group, sure, accepted long ago by virtue of my reliability as a go-between in matters of love and a fortress of neutrality in the (inevitable, and frequent) event of fallings-out. I was the Switzerland of our circle. A little too clean, a little too respectable for most people's taste, but safe, and remote, and unwilling to commit to either side in an argument. I have very definite opinions, but I don't like to state them publicly. I understand how that makes me useful, and how that usefulness is the basis for the general amicability of my relations with the members of our group. But I don't have any close friends—I never have, not even when I was small.

I was an only child, and my mother and I lived outside of Dayton, in a place called Lewisburg, north of town. We lived in a desanctified Pentecostal church, which had been renovated completely by my father before he died, when I was exactly three. I don't remember him at all except through the pictures my mother saved. There's one in particular where I'm in our backyard, on the verge of a stand of fir trees striped with the occasional birch, bent over a small fern with the concentrated interest of a botanist, or a child. In the background, my father watches me, arms folded. The photo's taken with a flash, so it's hard to tell the time of day, but my best guess is that it's late afternoon, in spring, two months before he fell off a roof he was retiling in Vandalia and impaled himself on the post of a chain-link fence. On my birthday, I always forget to say. He slipped—this is the way I imagine—because he was hurrying to finish work in time for my party, where we had chocolate cake with white and pink frosting, and little green frosting florets, and my name in frosting and three pink birthday candles. I don't remember anything about the party, of course. The description of the cake is from another photo, taken by my mother shortly before the policeman showed up to tell her the news. When she snapped this picture, of me looking small and confused in front of a cake too big for myself and two kids my age whose names I could not tell you if you held a gun to my head, if you pulled the trigger, if I died and went to heaven and my entire life were available for review—mom probably recruited them from families at church—she was doubtless angry or at least irritated that dad was late, doubtless ready to give him an earful of holler, as we liked to say. I don't know if we liked to say that, actually.

There weren't many kids my age in Lewisburg: there weren't many *people* in Lewisburg. I spent most of my time growing up alone, and then when I started at school, which was several miles down the highway in Tipp City, I didn't know how to talk to the other kids. At first I was the girl in the corner of the playground staring at dirt, but gradually I assimilated. I "came out of my shell," in the words of my third grade teacher, Mrs. Handerlich. I never liked that expression, with its reptilian or piscine associations. I was neither turtle nor hermit crab. I was a girl who did not like to talk to other people but who gradually accepted the necessity for doing so, on the condition that I not be required to form actual friendships. Thus, after a slow start, I became social, and even popular. My popularity was based on a simple principle: I did not care about being popular. I did not care about anything or anyone. I was never rude, I was never gossipy, I smiled readily and listened with attention to my schoolmates, even contributing a few gnomic comments when absolutely necessary to prove that I was not weird.

One girl I might have called friend. Her name was Eileen Gregg, and she could read 814 words per minute. I could read pretty fast, I could read pretty well, but I could not read as fast or as well as Eileen Gregg. She was ten years old, same as me, and had frizzy dark hair held in place with red barrettes, and tortoiseshell glasses behind which blinked narrow green eyes that never stopped moving down the page. Her prowess was no parlor trick, either—she could quote whole chunks of text, after reading, and showed by what she'd committed to memory an affinity for the same sorts of things (purply clumps of Dickens; Dylan Thomas's unfathomably luscious verse) I'd found and loved; and so by natural extension I loved Eileen Gregg, too. She was my first crush. Ours was not a showy love. Its depth and sublimity was expressed, by me (I'm not sure Eileen was ever aware of her part, but so hotly was our bond forged in the fire of my imagination that the less she acknowledged, the more I sighed), largely through a series of glances and gestures untranslated by anyone. I don't think we exchanged more than two sentences: "Did you drop this?" "No." "Okay." "Okay." Something like that. Something like this is what I heard: "There is nothing under round Phoebus's face so lovely to me as your smile, nothing so precious as your fingers, pale as swan's down. I would drown in any river at your command. I would and will read the book of your face at 814 words per minute for every minute my heart still beats, and beats, and beats."

Had I invited her over to my house, what then? She could come on the bus with me, but Mom would've balked at driving her all the way back to Tipp City (forty minutes round trip) in our embarrassingly ratty Primavera, which belched white smoke from the exhaust and overheated if you breathed too hard. Or if she hadn't balked, I would have, and probably long before the car subject arrived. Because the fuss my mother would've made over Eileen, over anyone-een, would've killed me sooner. (The subjunctive case—harbor of wishes and the flotsam of unseen futures—fills my sentences with would, which contrary to what I'd been led to believe doesn't float. I'm almost certain that's a good pun.) So the invitation remained unextended, and eventually Eileen Gregg moved away, or went to private school, or died of shock upon realizing the brutal truth of human existence.

No boyfriends, either. I go through periods of letting boys have their way with me, and once even thought I liked one for about two weeks who turned out to be gay (how absolutely banal, right?). Making things worse, I actually walked in on him and some guy. I almost never let anyone in my apartment except infrequently the Rose Scholar. Her real name was Cinnamon, which is bad enough, but I always called her the Rose Scholar—we have nicknames for regular customers at the library—because she knew everything about roses and seemed to have a genuine passion for botanical knowledge. I appreciate people with genuine passions, which in my experience are scarcer than *Albus honorifica*, a very rare varietal occurring only in the mountains of Peru, according to the Rose Scholar. I let her in my place to look at my botany books.

Thus I entered an apartment not my own to find my erstwhile lover humping another guy, or what looked like humping but what he claimed was "nothing, we were just messing around, it's not what you . . ." But, no, it's always what you think. I knew, on some level, even before I pushed open the broken screen door of that rat-trap(y) and followed the sounds of huffing down the dust-encrusted hallway. I had ascribed his reluctance in physical matters to a sensible disdain for my less-than-curvilinear physique, but turns out my boyish figure's exactly what drew him. The apartment, in any event, belonged to the hypotenuse of our brief, unshapely triangle. That's why the door wasn't locked—no one expected me, the base leg. I had stopped by to ask advice on a present I was planning to buy for a friend; as luck would have it the friend in question was already present.

That was two years ago. In hindsight, I'm guessing my attraction to the homosexual was based mostly on his indifference to me, which is a very nineteen-year-old-girl attribute, I think—to find indifference sexy. Since then I've been alone, and often lonely, but no lonelier than my childhood, which despite its under-population never felt particularly empty. My feeling's that the isolation of my upbringing was just a truer reflection of the Facts of Life—the bride stripped bare (I don't know why that article of rote popped up just now but we'll leave it)—and so rather than being deprived I had been gifted with a head start in the reality stakes. I remember trying out that theory on Kurt one night very late, at a stage of cozy drunkenness (cozy because I was curled up on an old carpet in front of a dying fire, drunkenness because I was drunk) that rarely fails to elicit from me bogus insights; I thought he would suffocate from laughing so hard. At the time I didn't see what was so funny, but now I get the joke: The joke's on me.

I lately wonder if my loneliness was why Kurt C— decided it was safe to unburden himself to me, or if he'd done his research and saw that I could keep a secret. If you'd asked me a couple of weeks ago for my chief virtue I might have said: I keep secrets. I'm telling secrets now, though—I'm slinging secrets like hot rocks into the sky-blue sea, now that nothing matters. Truth's its own consequence. The sun provides light but the sun is not itself light. I'll tell you another one: Kurt is dead. I killed him.

Notebook Two

Shot him in the head at close range. Do you want to know why?

Because he asked. Nicely. In a casual tone, the way you'd ask a friend to watch your cat, if you had a friend, or a cat. I'm not big on favors, but I did this one thing, this one time. It seemed to make sense, and still does, although I'm maybe using *make sense* in an unusual way. Kurt wanted an appropriate end to the story of Kurt C—. The end he chose matched the tenor of his story. That much I can aver, unreservedly.

Dredging up memories brings pain, and heat, and a weird taste in the back of my mouth, which may be related less to memory than to lunch, or more accurately the memory of lunch, since I have not eaten properly in some time. Things happen in the world objectively, that seems clear. But I can no longer determine the dividing line between matter and memory (the thing and the image of the thing, to complete the Bergsonian circle) with any self-confidence.

Kurt made a mess of himself, there's no getting around that, though the ripples of his exit will take some time to subside. While no anthropomorphic deity likely awaits behind pearly gates—God has been killed so many times by now it's considered bad manners to resurrect him again—the bulk of us, to judge from the available literature, still cling with childlike hope to some notion of immortality, to some idea of the soul. I know Kurt did, or he would not have handed me a pistol and asked me to shoot. I know I do, or I would not have shot.

I can't gargle or shuffle cards. The latter despite my mother's addiction to solitaire, and to bridge, and her patient efforts to teach me to cut the deck without looking, by touch—to take nonchalantly each half-deck in either hand and bend the cards until the bowed edges kiss, then interleave them with a rapid riffling sound like a gusty wind through ash leaves. I could never manage anything better than a lazy breeze. Considering my upbringing, I should be expert at solitary games. But: no.

My disability re gargling's a residual effect of my *religious upbringing*. I was raised as a Christian Scientist. Christian Science teaches that the world as perceived through our senses is an illusion, the creation of Mortal Error, and that by recognizing the illusory nature of reality and the consequent perfection of God's true creation—his image and likeness, as manifested by Jesus Christ, his terrestrial son—you will be able through the agency of the Divine Principle to heal the sick and raise the dead, just as Jesus did. Thus we had no need for doctors; if you know one thing about our religion that's probably the one thing, if you haven't in the first place confused Christian Science with Scientology, which is a completely different deal. It was founded in the late nineteenth century by a woman named Mary Baker Eddy, and probably because of its feminine origin has retained a matrilineal shape. It's often handed down from mother to daughter like a spiritual dowry, and the head office, so to speak, is called the Mother Church. My grandmother was a Christian Scientist, thence my mother, whence my mother's effort to raise me in the faith. Its tenets display a *proto-feminist* slant best exemplified by Mrs. Eddy's revisionist Lord's Prayer, which replaces "*Our Father, Who Art in Heaven*" with "*Our Father-Mother God, All Harmonious.*"

Replace is the wrong word: I think she intended her version as an interlinear gloss rather than a replacement. But for Christian Scientists, and so for me growing up, God was bisexual, or more accurately asexual—both male and female, but neither male nor female, because the Form of God had no body, no need for body, and no need for determinate sex. Which sounds sort of Platonic, and sort of Buddhist, and sort of German Romantic, and sort of American Transcendentalist, and sort of a lot of things but not very Christian, by which I mean that it espouses no inflexible dogma, and professes to draw wholly sufficient inspiration directly from the Bible without need for priestly mediation. You could maybe spot affinities to the Coptic gospels and Gnosticism, as well as with much Eastern thinking generally, too. I've always remembered my long-since-discarded religion fondly, as you would an eccentric aunt or an outgrown toy.

As a result of Christian Science, though, I never took medicine of any kind—not aspirin, not vitamins, not mouthwash—growing up, and so never learned how to swallow pills or gargle. I can now swallow pills, because once I discovered anti-anxiety drugs I realized that I needed them like some people need the light on at night, but I still can't gargle. I should also note that during the unmedicated portion of my life I never once fell majorly ill, and such diseases as I did manage to attract absented themselves in short order and with a minimum of fuss. Examples: I had chicken pox, but only for two days. Mumps, one day. Measles, my most recent disease, lasted longest, four days, and the first two were the only time in my childhood (lasting until I went off to college, in Yellow Springs, about twenty miles northeast of Dayton proper) when I was seriously ill, in the sense that I wasn't able to get out of bed. I ate a lot of grapes, which helped, and my mom read both the Bible and *Science and Health with Key to the Scriptures*, the main Christian Science text, which didn't.

Now I get sick all the time. If hungover counts as sick, I'm almost never not sick. To counteract the progress time and disease have made on my undoctored body, I've a) taken up hypochondria, more as a hobby than a career; and b) begun ingesting, regularly: vitamin supplements, bee pollen, spirulina extract, and pain relievers of every over-the-counter stripe. This in addition to whatever anxiety-related prescription medication I can obtain without prescription, or without resorting to doctors. Though my job carries health insurance (I'm almost certain), I've retained an aversion to the medical profession that, despite my deep conviction upon exiting the shower and seeing, in the infallible lens of my bathroom mirror, a dime-sized eggplant-purple shoulder bruise, that I had contracted the plague, prevents me from taking advantage of our nation's health care system. I do eat a lot of apples, however.

On the plus side, I'm very slender. My metabolism sprints where others crawl, and I have to make sure I eat enough to keep up a reasonable human façade, especially since in our social circle we look closely at each other for signs—like weight loss—which could indicate drug abuse, a subject to which we have become sensitized after three or four overdose deaths, presumed accidental. The two most popular drugs to abuse are methamphetamines and heroin. Either will kill you, but crystal meth will take longer, because you can't really overdose—I suppose it's theoretically possible that your heart could explode from the adrenalin rush, but the most likely result of taking too much is you'll shoot someone else or yourself or wake up two weeks later with an unnaturally clean apartment.

Not a drug-taker, me. One of the few in our town, or at least among my friends. Speed in any form's anathema to my constitution, and heroin's so perfectly designed for me that I've always been scared to try. Too many people I've known have tried, and died, or permanently scarred not just their own lives but the lives of the people in their calling circle. I watched it happen close hand, once. A summer roommate, Jeddah Tern, started as everyone starts, snorting an occasional line at parties, then snorting an occasional line in his room, then progressing to the needle and regular trips to West Dayton for his daily dose, which quickly increased from one to three to five to seven bags. At first, I cared. Rookie mistake. I took him to the methadone clinic on Brookdale Avenue, and tried to keep watch as best my schedule allowed, but after a week or so of vigilant care, I came home from work to find him nodding out on the couch. I slapped him, hard, on the cheek, so hard my hand stung for minutes. He just grinned at me—not sheepish, but not without a certain embarrassment, for the loss of his humanity. That was the only time I've ever hit another person as an adult.

Not until a month later—foolish Fiat—did I kick him out. Took me the better part of the next month to make a thorough accounting of everything Jeddah had stolen from me during that time, most of which I didn't mind and didn't miss (or it wouldn't have taken me a month): a good third of my CD collection; my CD player; a pair of expensive shoes, never worn, or worn only once, still in the box; a small camera, never used, also still in box; a fancy pen and pencil set, gold-plated, never used, s.i.b.; a framed print of a painting by the famous post-impressionist Darren Soon, stuffed in the back of a closet; several boxes of miscellaneous office supplies, which had been purloined from the library; a watch. The only thing of real value was a frail silver necklace that my mom had given me, and which had been (as these things inevitably have been) given to her by her mother, and so on, down to the tangled roots of my family tree, which lay buried somewhere in the dirt of Dayton. The necklace may have been worth a great deal of actual money, but its worth as a literal *memento mori* I could not then and cannot now bring myself to calculate.

Six months ago Jeddah Tern died of an overdose. I've spent some time since his death combing the pawnshops and thrift stores of Dayton for my necklace, unsuccessfully.

I'm not what you'd call good-looking—hardly any breasts, hips like a boy, dull gray eyes too small, too far apart on my face, which is one reason I wear glasses (the other's because I can't see without them). I don't wear makeup, and I hate messing with my hair, so I keep it short, but it sticks out in wild directions unbidden.

But no matter: I'm a serious girl, with serious aspirations that do not allow room for romance. As Hercules did by Cacus, he shall be dragged forth of doors by the heels, away with him! Not that I don't find boys attractive, or girls for that matter, but whenever I find myself tempted, whether theoretically or in drunken fact, I tend to shy away, envisioning as an aid to my impaired resolve the ugly consequences of a followed-through advance. Because those consequences, at least for me, have always been ugly, and painful, and worthless. I'm not the type who believes in learning from experience. Not my experience, anyway.

My main orientation has always been to books. I'm a bibliomane, which helps explain why I ended up a librarian. Part of my attraction is purely aesthetic—I love books as artifacts, and though I'm not a collector myself, I appreciate the attention to detail and respect for the texture of time exhibited by that breed. I have an aversion to badly designed books. I need to think that someone put a lot of thought and effort into every aspect of the book I hold in my hands. The other part's more straightforward: I'm in awe of the process—when rightly accomplished—by which thoughts can be ordered and expressed—whether profound or simply beautiful without apparent meaning. (For instance, I have spent hours mouthing Latin verse that I barely understand for enjoyment—for the music of the syllables pirouetting on my palate and out into the fetid air of my hot apartment.) Which doesn't mean I read poetry only, or novels, because my tastes are catholic even if my religion's not, and I've been imbued since birth with a thirst for the acquisition of facts that borders on pathological. So philosophy, of course, but also biology, chemistry, physics, linguistics, political science (in the general sense—as long as I'm left alone I don't much care about politics), the smatterings of about ten languages, with near fluency in reading three. Etcetera. You get the picture. I'm not bragging—of course I'm bragging, but I'm bragging to purpose, as a help to whomever stumbles on these notebooks and tries (and I'm hoping you'll try) to decipher, or better yet, edit my squirrelly scrawl. If a little learning's a dangerous thing, then the scattered ashes of great learning hold still more peril. What you hold in your hands, stands to reason, you hold at some risk. To what, I'm not exactly sure.

My favorite writer? Of all time? Really? If you speak, read, or write English as your native tongue and you don't say Shakespeare you're worse than a fool, because any fool knows what you pretend you don't. Okay, so him. But after Will, my absolute favorite is a fairly obscure Irish writer from the 1920s called Sean O'Hanlon, who must have used a tuning fork instead of a typewriter or pen, because his words have perfect pitch. His most famous book is called Miserogeny, which, though often described as a novel, is as much an epic poem, sketchbook, series of unconnected essays, apercus, epigrams, dicta, lists, formless only because it transcends form.

I once kissed a guy because he reminded me of the way I imagined Thomas Farrell, the hero or authorial alter ego in Miserogeny. I was drunk on whiskey and I went with the guy into the old gazebo in the park across from The Pearl. The cement on the floor of the gazebo was wet from summer rain, and so was the rotting bench where we sat making out. I could feel the seat of my jeans soaking through. Mist haloed the streetlamp on the corner which was the only light. When we started kissing he looked different, not so much like Thomas Farrell and more like someone I didn't want touching me, so I [passage deleted in text, scored heavily several times in pencil].

Afterwards, dizzy from drinking and flush from the humidity and the aborted arousal and the incompatible mix of substances in my stomach, I crawled to the edge of the gazebo and puked copiously into the weeds. The guy was sweet, he bent over and wiped my mouth with the tail of his shirt, but I told him I was okay and asked him to go back in and order me another drink. When he left I sat for a few minutes with my head resting against the wet wood of the gazebo's lattice. A perfume of azaleas made me think of the house in Lewisburg, which had a hedge of azalea bushes in front, facing the street. I carefully pulled a long stem of wild grass out of its socket and sat chewing.

Then I went inside, and thought everyone was looking at me and knew what I'd done, and for some reason that produced a feeling of guilt that would not subside for two or three drinks, even though no one had noticed, and even though had they noticed they wouldn't have cared, because you only notice things you care about, and you only care about things you notice. This was an epiphany I very clearly remember experiencing fully that night. Protected by my self-constructed paradox, I was free, and my freedom was a terrible thing to behold, if only anyone had cared to see. Outwardly, my behavior changed in no way: I chatted familiarly with familiar people, cracked a couple of wry jokes, destroyed an innocent stranger's self-confidence, possibly forever, with a withering put-down when he tried to strike up a friendly conversation. The usual, in other words. But on the inside, where all the important stuff happens, we're told, I had changed in fundamental ways, because I had come to a full realization of the power of my invisibility. The boy from the gazebo left an hour or so after I returned, without even looking to see if I was still there, as if nothing had happened between him and some drunk girl, not even bothering to point me out to his friends as a recent conquest. I know because I watched him go. I watched them all go. I know because I noticed.

Later that night we stood milling around in a soused clump in front of The Pearl at closing time, discussing whose turn it was to host the after-hours party. We were watching while Mary Valentine and Amanda Early made rash decisions about sleeping or not sleeping with whomever had bought them the most drinks that night (I know this sounds catty, but it's meant in the fondest way; also, it's the strict truth, more often than not—as either would admit, freely, unabashed, without rue). We'd grown used to Kurt's off-putting presence, and he'd grown used to ours, and he often stayed until the last few of us were left, although he had not yet acquired the habit of following us to after-hours. At first we assumed he was hoping for a ride, but too proud to ask, but whenever any of the few of us a) who could afford a car and b) were stupid enough to run the Dayton Police gauntlet at closing time, would offer, he always said no thanks and set off on foot, with a look of real happiness no matter the weather, which at the approach of winter was often bitter cold, and sometimes brought needles of frozen rain. Kurt would turn up the collar of his ginger-colored pea coat and walk into the dark, disappearing from the streetlit street by degrees.

Tonight, though—a night of firsts—something extraordinary happened: Kurt laughed. I didn't catch who or what had set him off, cackling like—well, like I don't know quite what, exactly. Which is partly what made the moment so formidable: the way Kurt threw his head back and unleashed (if you were there you'd know what I mean) his laughter, uncoiling the sound from his larynx in a way so unusual, and yet so natural, that his body transformed from a twisted, frail skeleton unsuited for any imaginable physical activity into a machine designed for laughter. The most compelling aspect of Kurt's laughter was that it became him, and that he seemed like a man who at one time had laughed often and easily, but not for a while. To me a discovery like this—a radical alteration of your initial impression about someone you've known for any length of time— was as exciting as the discovery of an unknown comet to an unknown astronomer.

In the context of Kurt's story, then, this was the second or third most important in his allotted basket of nights.

The only way to describe Kurt laughing would be to say he looked merry. Which I know is not a word used to describe anyone anymore, but it's the one that fits in this case. He laughed, merrily, and left with a wave of his arm, still laughing.

But you see the mischief: Many of us, knowing that merry company's the best medicine against melancholy, will neglect our business, and spend all our time among like-minders in a bar, and soon unlearn otherwise how to exist but in drinking: malt-worms, whiskey-fish, wine-snakes, *qui bibunt solum ranarum more, nihil comedentes*, "like so many frogs in a puddle."

My name is Fiat Lux. I work in the main library downtown. I actually went to college for that, if you can believe it takes a college degree to learn how to look after books. Of course that's not *why* I went to college, but it's what I studied. The reason being my already-stated near rapturous relationship to books (I grant the possibility of some unknown thing provoking in me greater heights of passion, but the way I live the chance of unknown things is slim). I picked Library Science, though, because I hate *selling*, which is what you have to do if you work in a bookstore. I tried working in bookstores. Plus side: you're around tons of books. Minus side: you have to sell. Library Science rather than Literature, though, because I hate theories about books. I hate mediation, generally, but especially with regard to things I hold dear, which are few.

Interestingly, you don't call yourself a librarian, anymore. *Librarian*, to most people, conjures an image of a fusty middle-aged spinster scouring the stacks to eliminate traces of pornography or, worse, Communism (you'd be surprised how long people cling to a shopworn shibboleth—we get all types at the library). And while it's true there's a disproportionate number of middle-aged spinsters, and even young-aged spinsters, on the whole we're discouraged—and this is part of a general trend of discouragement—from using the word librarian in regard to ourselves. We are not moth-ball perfumed custodians of wormy, well-forgotten tomes: we are highly trained technicians who specialize in parsing complex strands of fragile sense into manageable bits. We are scientists, each with a particular specialty in the endlessly subdividing organism called, for sake of argument, Book.

My field is Information Science. I specialize in the ordering of information. I am an archivist, a good one. Organization and cataloging, the ability to instantly find or know where to find a particular item—the precise thing required by the reader, whether scholar or child. Not the closest approximation to that item but the *res ipsa*. Sometimes we don't have the *ipsa*; sometimes we don't even have the *res*; but we know where it's hidden, we can ferret through the tunnels of any number of neighboring or not-so-neighboring libraries, linked like lovers' arms from here to eternity, and by use of the telephone or something called electronic mail with which I like to pretend I'm not familiar, request the item in question, which request is often granted, or else the whole system would collapse and I would have to find a new job.

In one sense, then, I'm an enabler. I enable people, whether artist or amateur, to exercise their epistemologies. Without regular exercise, these native philosophies tend to atrophy, and once that happens, I don't care how carefully you watch your diet of ideas, you'll go flabby and soft. In another sense, I'm an addict. The sensual rush I enjoy every time I have an excuse to wander through the closed stacks, down on the second floor, has only intensified with repetition. I don't mean the intellectual thrill of finding oneself surrounded by a dizzying assortment of the finest thinking available to humanity, but the actual sense-pleasure available to eyes (the combinations of colors), ears (the absolute silence), nose (the papery smell), mouth (the taste of the dust in your throat), and, most important, fingers: the texture of the buckram, in its infinite and infinitely subtle grains, dimensions, pliability, and heft.

Removed of their dust jackets, removed of the plastic casing that protects the dust jackets from dust, most latter-day volumes consist of any number of acid-free paper pages sewn or glued to buckram bindings in varying hues, from midnight black to virginal white. Arrayed on the steel shelving in our own modest stacks, the effect's overwhelming. I've yet to travel outside of Dayton, but I've seen pictures (in books) of some of the Greater Libraries of the world, and the sheer scope suggested by those pictures unmoors my brain. I'm honestly scared by magnitude—magnitude in everything, but magnitude in books just brings me, frankly, a little too close to the face of human ignorance.

In the Yule-Cordier edition of *The Travels of Marco Polo*, you'll find, somewhere in the footnotes, this explanation, here paraphrased: What was buckram? In the modern sense, sure, a coarse open texture of cotton or hemp, loaded with gum, used to stiffen certain articles of dress. But the medieval sense? A quotation in Raynouard's Romance Dictionary has, "*Vestirs de polpra e de bisso que est bocaran*," where Raynouard renders *bisso* as *lin*. It certainly was not necessarily linen, nor velvet, nor . . . I can't remember nor what else, but you see my problem. Either Colonel Yule or M. Cordier has provided a very good definition of the things buckram's not, or wasn't, but its origins, not only etymological but phenomenological, remain shrouded in velvet or linen.

I know: fascinating. The evolution of the librarian's role through history—the evolution of the library through history—is a fascinating subject, serious books have been devoted to thorough explorations of these evolutions, or revolutions, or what have you. In sum, I'm glad to say, these histories back my prime directive: Things as precious as books should not be sold but given away or at least lent. Ancient authors—in the days when books were scrolls or wood-bound codices—had to pay for copies at their own expense, and booksellers employed troops of scribes to produce further copies, which, when sold, derived no profit to their authors. You wrote a book: you made a few presentation copies for friends and patrons: and you were done. In other words, to find readers you had to pay, from your own pocket, to make copies of your manuscript, or direct the would-be fan to the nearest store. Imagine the slighted sensibilities of those so directed! Untenable. In time, then, the library, at first an empty *beau geste* by emperor or king bent on bolstering his profile, then a religious scholar's refuge, and still later, after too much irrational blood and burning (nearly as many books have been burned or buried or pulped as have been printed, and every book burned or buried or pulped is a murderous act, both in the obvious, hate-fuelled fact and in the fundamental irreplaceableness, word choice, of the book-as-artifact), a publicly funded institution whose methods and purpose have been vigorously debated over the last couple of centuries, came to occupy a place in the common consciousness so ubiquitous and well-deployed as to have achieved the height of stability: an unarguable good, a necessity. Even when underfunded and overlooked, even when closely circumscribed by the whims of autocratic rulers or (not so very long ago) pernicious race laws, the library survives.

At the library, we almost never have to sell anything. The only exception is the annual discard sale, where we get rid of books that have outlived their usefulness for one reason or another (superseded textbooks, outmoded translations, dogeared classics). But even then—I'll tell you another secret—I feel bad for the unwanted discards at the end of the sale, the two or three cartons overflowing with torn and soiled and unloved books. I'm supposed to haul them to the recycling center but I never do. I keep them in the spare room of my three-room apartment on Hickory. I keep them arranged in an abstruse filing system of my own device—I'm frankly sick of the alphanumerical Library of Congress method, as well as dropsical Dewey Decimal, and I'm convinced my system's more intuitive and commonsensical, and generally better, but try telling that to the Library Administration or the Board of Directors. These orphans, though, sheltered in orderly ranks on planks of wood balanced on cement bricks, are the only books I permit myself to own.

Because no one else wants them, you see. They have no value except what I've given them. I would not have picked many of them—I've got fifteen volumes on botany, for instance, and no garden. I have a nearly complete paperback collection (twenty-three luridly decorated books) of the Western novels of Red Hand (pen name of Armitage Shanks, of Uxbridge, England). I hate Western novels. I have graffiti-filled high school calculus textbooks in triplicate, a police manual on crowd control from the '50s, and four different Spanish-language vegetarian cookbooks. I'm not a vegetarian. I don't read Spanish.

There are some treasures, however. I have a book in German called *Das Bienenzüchter sucht nach Ruth [Beekeeper Seeks Ruth]*, by an Austrian biologist called Wilhelm Kneissl, privately printed (and much damaged by water; the cover and first few pages are missing) in 1963, which may be the finest love story ever written. I also have a beat-up two volume set of *Gargantua and*

Pantagruel, and a copy of R.L. Stevenson's *Memories and Portraits*, Chatto and Windus, London, 1904, Pott 8vo, cloth binding, gilt top. But I don't rank the books, most of the time. I would never hurt the other books' feelings by considering them somehow inferior to the ones I (privately) cherish, because everything I keep, every book—every one I don't keep, too—that's written with any kind of open mind represents human striving toward its unnamable essence, right? So nothing's wasted, and nothing's worthless. I'd advise you to bear that in mind.

Notebook Three

Record 1 (1:49)
The Hunt for Proper Diction (Abandoned)
Context
An Epic Poem

Come here. Look, do you see that? There, past the small stand of hickory trees, past the cornfields baked the color of straw in the buttery sun, past the empty office buildings and the cracked asphalt of the downtown sidewalks. We're close enough now to smell the sickly sweet cloud from the corn syrup plant, to hear the train lowly moan through town. But mostly it's the view: a sky like shaved soap, ashes from imaginary bonfires floating in lazy gusts from the dingy brick warehouses on Third Street to the webbed clouds, the veiled sun, and the horizon of the next thousand years.

Welcome to Dayton, Ohio, Nineteen Something and Five (by the old reckoning), birthplace of aviation, home of Orville Wright, whose extant mansion sits on a small hill not far from our apartment; and of Hangar 18, reputed storage site for the Roswell, NM alien crash

remains; and of Wright-Patterson Air Force Base, where
the Bosnian peace talks were held. Origin, too, though
no real proof exists, of the Great Change. But we're not
here to speak of recent events. Our concern is a thing no
longer much accounted useful: history. Not history in
the old sense, of course, because we've done away with
that, and good riddance. Better to say *context*.

Few of us are left who remember the days before the
change. Which is why we have decided, before we take
our leave, that a record should be inscribed for those
among us still interested in peering through the lens of
time at the patterns imprinted on the palimpsest of
what we once called the past. We have no further use
for our memories, and we can't imagine any better
general use than as an artifact, a Thing, to use the old
nomenclature, or a Tool, in the modern parlance. So we
have set ourselves this task: to reproduce as faithfully as
possible, given the inherently liminal nature of human
recollection, the fabric of a certain (to our mind)
turning point in events, which went almost without
remark at the time and which, after a few decades of
tumult, proved crucial to the progress of our common
humanity.

No one who reads this now will need to be
reminded of the way in which our society changed, or
how quickly, and with what confusion and hope we
greeted the dawn of a new era in human relations. That
we can now trace this change to the collapse of the
entertainment industry in the third decade of the new
millennium is, we think, a widely shared view; we have
moved far and fast from such an inauspicious
beginning, through a global economic collapse, a period

of confusion and chaos, even violence and fear, to the slow dawn of realization that our nature itself had somehow subtly but dramatically changed, that we were no longer enchained by the petty desires of our individual ego and that, further, by liberating ourselves from that ego we need not destroy our individual essence, that we were enhanced by the connections that grew in place of our fetters.

We mention this only to prepare those who might wish to read further, and who did not live through those turbulent times (nor the turbulence preceding the turbulence), for the strange rhythms and language you will encounter here. Terms long out of use, references to people and places that no longer exist—more importantly, to forms and functions that no longer exist—you will find in abundance, but that is part of the reason we have decided to record them, before they pass out of all living memory. It may seem an odd thing to do—it *is* an odd thing to do—but you will perhaps be surprised that it was once the custom to record the thoughts and deeds of a particular person for the use of posterity. At least, in its initial intent. You will not be surprised that this practice swelled to absurd proportions not long before the change, and some will even remember the deluge of memoirs (that was the term), sometimes from children and pets, or sometimes ghost-written (another term) on behalf of these people or animals if they were not judged sufficiently skilled memoirists (may not have been an actual term).

What follows here has been extracted from a book we were engaged in writing at the time, a book we had been contracted to write—in other words, that we had promised to write in exchange for money, which as many will remember was the word for the currency then in use. While we have tried to the extent possible to expunge as many remnants of ego as we could, the ghosts of Capital I are everywhere in these pages, and for that we apologize. We were convinced, then, that what we were writing was important, that what we had to say would fall on receptive ears, and that, frankly, we would be lauded and rewarded for our ability to shed light on what, then, was an abstruse subject (and which is now merely irrelevant). In an irony that we would even then have appreciated, the importance of what we wrote now seems purely accidental—a footnote to what we considered our real subject: a specific sub-genre of rock music, then at its apex, soon to fall, for specific and general reasons, out of favor with the consumer.

You will also note a jejune obsession with the consumption of alcohol, a widespread practice of abusing which afflicted too many of us in those days, as we attempted to reach through habitual intoxication those altered states of being now obtainable easily by any of us through simple application of proper focus. We ask you to forgive us, as our ignorance had the best part of our better nature. Apart from that, we have tried to present an undiluted excerpt from a diluted time. We begin, as all stories must, with a tragedy.

Named after Jonathan Dayton, a U.S. Senator from New Jersey, who was one of four out-of-state worthies deeded the land—which occurs in the southwest corner of Ohio, about fifty miles north of the Kentucky border—in 1789, Dayton was first formed as a township in the winter of 1796–97, and incorporated in 1805. The area had originally been settled by different tribes of Indians over the millennia, some of whom left elaborate and imposing burial mounds (most famous is probably the Serpent Mound in Adams County, concerning which all sorts of occult theories have sprouted) which exist, still. Prostitution was legal until 1915—the city's most famous madam, Elizabeth Richter, better known as Lib Hedges, died in 1923 and is buried in Woodland Cemetery alongside the cream of Dayton's crop. Plagued over the years by periodic flooding of the Great Miami River, the town raised two million dollars in the aftermath of the catastrophic 1913 flood (which was followed by an equally disastrous fire) to help construct a series of five dams. Pictures of the flooding are obtainable with a minimum of digging at the Dayton Public Library.

In addition to the invention of the airplane by favorite sons Orville and Wilbur Wright, Dayton has contributed these several items to American culture: the cash register; welfare; ethyl gas; the portable electric generator; the electric ignition/electric self-starter; the original pop-top. We are justly proud of these inventions, if only because their legacy is a reminder of the sort of individual achievement no longer viable (or, perhaps better: no longer *desirable*). We were even more justly proud of them decades ago, when they were all we had left after an economic downturn that had severely depressed the entire region's economy. Nowadays, when no one bothers to study economics anymore (a lost art, and sadly so, we think), the causality of the downturn lies shrouded in a fog of meaningless terms and phrases—interest rates, inflationary pressures, job claims index, the Fed—and those of us old enough to remember can speak only to effects, which were certainly widespread, and noticeable. *Felix qui potuit rerum cognoscere causas.* We were never so lucky.

Most importantly, for our purposes, the general economic slump left downtown lying fallow. Which was good for us, for youngish people who disdained regular employment and liked to drink a lot and pretended to aspire to more important things than material success. Decay and emptiness once lent the area a seedy romance of the sort that engenders bad music and worse poetry. We had a lot of the former, not so much of the latter, because poetry was considered fey and affected by most Midwesterners. On winter afternoons, the late light snagging on the edges of a broken window high up in a deserted downtown church could make you a believer in nonreligious things.

Several decades ago, in the year we're thinking of, the church we're thinking of—an honestly majestic Roman Catholic semi-cathedral of stone—was torn down and replaced by a parking lot. A few general facts concerning Dayton in the decade before the last millennium: Population: 948,000 (including the General Metropolitan Area); median age: 32.9 (10.6% between 18 and 24); average annual income: $24,572; number of churches: 900; percentage of vacant office space: 22; number of drive-by BB gun shootings: 1; number of decent bars: 3; number of okay record stores: 3; number of rock bands: at least 100; number of decent rock bands: 2. Nicknamed the Gem City for obscure reasons, once called "an American microcosm" by a national magazine, Dayton was at that time largely dependent on two industries, auto manufacturing and defense, for its citizens' employment.

Although its proximity to the University of Dayton provided Brown Street with a vaguely collegiate air, very little of the usual "college town" atmosphere infected the relentlessly lowbrow town. UD was a Catholic-run school (Catholicism was a religion whose main themes were: belief in a trinity of Gods; belief in the teachings of Jesus Christ, filtered through the Apostle Paul, whose main writings can be found, still, in what used to be called the New Testament of what used to be called the Bible; and a somewhat perplexing opposition to any type of birth control), dominated by a conservative faculty and students who considered the town itself more or less grubby and beneath them. UD's inmates, in general, regarded the weekend keg party as the highest culture to which one might aspire. Natives with a shred of intelligence or ambition left town as soon as able. Those who remained were held in place either by inertia or by the lure of cheap rent and cheaper alcohol.

We never went to any of the other bars, which were more exclusively the province of the students, except occasionally to The Hangar, which opened at 6 a.m. to take advantage of the many third-shift factory workers in town (General Motors, mostly). These swarmed the bar from dawn until late morning, when they would slowly disperse like a cloud of impermeable alcoholic vapor. From time to time, when under the influence of various illicit substances, some few of us would find ourselves still conscious as the sun began its slow climb in the Midwest sky, we would stagger or sway over to The Hangar to join the crowds of weary workers slumped over their beers and shots. Which was never an uplifting vista.

We lived then, and still, in a large one-bedroom apartment in an old brick house, on the corner of Morton and Hickory Streets—about two hundred yards from the Hive—that had been divided into three similar spaces. We have a tin porch, rusting at the edges and intolerably hot when the sun beats down. The bricks, faded to a dusky yellowish-brown over the years, serve a little too well as insulation, meaning that in the summer the inside of the apartment remains sweltering until the very earliest hours of the morning. The bricks radiate heat even in deepest night; we sometimes wander out on the porch late and place the flat of our palms on the walls to feel their warmth.

There're three rooms and a smallish bathroom, all painted a sickly yellowish-brown, presumably to match the exterior. The ceilings are very high, which we like, and the windows, at least the ones which face the street (three facing Morton and two facing Hickory) are likewise tall and somewhat imposing. We've festooned them with strings of white Christmas lights which we never turn off. In the living room is a small desk, a busted mustard-colored couch, two similarly hued easy chairs, three rickety bookshelves, and a blue aluminum trunk which serves as a coffee table. The bedroom features our bed, two motel-room-style dressers, and a large dusty mirror. The kitchen has a gas stove, an ancient refrigerator, and a small folding table. Various carpet remnants, ugly dark red, are laid over the darkly stained hardwood floors. We're a bad housekeeper, in general. Although the apartment is usually neat, it's very rarely clean. There's a song called "Opalescent" by Sad Blue Moon which is also neat but not clean. If you listen to the song, imagine our apartment. Or don't. Either way, we still live here.

Notebook Four

Manuscript, unruled paper bound in brown leather, Box 113, File 5, the Wright Brothers Collection, Wright State University Archives, Dayton, OH. Temporarily relocated to Hickory Street Satellite.

1.

• Around noon took it into my head to determine the workings of Miss Beck's electric typewriter, which had been tormenting me by its presence since arriving less than two weeks ago. I took the thing apart with nothing more than a screwdriver, and had carefully spread its components on a sheet of newsprint on the floor of my laboratory when Miss Beck, returning from lunch, surprised me at my work and expressed a certain understandable dismay. It was agreed that if I could not successfully reassemble the machine by the end of the business day we would call the man from International Business Machines. However, engrossed as I was in my task and, sad to say, somewhat bewildered by the array of small springs and switches (many with no immediately apparent function) that turned out to be hiding inside, I was unable to finish the job in the agreed time. In fact, I only managed to further dismantle the device, so that it now resembles a puzzle of a typewriter. Miss Beck says the company man will be here in the morning, from Columbus, and in the meantime is rather cross at having to resort to her manual machine.

• I was always better at the inner workings of things, but I could never see the long view, the overall picture, the way Will did. More than thirty years gone I miss his perspective. Will would not have had it back together before me, but he would have had the sense not to take it apart in the first place. I cannot resist the lure of the smallest and most complex devices. A corollary: We developed lateral control of the wing-warping (the application of the lift balance) because of Will. I would not have thought of that.

• Another letter from Lindbergh. Insists that an autobiography would be a chance to set the record straight, to repair the damage wrought by Curtis and the Smithsonian crew. But I spent better than twenty-five years repairing that damage, and no longer have the energy to fight the calumnies and distortions provoked by greed and jealousy of our accomplishments. Perhaps I am guilty, too, of an untoward pride in those accomplishments, which after all amount to little more than the usual duties of a midwife.

Attention to detail was our only advantage, and ceaseless industry, which are fair uses of the gifts of divine Providence given to every man; our success therefore less the result of any arrogance or unseemly ambition than a reflection of God's glory made manifest in His humblest creation.

• Hard to believe that only fifty years ago, the very concept of powered flight was considered not only impossible but absurd, and moreover, to some, an effrontery to Nature. Whereas the pace of flight's development in that time has so accelerated that the terrible war just concluded was altered in its balance and duration considerably by the application of the basic principles established by my brother and me. Oppenheimer grew to regret the atomic bomb he had labored for so long to construct; but it was my invention that delivered his device. Who bears the greater responsibility?

2.

• Difficult sleep last night, dreams of flying again. Always the same scenario: the crash with Lt. Selfridge. The shudder of the plane, and sudden swift descent. Smack of the green earth. There's a detached, newsreel quality to the dream, very similar to how the actual event filtered through my senses. The twisted fabric of the wings at a crazy angle above my head, acrid smell of the still-sputtering engine, clumps of Virginia turf gouged by the iron bars of the frame. I'm trapped at the controls, the absurdly complicated but precise controls, while men work frantically to lift the wreckage and free me. If I strain my neck, which isn't easy because of the injury to my back, I can see a cluster around the prone body of Selfridge, who was thrown clear on impact. The first death by airplane. I remember the sharp crack of the overstressed propeller announcing our doom, the immediate wobble of the craft, the downwards spiral. I struggled to regain control but we quickly fell, too quickly for me to register the danger. I felt nothing, not even pain, for several days. In my dream, I see Selfridge's gray eyes staring back at me, calmly, with a cold accusing gleam. I'm not even sure he had gray eyes. There's so much I cannot remember clearly, so much that's been lost. Selfridge was a last-minute substitution for old Charlie Taylor. His loss I could not have borne.

• Had we not cracked flight's stubborn code, someone else would have, and soon, and almost did. If we had the advantage in anything, it was in common sense.

• I have other dreams of flying, too, similar to the daydreams of my youth, when manned flight was still a fantasy only. These are my favorite, because they come closest to the original feeling, when I would lie in bed unable to sleep with the excitement over our latest discovery, however small, which brought us that much nearer to our goal. The imagined flights I took those sleepless nights, in their purity and sustained thrill, were more real to me, then, than the memory of our many actual successes, now. The experience itself never matched the anticipation of that experience. I suppose what I mean to say is that the enabling flight was one of fancy and not of iron and linen, elevator and rudder, wing and warp. The ground rushing beneath me during those early experiments was formless and abstract as it had never been in my reverie of flight. I'm not sure I ever fully adjusted to that initial disappointment.

3.

• When we first went around Europe demonstrating our Flyer, the crowds were enormous, frighteningly so. In Berlin, nearly 200,000 people. I flew nineteen times from the military parade grounds there, Tempelhof Field, to Potsdam and back. I took the Crown Prince on a fifteen-minute flight, and he gave me his stickpin. Met the Kaiser—this was before the war, of course. When I look back on that exhilarating period of my life, a great sadness overtakes me, not for the passing of such excitement, but for the loss of those without whom the experience would have meant nothing. Mother, of course, but bless her, she passed many years before our labors bore fruit. Dear Will first, then the bishop, and last of all K., whose death, while devastating, hurt less than her defection by marriage three years prior. I have wasted many hours in the twenty years since with self-recrimination, but no matter how abjectly I prostrate myself before the altar of regret, I cannot wipe clean my heart. She was everything to me, and when she left I shunned her. The sight of her lying on her Oberlin—so far from home!—deathbed, the painful wheezing of her breath, unable to speak, eyes wet with tears . . . and I said nothing. I forgave no one. I was cold and uncaring, and could think only of the slight to myself, that I had been left alone. She left me twice, and neither time did I say goodbye.

• I was closer to K. than to anyone, even Will. It is easier, sometimes, to discuss introspective matters with a woman, especially one in whom the faculties of understanding were so advanced. K. understood what there is to understand of me, which is, centrally, that I have always preferred the small life to the important one. Events were thrust upon me by the success of our invention, but I never enjoyed myself without the company of such of my family as could make the voyage. Chief among these, always, K. My sister was one of the first women to fly, not many people remember that. At Pau, in 1909, I believe. There's a picture of it somewhere. Wilbur took her up. She grasped the strut so hard with her little white-gloved hand I thought she might tear it right out of the base. She wore a billowy white kerchief over her hat, and her customary polka-dotted veil, which I never liked. Made her face look like she had the pox. Suppose it was the fashion for ladies at the time, however. Not that K. was caught up in that nonsense, but when we spent time in Paris, around the same period, I did notice various small additions to her wardrobe. Hard to resist the example of the glamorous *parisiennes*.

• When we made the move from Hawthorn Street to Hawthorn Hill, to Albion, I'm not sure K. entirely approved. We had lived our whole lives on Hawthorn Street, but with both Father and Mother gone, and then Will, and Lorin and Reuch married and moved away, the place resembled less to me the home of my upbringing and more the museum it would eventually become. When Ford came and wanted the house and the bicycle shop for his Greenfield Village, I was glad to be rid of both. Memory is far richer than the physical evidence of the past, in any case. But K. always claimed to be happier on Hawthorn Street than ever after. I have grown used to Albion, and it has been my home longer than any other. But it will never replace our familial home in my affections, for the simple reason that a house is not merely a con-struction of wood and bricks, but of the bonds between parent and child, and brother and sister. I can remember sitting on the front porch at Hawthorn Street with K. when we were very young, perhaps I was ten, which would have made her seven. It was summer, and late in the evening, and the most extraordinary thing about late summer evenings in this part of the country is the massing of fireflies all along the hedgerows and bushes and even in the tangled ivy growing up the bricks of the hardware store opposite our house. There are few sights on earth more peaceful, and more beautiful, than the winking of these fluorescent armies as they move, together yet separate, over the cooling earth at sunset. K. ran from one end of the porch to the other, leaning over the railing, pointing at one and then another and another, shrieking with happiness, as if to miss one were to miss them all. Her joy turned quickly to tears when she accidentally crushed one of the poor insects in her tiny hand.

• I am a religious man, but not a reflective man. I believe that one should conduct one's life in accordance with the principles inscribed in the Bible. I recognize that despite my attempts to lead a virtuous life, I am a sinner, and repent of my many sins, and hope that Our Lord Jesus Christ will find room in His infinite heart to forgive my transgressions. I believe that my repentance, if sincere and heartfelt, will enable me to enter the Kingdom of Heaven when I die. I am a religious man, but not a reflective man. It is with full knowledge of the requirements of my faith that I say I would trade the Kingdom of

Heaven without a moment's hesitation to have her by my side right now.

4.

• Writing from my specially constructed chair at night, about 9:30. There is nothing I hate more than enforced idleness. Disabled by a sciatic flare-up—more common, these days, and more troubling—I have spent the better part of the day designing a more efficient vacuum system for Hawthorn Hill. The problem, I now believe, was in the pinions for the pump mechanism, which were too small and inflexible to provide the necessary leverage. I have designed a new pinion, to be constructed from aluminum rather than stainless steel.

• I rarely fall ill, but whenever I do I am put in mind of the terrible time fifty years or so ago when I contracted typhoid fever. I was bedridden for nearly six weeks, unconscious or delirious for over four. K. and Will took turns feeding me milk and broth, to which ministrations I was nearly insensible. Even when the fever finally broke, I was too weak to return to the bicycle shop for some few more weeks. This was about the time, in 1896 or so, that Will and I first undertook seriously to look into the problem of flight. Lilienthal's death set Will thinking, coupled with a banal remark I am supposed to have made in my delirium: "Mark the buzzards circling." Our researches, soon thereafter, into matters ornithological received its initial spark from that febrile outburst, which led, before long, to Pettigrew's book, the source of all our later investigations. Inconceivable that man could not achieve on a larger scale what God had provided for His winged creatures. Nothing worthwhile ever comes easy, and anything useful runs up against the usual gamut of fools and knaves. Had I not been taken ill just then, had notice of Lilienthal's death not appeared in our local wire service, had I not uttered a random remark that reminded Will of our childhood fascination with the toy helicopter and with the romantic idea of flight— had any one of these things not happened, or had they happened at a different time or in a different order, we would not have been the first to invent the airplane. We would not even have been the first to discover wing-warping. The achievement, I have said before, was an achievement of all mankind, the massed learning of every preceding student an enabling weight, and one that would have succeeded quite without us if necessary. The time had come to advance to the level of manned flight. That is quite evident. Whatever principle drives history forward chose us as its random instrument. Sometimes I wish God had chosen someone else, though.

• I am seventy-six years old. Every once in a while some would-be biographer writes to pester me with the same question: Is there anything you regret? I answer, always, the same. I regret nothing except the time spent answering fool questions. Kelly, who started as a friend, made an enemy of me by including all sorts of pointless conjecture in his book. I tried to keep him to the facts, but there's something about a writer that makes him want to get inside a fellow's head and find out exactly what he's thinking. I understand the impulse, it's doubtless related to the impulse that drove me to take apart Miss Beck's typewriter. But you cannot ascribe thoughts to another human being without that person's knowledge or permission. Such fancy inevitably distorts the true record of events, the sequence and development of ideas, the intricate pattern underlying and leading to the final inspiration. One cannot see into another's heart and mind. That insight is left to God alone.

- In truth, I do have regrets. I regret, as I've had cause to reflect recently, the treatment K. received from me after declaring her intention to marry. I regret, moreover, never having married, myself, or rather never having found one to whom I might make such a commitment of life, love, and property. While I might argue that my work consumed so much of my being that the meager portion left over would, however bound by devotion, have made me a poor a husband, who knows what joys might have ensued from a union of my own, and from children of my own issue?

- I helped invent the airplane, true. I gave men wings. But I could not lift my own heart above ground level.

Notebook Five

The setting sun hung like a viscous, glowing pear low in the pale sky, occluded from time to time by wispy strands of gold-and-gray-tinged clouds. Slender, sinuous Mary Valentine selected from the bunch of keys in her hand the one, color-coded with an indelible red marker, that slid with some effort the ancient dead bolt into its groove and permitted her to swing open the heavy door on its tired heels and exit the musty cool of the store's interior. In the sunset heat she turned and performed a reverse image of the same sequence, a movie rewinding in a mirror.

She was dressed in a heavy dark gray sweater and black jeans, as usual during the winter months. She had short, bright blond, tousled hair, sometimes held in place with a couple of cheap ornamented hairclips (mock tortoiseshell, ironic ivory). Around her neck was wrapped a robin's-egg-blue cashmere scarf. Her shoes were open-toed, with short wooden heels that clacked noisily on the veiny sidewalk as she crossed the street back to her apartment.

Mary hadn't taken any speed since before work, and was feeling strung out and hollow. She walked up one flight of carpeted stairs, unlocked and opened the gray-painted door, and entered the small room, divided neatly in two by a Japanese screen, behind which lay an old mattress piled with magazines and disheveled sheets. She decided to take a bath, and stripped off her clothes while running the water, leaving them in a heap next to the bathtub. From a drawer next to the bathroom sink she took a tiny plastic baglet half-filled with a white powder, and poured a little out on the cover of a paperback lying on the counter next to the sink amid a jumble of cosmetics and costume jewelry. Perched on the edge of the toilet, she arranged the pile into a short fat line with the unfolded edge of a matchbook, and, taking a bit of plastic straw scissored from its now-discarded parent, snorted the line with her left nostril.

"Goodness," she exclaimed, straightening, as the crystal meth burned into her nasal passages. She sniffed twice, as if trying to identify the stale smell inhabiting her discarded clothing, and shivered her naked shoulders. Her eyes teared, and she wiped them one at a time with the back of each hand.

Mary stepped into the bathtub, hardly sensible to the scalding heat. Her hands and feet tingled pleasantly as she sank up to her neck in the soapy water. She loved floating, her limbs light in the water's buoyant grip, sweat beading on her upper lip and at her temples, running in uneven rivulets from forehead to chin, to drop at irregular intervals into the garland of suds around her neck.

She sat soaking with her eyes closed for some time. Upon opening them, Mary gazed blankly at the tiles of the bathroom wall, sea-green and slick with soap scum. The wall clock in the next room ticked audibly as she lay still, gazing. At length she sighed, and shifted to a sitting position. The suds slid down her shoulders and arms to the steaming water. She drew her legs to her chest, running her hands down the length of her shins and over her calves to gauge the growth of stubble, and reached for the razor perched on the sill of the tub. Around her upper left arm wound the dull green band of a tattoo, a reproduction of the border around her favorite edition of the I Ching.

Propping her right foot on the rim near the faucet, Mary moved the razor over the smooth curve of her calf, using the soapy foam as lubricant. When she reached the kneecap area, she was careful to navigate around a narrowly-striped pattern of scar tissue, the result of having tried to hop on Joe Smallman's back two weeks ago outside the Hive. She smiled at the memory of tumbling from Joe's thin shoulders, taking him down, too, both falling to the sidewalk in a tangle of flapping limbs, too drunk to register the bruises and abrasions until the next day's rueful inventory. Joe got the worst of it, twisting his left ankle badly. When he stopped by the store earlier today, she recalled, he was still limping.

Distracted by her reverie, Mary's hand slipped and she sliced into her shin. She watched the trickle of blood trail down her leg with detached interest. Blood is thicker than water, she thought, but the body is mostly water. And so blood is mostly water.

Having finished her legs, Mary gave a cursory scrape to her axillae, extending each arm skyward with unself-conscious grace. She then examined the pilosity of her pelvic area by resting her weight on her elbows and thrusting upwards through the bathwater. Mary was not overly fussy with regard to pubic topiary. If that was what boys wanted, she thought, they could try Rosy Cramp, who was rumored to shave her stuff completely, possibly because of crabs. She preferred a more expansive growth, and saw nothing now that required trimming or alteration.

Her awkward position provoked a memory of sex, and she flushed with sudden heat that compounded the flush from the heat of the bath. His face there, she remembered. She moved her fingers through the soft hairs slowly. The pang of regret in her stomach was related to the remembered desire, but its greater component was the loss of a deeper, more permanent connection, the removal of which had been unaccompanied by the usual post-coital relief and self-disgust.

Occasional bouts of intensity in her emotional life irritated Mary. She sat up and splashed water over her face, then reached for the bar of blue soap caked to the tub's rim near the hot water cock.

If tonight were not the same, if something different and definite were to happen, she thought, slouched on her mattress flipping through the pages of her sketchbook, I would have to be the one. After so long of pretending. On the one hand something would happen and I wouldn't be so bored. On the other my heart might get rebroken, a thing I could not bear.

She took a red drawing pencil and filled in the outline of a cartoon heart she had unconsciously outlined. The main point is to get out of this dreary place. Sometimes I try too hard to keep my heart out of the way, and then sometimes I don't even know if my heart works properly. As in, can I love someone completely or do I care too much about keeping my options open? Mistake I made with Michael, but also his mistake. We both made the same mistake. Isn't that more evidence of our compatibility?

She laughed, or made a noise like a laugh that almost immediately brought tears to her eyes. Mary took a black drawing pencil and scored heavily the red cartoon heart in her sketchbook. I am ridiculously literal. Tonight I will dress literally and go to the bar literally and avoid most of the people I know literally and see if a metaphor happens.

Mary sighed and rolled over on her back. She folded her arms behind her head and closed her eyes. Can see every bland facet of this room with eyes closed. If I were blind I could walk across the street to the store, walk back, use the telephone to order food and drugs. Does that mean a life? The way I've constructed my life, it could be lived by a blind person. Could even find my way to the Hive. Think of the more free drinks out of pity for the poor blind girl.

She couldn't remain still for long because of the speed. Took the pillow and hugged it against her abdomen, curling sideways into the dirty sheets, the smell of them both repellent and comforting. That girl Amanda and her stupid rocks. Probably the right idea. Wish I could get interested in something, a language or a leap of faith, but everything bores me to giggles.

Someone like Joe, works in record store for three

maybe four years now out of school, doesn't seem to mind. But even he has ambition, to open his own store. What if a person doesn't have ambition? Not in the ordinary sense like having buckets of money without having to work. But ambition to be, in any sense other than in relation to another person. I don't stand alone and I don't want to stand alone because I don't know what that would mean: alone. Afraid I would stop existing. Not that existence itself is a peach, but the devil you know, and so on.

Mary, restless, stood up from her mattress and walked over to the small table where her phone was positioned next to a dusty glass filled with drawing pencils and brushes. In a drug-induced smog she had one very long night painted her phone in hideous fluorescent colors. He never said the word. I never said the word. You say the word and the abstract's set in concrete. But if I had said the word, would he have said the word back? And if he had, would that be because he felt obliged, or just *felt*?

These are all good reasons, thought Mary, never to say words. All words lead to trouble: why I never read books. He reads all the time, the same books from school I skipped or lied or flirted my way through to my degree. Don't trust a man who reads too much. Self-involved. Exclusionary. Just Michael and his little thought world like those helium balloons that one night after we first started going out. Just air that makes you sound silly when you talk.

She picked up the phone's handset and scrolled through the list of recent callers. Boy, boy, wrong number, boy, work, boy. None of them the right boy because the right boy never calls, never used to call, which is a game you play when you're scared. Know because I never call unless something means nothing, or I need something from someone. Because in other situations I'm scared, like everybody. Why I try to keep other situations to a manageable few.

Mary Valentine returned the handset to its cradle. There are things you have to learn to get by, and I have learned them all, she thought. I shall illustrate. Out loud Mary said these words: "I shall illustrate." Dressed in a white T-shirt and boys' briefs, she walked over to the rack where her clothes hung in disarray, a scrum of mismatched colors, flimsy fabrics draped over heavier, darker items. Pulled a periwinkle-green skirt from the rack, dislodging a teal sweater and a gray, long-sleeved wool-blend shirt.

She stepped into the skirt, pulled it up around her waist, and zipped the side zipper. Then she pulled the T-shirt over her head and slung it across the room onto the bed. It's too cold for this skirt, which is the reason for wearing it, she thought. Then bent down and picked the teal sweater from the floor, turned and held the sweater against her chest, appraising in the mirror tacked to the back of her front door. You wear a skirt when it's too cold, no one else will wear a skirt. This provides immediate access to easier targets, the boys whose brains are frozen and wallets are humid with desire.

She dropped the sweater at her feet, turned back to the rack, and unlooped a white bra from a hanger. Most of the time for drinks you have to flirt or even more, although comes a point where the flirting is no longer just flirting, which is how I know I've had enough drinks. Problem being: I enjoy the part where flirting is no longer just flirting. Mary hooked the bra in back, using both hands to adjust the hooks properly, then adjusted the front so that her breasts sat comfortably. My name is Mary Valentine, and I am an addict. Addicted to the thrill of conquest, to confirmation of my ability to attract. The rest is motion only, silent *e*. Sometimes pleasure, sometimes pain, but simple, uncomplicated, inhuman. As stave against boredom, keep two on a string any given time, more thrill in pretending to avoid or avoiding or trying to conceal the one from the other or more than other. Like hide-and-seek, where getting caught is the point, and most of the fun.

But with Kurt, there's no real flirting except the kind all humans perform, called charm. In his way charming, and beneath or behind the aloofness, the old-fashioned courtesy which is even more funny but at the same time charming. With him I can be charming, too, or seems like charming, because removed from sexual sphere. And why is that? Because I have no interest, but he can't know that: no. He has no interest, and I can tell. And he knows I can tell. No explicit statement of uninterest, but in his presence I'm disarmed. Intensely liberating. He buys me drinks anyway.

Some grumble Kurt's got motives, an angle, too good to be true, perhaps angling for demotic credibility by pretending to hang with the people. But how can you say *too good to be true* about a guy that rich and famous already, and who never asks for a favor, not one, ever, and only's ever kind no matter what. What angle, however oblique, draws itself with such bold, uncomplicated lines?

Mary shrugged into the teal sweater, pulling along the bottom edge to smooth wrinkles. She walked into the bathroom, flipping on the light switch to examine her face in the mirrored medicine chest. Skin's a little mottled from the speed, she thought, applying a thin coat of foundation from a nearly empty jar. Why is the Hive so well-lighted? Bars are meant to be dark. Meant to conceal secrets and possibly revelations. She unscrewed a slim tube of lipstick and drew a rosy line across her lips, blotted with a square of toilet paper.

Walking out of the bathroom, she went to the window where winter dark had descended and the bluish tint of streetlight illuminated people walking by below, bundled against the cold. You can see their shadows more clearly than their features. The outline of a person's probably a true indicator. When you throw in expressions and ugly lies you just end up more confused. Are all of these as confused and as lost and as unutterably alone as me? The sudden gush of melancholy reduced Mary to giggles.

She shook her head and moved away from the window, covering her mouth, an oddly girlish gesture for an oddly girlish girl. He wasn't so famous, I'd marry him. He wouldn't have me. But I'd marry him. The perfect husband, always least suitable of suitors. You wouldn't guess, but I'd make a perfect wife. Unfaithful, probably, but discreet, and uncomplaining, and supportive. Ask you to keep me in food and clothes and a car and house, that's all. Will use my powers of sexuality to ensure that when you want me, I will be difficult to lure, so you will always want me. Not always as in all the time, but as in continuously over the long stretch of years before I decay and we no longer use sex as currency.

She took the robin's-egg-blue scarf from the hook on the back of the front door, started to turn the knob, started to leave, to go out, paused.

The right skirt? Black absorbs more heat. Absorbs or attracts? The difference is important.

Notebook Six

Record 2 (5:11)
The Calling
Typology I
Aesthetics of Alt-Rock

All rock is divided into three parts: repetition, repetition, repetition.
—Stanley Shorbuck, I *Shit You Not: A Rational Guide to Irrational Music* (Vintage Classics of Rock Criticism, 1989)

Once upon a time, we were offered the world. We turned the world down, of course. That's just our nature, we don't like to be burdened, though we thought at the time our motives were nobler. We thought our refusal had a philosophical underpinning, a rejection of transitory *gloria mundi* in favor of enduring verities.

We're referring to a tiny subset of popular culture in the early 1990s, a community—though one of the important traits of this community was that it refused to be identified as such—that came to be known (after it had ceased to exist in any meaningful way) as "alternative," defined to a certain extent by the style of music to which it listened.

The history of alternative music dates back to the punk rock eruption of the mid- to late-'70s, and even before that, back to the counter-countercultural movements of the early- and mid-'60s (La Monte Young, Fluxus, Warhol, and the Velvets, etc.), and before that, still, to the weirder Beat offshoots and possibly even to post-WWII jazz culture (or at least many alternative types in the time of our subcultural flowering liked to affect an interest in bebop). The history of alternative culture could be read as an attempt by a small group of similarly middle-class, educated people to come to terms with its basic, and basically unalterable, lameness. Of course, some things of real beauty were created within this environment, as inevitably happens when enough people sit around with enough drugs and no pressing need to work for a living. You can see, though, how such a group, when presented with the world, would feel highly ambivalent and unworthy of such a gift. The idea behind us— behind our culture-that-would-not-be-named—was an enormous sense of entitlement-deficit, after all. Our credo was lifted from Yeats's "Second Coming": "*The best lack all conviction while the worst, Are full of passionate intensity.*"

We eventually self-destructed, shattered into ineffectual fragments, became useless and frustrated and bitter and hopeless. This you could probably have seen coming, and, in an unfairly simplistic way, can be reduced to one word: money. As soon as the big record companies sensed or decided that hitherto hidden or underground artists might also harbor hidden riches, the game was more or less over. Took us a few years of compromise and rejection (by the public, by the companies, by ourselves) to understand that easy lesson. By the time we did, it was too late for us. A new sensibility gripped the music business, frustrated with the anti-star mentality of its biggest artists; many of those same artists, unused to any attempt to exercise control over the content or presentation of their music, soured on the major label experience and were either dropped and went back to their underground hideouts, or dropped themselves and did the same, even in rare cases disbanding for good, having decided that careerism was not a good ploy for a musician with artistic pretensions. The music business then moved on to molded and preformed pop acts who were more easily controlled, and began to experience a decline from which it may never recover.

When we think back to those years, we mostly remember the drinking. We drank a lot then, and we weren't the only one. The reckless consumption of alcohol was a basic feature of our social life, the centrifugal force that kept us together. At the time, we had arranged a host of theories in defense of our drinking: that an altered consciousness was necessary for a proper appreciation of the rock experience; that alcohol's proven health benefits outweighed any supposed drawbacks; that people who didn't drink were not to be trusted; that without alcohol life was not worth living.

We don't drink anymore, but we are not against

drinking in principle. Just the opposite, we are very pro-drinking. We understand completely and love dearly those people for whom drinking is a centerpiece of their lives, and always will be until they die (from drinking). We realize this is an old-fashioned view, long-debunked and held in contempt by adherents of addiction support groups and a society conditioned to view heavy drinking as pathetic and incontrovertibly lousy for you. But we cannot help the way that booze appeals to every still-functioning sense we own, on both metaphorical and actual levels. We love bars, we love everything about them except the plastered assholes who sometimes inhabit them, not excluding ourself. But there's nothing as bathos-ridden as a rundown bar in the middle of the afternoon with snow drifting past the grimy windows. Do you know what we mean? Ripped red vinyl booths, tables graffitied with pens or penknives or the acid drool of broken-hearted drunks, jukeboxes that play pop hits or obscure Las Vegas bump-and-grind songs from the early '60s. It doesn't matter what songs. The music in bars is always soundtrack music, carrying as many shades of emotion as the drinking heart is capable of sustaining, probably an infinite number, though those infinite shades are compressed within an intolerably finite moment of joy, or intense sadness. The ability to visit extremes of human feeling is the great thing that the conjunction of music/booze confers upon the regular drinker. The inability to render those emotions useful in the context of quotidian life is the awful, the finally defeating thing about the music/booze conjunction. When you're drunk, and you hear a great song, your expectations are inevitably raised. You're granted in that instant a glimpse of another life, with a pervading amber tint not merely of sound and vision but of texture and emotional tone. Everything goes gentle, and you can't move because the joy inside you is trying to escape. (This happens most forcefully at moments of black despair.) It is the most perfect feeling possible, and it happens not because of music or booze but because something larger than life is trying to use this moment of complete receptivity produced by the music/booze intersect to tell you something ineffable, and ineffably important.

A minute later, the feeling passes and you want to hit someone. If you're not the physical type, you will, like us, lash out in brutal/cowardly passive-aggressive ways at whomever happens to be nearest. The cruelest thing about fighting with your friends in a bar is not the public display of your worst character traits but the way those traits always seem, upon reflection, to be the truest expression of your always-shifting notion of selfhood.

That's the obverse of the drinking paradigm; the skin of self-disgust that covers your life, that colors every word or action you attempt whether sober or drunk. Feeling hopeless, you drink, which makes you feel transiently hopeful. The removal of that fleeting certitude— by ineluctable sobriety—destroys you. Pulls you down farther than you can imagine crawling back, which feeling has charms of its own. That's the thing with drunks: We don't drink to feel better, we drink to feel.

Somewhere between the time of great drinking and the

present moment—not long, but long enough—we were engaged to write a book about our life in rock. The book was not meant to be about us, you understand, but about the things we had done and witnessed that involved book-worthy people or events. The idea was not our idea, and would never have occurred to us independently, but was handed down from above, or up from below, choose your poison. We were minding our own business, which consisted at that time of not much: desultory research and writing for our Orville Wright biography (about which, more soon), and a lot of sitting around rethinking our decision to quit playing in the rock band that had provided us with the material to write a book about our life in rock—shall we call that irony? (Will have to consult our editor about shadings in the irony area; on second thought, will not call editor because we are, for reasons [again] soon to be revealed, avoiding our editor)—when we suddenly acquired a literary agent. We acquired an agent by mistake—that's to say, not accidentally, but by making a mistake we rarely made: We answered the phone. And while at first we thought it would be funny—telling people we had an agent, saying we would have to check with our agent before going to buy a round of drinks, complaining that our agent won't leave us alone—the joke, as with all good jokes, turned out to be on us.

Because, as it turns out, our agent *won't* leave us alone. We think she's in love with us, which is fine, even sweet, but she's a 250-pound Jewish girl from Long Island with one eye and we are a superficial Midwestern prick with four. It would never work. Our one-eyed agent called us up almost exactly a year ago, about two months after we officially quit Whiskey Ships, which is the name of the band we used to play guitar in, not lead guitar but lead rhythm, if there is such a thing. We were a very good, even great band, but we weren't very good musicians. We quit, and then one day around 3:00 in the afternoon Gail called.

"Is this Trip?" asked Gail, who has a not-unpleasant, flat, nasally voice, almost motherly sounding.

"Yes."

"Trip Ryvvers, from Whiskey Ships?"

"Uh, uh-huh." We were starting to tense up. We'd been receiving a number of bill collector calls, and the collectors had begun resorting to just this sort of fake-chummy tactic, doing just enough research on us to put us off guard, make us think there was no way a bill collector could have heard of Whiskey Ships, who only barely sold a hundred thousand copies of any one record, and hardly ever appeared on TV or got played on the radio, and even if by some miracle they had heard of us, the odds of their knowing the names of even one band member, especially a fairly anonymous guitarist who didn't write songs except for on one EP and a couple of cowrites for which we still hadn't received a dime of publishing money, were extremely slim. It was the very unlikelihood of any bill collector having access to this kind of information that made us think we might be dealing with one.

"Oh my God, this is so great!" squealed Gail, who turned out not to be a bill collector, but a literary agent from New York City, who not only knew of our band but claimed to have met us.

"You probably don't remember. It was backstage at the New York festival, the one out at Randall's Island, where you guys were playing, and Rooftop Kings, and Frail. That one. It was back by your trailer. You were talking to the guy from Five Angry Jews. Ring a bell?"

Because we have no way of knowing at what future time you may be reading these words, and because we assume that the words "Rooftop Kings" will mean nothing as a cultural signifier, because the band was not very good and will not be remembered for very long, we will explain that any and all references to bands or persons with which readers are unfamiliar may be passed over without worry. They are tokens, merely, and mean nothing, or maybe a little something, but usually that something will be a joke the humor of which is so ephemeral it needn't trouble you if you miss it. So don't worry. Half the band names we have made up anyway because we couldn't remember the real band name and the imperfectly remembered name seemed more appropriate. This goes double for people's names, too, some of which may be ciphers (even when historical names are used) for actual people, some of which may not exist, and some of which, like Gail, for instance, may just be ordinary real human beings who happen to figure into the story in question.

"No, uh . . . no," we replied to Gail's question about whether we remembered meeting her. We didn't remember for one of two reasons: 1) We were drunk. 2) She was lying.

Number two's the most likely explanation, believe it or not. First of all, we have a near-eidetic memory for names which only increases when drunk, so the odds of our not remembering Gail's name had we actually met her backstage at a rock festival in the mid-'90s were slim. In addition, the details she used to lend her story verisimilitude, while plausible enough, had a generalized, too-obvious quality. They had the aura of specificity but lacked true detail, and the circumstances she sketched out could have occurred at pretty much any large festival-type show in any geographic location over a three- or four-year span.

So she lied, as many people do when they want something from someone but don't want to seem like they want something. She lied to make the transition easier from saying hello to pitching her idea, which was for us to write a book based on our "experiences." The idea, especially since we could practically see her making quotation marks with her fingers, naturally repelled us at first, and then, as with all things that we find repellent at first, sprouted claws, attached itself to the inside of our throat, grew irresistible. We became, within a very short time, insanely attracted to the idea of writing a book about our "experiences." We were not sure at that point what those experiences were or how we would go about organizing them into a coherent format, but these were not things with which in general we concerned ourself in those days anyway. We may as well confess that we became insanely attracted to the idea of writing a book as soon as Gail uttered the word "advance."

"Advance" is a word musicians are very familiar with, usually to their eventual dismay, as in the music business it's a synonym for "devious way the record company gets you in their debt so you feel guilty about not working as hard as you possibly can every single day of your foreshortened life to pay back the absurd amount of money the company spent helping you make and promote your record." We knew that, but we also knew that we had not worked in six months and had currently neither prospects for work nor desire to work. (In addition, certain rumblings in our personal life were rapidly nearing the eruptive stage, so we were maybe in the mood for distraction.) We had done some writing, off and on (more off than on), for a few general interest magazines both before and during our tenure in Whiskey Ships, which was how Gail came to the somewhat hasty conclusion that we might be able to parse the complexities of book writing. What she did not know is that we have since the age of twenty-three been working on a biography of Orville Wright, the co-inventor of flight and native Daytonian, and that we're now up to Chapter 14. It's got all kinds of new revelations, based on material we unearthed at the Wright State Library while we were still a T.A. there, in our first year of post-grad work in the history department. (We quit before our second year out of what we like to call boredom.) We managed to borrow a milk crate's worth of notebooks which turned out to be Orville's secret written-in-code diary, which had lain undisturbed for years, misidentified as his schoolboy Greek and Latin exercises.

Our point is that we know how to write a book, which is a thing Gail did not know when she offered her services to shop around the proposal for a book about our "experiences" (we'll drop the quotation marks soon, we promise.) There's also the not entirely ancillary point that in mulling over Gail's phone call, her notion that our as-yet-barely-lived life might have value, not just in an abstract sense but actual monetary value, provided us with a fillip of pride. We were not worthless, despite what our soon-to-be ex-girlfriend had recently told us, if someone would pay money for the story of at least a part of our life. As you can imagine, the more we thought about it, the more depressed we got, and as a result found it necessary to get even drunker than usual, which meant having to sell off another small piece of our record collection, which was basically a weekly or twice-weekly occurrence at that point. And then after we got even drunker than usual, we ended up trying to make out with Mary Valentine again. We may have done more than just try to kiss her, there may have been confessional words spoken—in the clear light of sobriety we're almost sure there must have been—shameful, dishonest words about undying love and the skin-cleansing properties of certain love-related fluids. We may also have used the line, "Like all poets, I am an inarticulate man," which we read somewhere was a line Joyce had used on Nora, early on. We're fairly confident that pronouncing the word "inarticulate" after fifteen or twenty strong whiskey drinks is the definition of inarticulate, as well as of several other less complimentary words.

After sobering up, which is as deceptively easy a prepositional phrase as we will ever write (the world of hurt contained within the one word "sobering" deserves a book of its own, a book we may well one day write), we reconsidered. It now seemed to us, or rather began to seem as the throbbing in our temples receded under the influence of a dozen ibuprofen, that a book about our life might serve as proof that our life had not been entirely wasted. After all, look, here's a book! This thought enabled us to get up for the first time that day, which was a mistake, as we almost immediately felt nauseated, and had to lurch back to our one piece of decent furniture, the bed.

As we lay in bed thinking about our bed, the phone rang, forcing us to get out of bed and grab the phone and get back into bed. We almost missed the call. It was Gail (we knew it would be Gail), and we said yes, we would like her to shop the proposal for a book about our experiences to various publishers. What we neglected to consider when answering Gail's phone call was that this book proposal would not, however much we might wish otherwise, write itself, which meant that before we could receive an advance we would have to actually come up with what Gail now terrifyingly described to us as "nothing major, a sample chapter and an outline, maybe twenty-five pages." The prospect of writing twenty-five pages about anything except the concept of wing-warping by which Orville and Wilbur Wright solved—without the benefit of government funding or even college education—the problem of heavier-than-air flight seemed not just painfully difficult but absurd. We didn't understand why Gail couldn't just call up one of these publishers and promise them that we were going to write a very enter-taining book about our experiences. Based on our agent's verbal assurances, said publisher would then forward us a check that would fund our drinking for as much as a year, which is the longest stretch of time we were capable at that time of imagining.

When it became clear that this was not going to happen, we set about in that section of the day we came to think of as our "sober window," a not-inconsiderable slice of daylight extending from somewhere around noon, which is when we would generally wake up, until 9 or 10 at night, when we would go to the bar, working on what became quickly known among our group of friends as "Trip's book proposal." Our friends were not notable for their imaginative powers. It's not what they were good at. What they were good at, drinking, was why they were our friends.

> All rock is artifice—artifice is the basis of at least the kind of art that anyone wants to see, hear, feel; to the extent that this artifice succeeds in creating an alternate "reality" convincing and/or illuminating enough to sustain the attention of the listener, it can be said to have succeeded. Success in rock is therefore measurable by the depth and duration of the enchantment it creates. So maybe it's more accurate to say that rock is magic.
> —Shorbuck, op. cit.

We figured that if we were going to write a book proposal, we might as well write a book proposal designed to produce the largest possible advance. In order to do that, we would have to promise, in the proposal, to deliver things—revelations, exposés, scintillations of gossip, bouquets of innuendo—concerning the demi-celebrities with which we had been associated over the years. Because we have no soul, we went ahead and promised to deliver these things, despite the fact that we had no intention of fulfilling delivery, and despite the further fact that even if we had intended to deliver the promised material, we couldn't. There were no revelations, exposés, any of that stuff, nothing. Or if there were, they happened outside our purview, or while we were passed out. We did not let this inconvenient truth stop us from adumbrating the fantastic stories of debauchery and heartbreak that would fill the pages of a book we had no intention of writing, however. On the contrary: We got carried away, and started promising disclosures about people we did not know and had never met. We ended up, after a two-week period during which we did little else but drink, wake up, invent more spurious details, and drink, with a proposal for a great book, a book we would certainly be interested in reading, called *Exit Flagging*, after a song by Whiskey Ships. We promised an inside look at Kurt C—'s house the day after he died, for instance. We promised to explain who killed him and why. We promised that the mystery of several prominent rock stars' rumored drug addictions would be thoroughly plumbed. We promised that we would tell who was gay, and who only wanted to be gay. The actual ages of several people who would be found to be lying about their ages. This one guy who knew this other guy who heard from the tour bus driver that someone who ought to know better had had sex with a number of underage girls and one underage boy. We made so many promises that we began to think that instead of writing the book, we wanted to sleep with the book. We would say anything to get this book into bed, and we did, and in the end, because if you try hard enough most books will eventually surrender, we succeeded, and of course almost immediately regretted everything.

Two problems arose as a direct result of our unwise burst of energy and ambition. Neither seemed, at first, to be problems. One was that our proposal received a certain amount of interest from some of the larger publishing houses in Manhattan (it had been our understanding that, as is the case with record companies, there's only one enormous publishing house, which operates, by a sophisticated system of barely legal tax dodgery, a network of subsidiaries who go around pretending to compete with each other, the whole thing a sophisticated twenty-first-century parodic masque of capitalism's cuter but no longer viable aspects; but we've been told that that's wrong.), so that by the time Gail was done playing them off against each other, we received an advance the size of which, when it became common knowledge (as anything that happens to a heavy drinker soon becomes common knowledge, because he cannot keep his fool mouth shut), caused entire neighborhoods in the part of East Dayton where we lived to riot. This, as we say, did not at first seem to be a problem so much as a cause for celebration, but there arose complications. Firstly, our friends somehow formed from the premise of our enormous advance the syllogism that they would never again have to pay for a drink. We were not quick to disabuse them, because we're a guy who likes to be liked, even if he has to pay for the honor. Secondly, it soon became clear that the Enormous Publishing House who had sent us the generous advance check, a portion of whose proceeds were indirectly paying for the new pool table in the Hive, expected in return timely delivery of a book more or less like the one we had breathlessly outlined mere months ago. Furthermore, since the subject matter of said book could be fairly described as time-sensitive, as is the case with all pop-cultural material, the market for which is at the best of times a dicey prospect to predict, the sooner the better.

It is convenient from time to time to make the world go away. If someone or something was bothering us (for instance bill collectors), we simply turned the ringer off, and the answering machine, and the world went away. So the occasional nervous phone calls from our editor at Enormous Publishing House were easy to avoid, especially since we could predict them: They would occur a day or two after the date we had last given as the likely day when our editor could "expect to see something," as he very politely and never-less-than-professionally put it. That's where we had him. He was a professional, and we could always rely on his profes-sionalism, whereas he could not rely on us in any capacity, and despite the fact that we think fairly early on he realized this (we're not the only unproductive author, real or fake, so it's not like we crushed his ideals about writers), we don't think he ever quite realized the lengths to which we were prepared not to go.

Gail, on the other hand, pursued us with monocular singularity of focus, somehow transforming herself by force of will into an Argus-eyed tracker of tremendous patience and perseverance, two qualities we find irritating in the extreme in other people because of their irritatingly total absence in our character. Gail called at all hours of the day and night. We might unplug the phone in mid-ring, knowing it was her, and wait five or more hours before reconnecting the phone, at which point it would resume ringing as if time had suddenly accordioned shut at the two ends of that similar action. It was creepy, and we took to drinking even more than usual in an effort to stay away from the house, and the phone, which helped a little until Gail— doing the bare minimum of detective work, it wasn't like we were actually in hiding—tracked us down at the bar and kept calling us there, which didn't piss us off as much as it did the bartenders who had to answer the phone and pretend we weren't there. The threat of being banned from the Snafu Hive—which would have meant walking about thirty or forty feet to the next bar, but that's not the point, your choice in bars is like your choice in anything else, it defines you, and if you lose the ability to define yourself you've lost everything, plus we had put in a lot of effort cultivating occasional free drinks from the bartenders at the Hive before they got pissed at us—finally drove us to pick up the phone and talk to Gail, which was a big mistake.

Turns out Gail's nuts. Our agent: insane. Had we done any asking around (but who do you ask about these things?), we would have discovered that Gail was, in addition to obese and one-eyed, a notorious heroin addict. Her addiction was related to both her obesity (because smack rendered her immobile and non-metabolic and yet somehow, in contradistinction to the vast majority of opium-eaters, did not affect her appetite) and her cyclopticism (a bad case of cotton fever, left untreated, which in the first place had derived from a needle Gail had dropped in a plate of spaghetti and neglected to clean before using), and that moreover in the book publishing world she was regarded with great suspicion as a result of such junk-related exploits as pissing on an editor's desk in a fit of pique (which begs the question of how did she climb up on his desk in the first place, encumbered triply by heroin/gross bodyweight/no depth perception) and setting fire to a ficus tree in the lobby of Simon & Schuster (to say nothing of the drug problem itself, which no one exactly smiled upon). These are petty exploits, but heroin addiction is a petty thing, indulged in mostly by cowards and rock musicians.

We didn't know about Gail's predilection for hard drugs, but then again we didn't know anything about her morbid obesity or her creepy one-eyed face either, until she started mailing us semi-nude photos, but we're getting ahead. When she first started calling with rabid regularity, we assumed it was because she was worried about the extremely inchoate condition of the book we were purportedly working on. Our assumption took on further form and heft when we discovered that we were Gail's only current client, and that her share of our advance had been almost immediately spent on a massive shipment of Malaysian tar that explains why for three weeks our phone didn't ring. Meaning, however, that Gail would not get paid again until we turned in our manuscript, because the way advances work is slightly misnomerical in that you only get half of the advance in advance, and the other half when you complete the work and it's accepted by the publisher, which is a time-honored incentive program, and works just as well with writers as with hit men.

We discovered, though, after a few months of enduring these any-time-at-all phone calls about usually nothing, that Gail could not care less whether we were writing or not, or how much progress we had or hadn't made, or whether what we had managed to eke out was any good or not or even readable. Her inquiries on these subjects were perfunctory, dutiful. Nor did she seem to care about the money. We discovered, after trying unsuccessfully on a rare trip to New York to track her down at the office address she gave us, which turned out to be the address of a methadone clinic on Bowery, that Gail had a somewhat peripatetic lifestyle. To put it bluntly, she was homeless. Our agent was a homeless drug addict, which on the plus side left her with a lot of free time, and cut way down on her overhead.

We're pretty sure she was only recently homeless, because at some point she must have been a legit agent with at least a grubby meatpacking district office (before the meatpacking district became chic and ungrubby), or else how could she even get our proposal through the door at Enormous Publishing House, or any of the satellite houses that sparked the bidding war. Nevertheless, the proof we assembled during our brief visit—going so far as to call our editor and undergo the conversational equivalent of a rectal exam in order to discover, after five highly uncomfortable minutes, only that he hadn't spoken to Gail in three weeks and had the same methadone clinic address we had for her—proved, at length, conclusive. Our search was hampered both by our complete lack of information about her physical makeup (this was before the pictures) and by our not caring all that much and by our need to spend most of our time in the horseshoe-shaped bar on the corner of 7th Street and Avenue B, which is our favorite bar in New York, or was when Avenue B was an adventurous and unwise part of town to visit. Eventually, by talking to the orderly at the methadone clinic who was nice enough to hold Gail's mail for her, we discovered that as far as he (Leo, a chain-smoker with a weirdly high-pitched voice) knew, she was homeless, or at least looked to be—unwashed, clothes in tatters, bad smell of urine. Leo neglected to inform us of her astounding girth or the gaping hole where her left eye used to be, but in all fairness we didn't ask.

So Gail was homeless, and yet seemingly happy that way, at least in the sense that she did not seem perturbed by our continuing failure to deliver material in a "timely manner" (quoting from our book contract) to Enormous Publishing House. You'd think, standing in her worn-through shoes, squatting in her trash heap, she'd be on the phone to us three, four, twenty times a day, whatever it took, screaming, cajoling, pleading with us to write something, anything, and send it to our editor so she stood a chance of getting paid again. And she was on the phone three, four, twenty times a day, but she wasn't calling to beg us to write. At first this confused us.

Gail was calling, it at length became evident, because she had developed somewhere in her overweight, smack-addled brain the notion that our relationship was something more than professional. At first her less-than-pro inquiries into our personal life, extending to casual sex-life banter of the sort that probably now could get you sued for sexual harassment but back then, in the carefree early '90s, still passed for harmless, did not bother us. We enjoyed our conversations, more so when we were somewhat drunk than when we were sober, but we're hard-pressed to come up with any conversation that wouldn't be true for, and it wasn't until a few of these conversations took an especially intense turn that ended up with Gail in tears and us mumbling excuses to get off the phone that we noticed anything wrong. We weren't sure why she'd started crying, exactly, the first couple of times, but we thought it might be related to some hormonal mood swing.

> To apprehend rock you have to speak around it, if you will, to come at it in terms of metaphor and indirect experience of the thing. So that the more appropriate question is perhaps not What is it? but What does it look/sound like? Or what is it most like that we in our direct experience may relate it to? Which is why writers so often resort to similes/comparisons as a method of describing both its nature and its effects. The two are distinct and yet closely related— nature and the effect of nature upon human sensibility.
> —Shorbuck, op. cit.

After enduring without complaint months more of this long-distance stalking, we cracked. We were down at the Hive, somewhere near closing time, and we were already uneasy because our friend Magnetic Tom had thrown an ashtray through the TV set hanging from the ceiling in the back, and even though the TV hadn't worked in years and was purely decorative, Billy the bartender threw Magnetic Tom out and threatened to throw everyone else out who even laughed at the imploded TV skeleton, since Billy was the one who had to clean up the shards of screen littering the linoleum floor sticky with beer, and of course we were one of the ones laughing hardest, and may even have been the one who dared Magnetic Tom to throw the ashtray, knowing full well that he would do absolutely anything at the slightest provocation. Right then the phone rang, and it was of course Gail, and Billy handed us the phone with a weary shake of his fed-up head, and despite our attempt at not-listening, we clearly heard Gail's nasally but not-unpleasant voice asking us how things were going and she hoped it wasn't a bad time to call, she just wanted us to know she'd been thinking about us and wishing all very good things for us and did we happen to get the last thing she sent us, some semi-important legal papers relating to (fictitious) paperback rights in Scandinavia which she was *this close* to closing the deal for, also the set of prints of her posing with her shirt off in what looked to be a dressing room in Bloomingdale's, also the eighteen-page letter declaring us her best friend for life and the only one who truly understood her; we hung up the phone without saying a word. We walked back to our booth and buried our head in our hands and then looked up, tossed back the remains of our whiskey drink, and announced that we "have to write this goddamn book," though of course the booth was by now empty so we were making this announcement to the framed picture of ourself and some of the guys from our band and Kurt C— and Michael Goodlife and some other guys from maybe some other band, which had been placed on the wall over the booth as a token both of our local celebrity and of our outstanding patronage. We would have preferred more free drinks, but the framed picture was a nice gesture. We came to think of that booth as *our* booth, because it had our picture above it, even after the elements constituting that picture, captured at that mostly happy moment in time, no longer existed and never would again exist and consequently that picture became both impossible and a lie.

But we think things that are both impossible and a lie are the basis of most worthwhile human effort. So we began to consider that while the impossible lie of our book proposal was clearly beyond reach of both our abilities and ambition as a writer, we might attempt something that in general shape would not look entirely dissimilar to the outline that had won us the big-bucks advance. The irony of us sitting in a booth underneath a picture of everything we had lost or given up was not wasted on our wasted brain. We spent our hours now in a torpid fog through which we regarded every angle, every mistake of our failures in life. Which is why we have decided to get through this. Okay: excise the scar tissue and expose the wound to the healing breeze of memory's fresh breath.

So we have two reasons, then, to get on with *Exit Flagging*. The first is purely prosaic, and hardly worth re-mentioning: to save our life. The second is rather more difficult, and infinitely more valuable: to get Gail to stop calling us. In order to accomplish this latter task, and in so doing to release from thralldom whatever demons have possessed her, we have to write *Exit*

Flagging. We hope these demons do not then turn around and inhabit someone else, because we would feel bad and partly responsible, but instead return to the nether regions of universal consciousness whence they originally crawled (the happy ending to our life's horror movie). We think that the demons inflicting Gail, that bade her believe she's in love with us or that something in us is necessary for her bare-bones survival, as if we were bread or water or whiskey or heroin, we think these demons have something to do with our quitting Whiskey Ships, and Kurt's suicide, and Michael Goodlife's death by misadventure, and the disappearance of both Amanda Early and Fiat Lux, and maybe with the larger phenomenon of the death of rock music in any meaningful form. We think these demons are somehow contained in this book, in the words themselves, the actual writing, and the only way to exorcise them is to spell their names, i.e., write the book. So we will write the book, and we will be rid of the demons and so will Gail, and then we will be rid of Gail.

We'll say this much for her, though: She believed in us. She believed when no one else would have, especially not ourself. That measure of belief is rare in an agent, rare in a human being, these days, sadly. We may be writing this book, finally, mostly, in an effort to get her off our back, but when that sad day inevitably arrives, we will miss the hell out of sweet Gail.

Notebook Seven

Albion stands south of downtown on a small hill, approximately 275 feet higher than sea level, which gives, from the second floor or the roof, "sweeping views" of most of the city to the north. I put sweeping views in quotes because I don't know what that phrase signifies but it's in most of the real estate listings I used to browse on Sundays, pretending I'd ever have enough money to buy a house. You can buy one here for cheap— I know a bartender at the Snafu Hive who bought a split-level in East Dayton (the redneck section) recently for about twenty grand. According to the listings, the asking price for Albion was around $180,000 reduced over the past five or so years from an originally absurd $350,000. You might consider that's not much money for a place the size of a high school, but two things militated in favor of cheapness: 1) as the purpose-built home of Orville Wright, cofounder of flight, Albion held an insurmountably High Historical Value, meaning that despite that Wright had designed its working parts in a way befitting an eccentric inventor—none of Albion's systems of lighting, heating, or plumbing worked the way standard such systems worked—you could not touch or replace or do anything but restore these systems. Which for the most part did not work. And 2) no one had lived there for over ten years and the property was a mess. You would have had to put at least another hundred thousand in renovations into the house in order to render it habitable, never mind the cost of heating and lighting and merely maintaining the place.

In back of the deserted manse there grew a tangle of untamed shrubbery (wisteria, lilac, azalea), weeds, wildflowers (snapdragon, tickseed, beebalm, aster, hollyhock, heliotrope, cornflower), and, unexpectedly, roses, among which, according to season, bloomed a Black Jade miniature rose and several rogue Hybrid Teas (Crimson Glory, Double Delight, Fragrant Cloud, Mr. Lincoln) and a cream-white single bloom Sombreauil Tea (all this according to the Rose Scholar. To me, a rose by any other name looks as complexly creepy). The Rose Scholar claimed that the Cox Arboretum over on Springfield Pike was a desert of thorns next to Albion's accidental rosaceae. I'll take her word for it—she once journeyed to the Toledo Botanical Gardens in search of a rare Damask in the petalled flesh. She had of course seen pictures in books. I'd checked out many of those books for her.

The property had been held in trust for an absentee owner who was in no apparent hurry to sell. After Wright's death in 1948, Albion had been purchased by the National Cash Register corporation to use as a guest house for corporate clients, but that didn't last very long—the expense of maintaining a National Historic Residence didn't justify the benefit to its clients, especially as the company's resources shrank over time—the cash register, its notable proprietary invention, gradually superseded by computer-driven devices that NCR failed to take seriously. Its last resident—Oscar Siebenthaler, an old-growth Daytonian (I researched Albion's history in an off-hour at the library)—had been an amateur horticulturist, which explained the proliferation of flora, but in the ten years since his occupation (ended, as with many things, by death), his carefully organized garden had exploded, migrating willy-nilly over the two acres of partially wooded property. In areas thickly shaded by trees, flowers that flourished in shade grew. In sunny spots grew heliophilic things. Where conditions were right (neither too much nor too little sun, for instance up near the house itself), a scumble of colors occurred in spring, attracting swarms of bees and butterflies— among these: Silver-spotted Skippers (Epargyreus clarus *clarus*) and American Coppers (Lycaena phlaes *americana*)—in abundance. Sadly, we did not have much chance to enjoy our skippers or our coppers or our ad hoc apiary, as by that time things had changed.

After Kurt C— purchased the house, he exhibited no interest in clearing away the dead brush from the backyard or mowing the front or back—as a result wild grasses flourished, which proved a boon to insects and to the birds who fed on them (Acadian Flycatcher, Barn Swallow, Horned Lark, Red-Eyed Vireo, Cedar Waxwing, as well as the usual sparrow, house wren, and starling crowd). The unkempt grounds and the general disrepair of Albion's façade (paint cracked and flaking, gutters askew, unhinged shingles, broken flagstones on the path leading up to the front porch, which featured a porch swing as rotted and tenuous as the gazebo across from the Belle) kept neighbors tut-tutting and most strangers at bay. The place was thus ideal for late-night convocations, once Kurt started to invite us to Albion for after-hours. The only real drawback was that he never figured out or bothered to try more accurately to figure out the electricity situation, so there was none. For light we used many candles, placed in multiples on octopus-armed wrought-iron stands, and the effulgent fire.

> Now it is more noble to sit like Jove than to fly like Mercury—let us not therefore go hurrying about and collecting honeybeelike, buzzing here and there impatiently from a knowledge of what is to be arrived at: but let us open our leaves like a flower and be passive and receptive
> —Keats in letter

> diligent indolence
> —Ibid.

> NEGATIVE CAPABILITY, that is when man is capable of being in uncertainties, mysteries, doubts, without any irritable reaching after fact & reason.
> —Keats, in different letter; famous description, referring to Shakespeare

Inside, the house was sparse and falling apart. Most of the place was uninhabitable, so we spent the greater part of our drinking time in a decrepit main room the size of a gymnasium, with no furniture except two mildewed, sagging armchairs arranged on thick, worn carpets around an enormous stone fireplace at the farthest end of the room from the double-doored entrance. A pendulous chandelier hung from the center of the peeling ceiling; its cut glass facets chimed airily whenever anyone opened the double doors or when a gust of winter wind came through the chimney flue, which we always kept open, so that when the fire was dead the wind blew up a twister of ashes. If you fell asleep in front of the fire, as I often did in the weeks when Albion became more my home than my own apartment, you would wake with a fine silt of ash covering your clothes and skin. On top of the hill where Albion sat the wind was often strong.

Over time, the ash collected in layers around the huge stone hearth, drifting like gray snow, and was left undisturbed until replaced by real snow (also gray, in the ashen light of dawn) later in the winter. One morning we woke up to find a snowy semicircle had formed around us while we slept. It's not true that we then built a snowman and waltzed around the frozen ballroom, as Mary tried to say—and who can blame her? It's what we should have done, not just then but the three or four other times the snow repeated its nocturnal trick; but hungover first thing on a cold winter morning is maybe not the best timing for a waltz. I do remember that one day Joe Smallman tried to start a snowball fight. His effort went unloved by the recently sleep-enfolded rest of us. First task in the morning, for those of us who hadn't managed to stagger home before passing out, was almost always rekindling the fire, which most of the time was the sole source of heat in Albion.

The ballroom wasn't the only room, obviously, just the biggest, and the one I knew best. The kitchen was as oversized as everything else at Albion, and as rust-riddled, dappled with dirt, dusty, and disused. I doubt anyone could have cooked in that kitchen. When we got hungry, late at night, we ordered food delivered—usually sandwiches or similarly simple stuff, but sometimes sirloin or burgers from the Pine Club, a nearby steakhouse. Most often somebody called The Sandwich Champ, our local deli (which, conveniently, kept late hours because of its proximity to the University of Dayton—UD was a Catholic-run college specializing in churning out narrow-minded philistines; I'm generalizing, of course).

We drank and ate and smoked and talked in the ballroom, happily, greedily, backlit by the ruddy glow from the fire—white ash *(Fraxinus americana)*, Chinquapin oak *(Quercus muehlenbergii)*, and buckeye *(Aesculus glabra)* gathered from Albion's two acres of semi-wooded backyard—which Mary Valentine could not resist worrying, constantly, with a long polished stick (some kind of hardwood, possibly hickory) that served us in lieu of a standard fireplace tool. Kurt always paid for the meal, which was one among many reasons why Albion's popularity grew so swiftly in the brief period of its ascendancy. In addition, he would produce, to augment our own cheap beer or liquor, wine from an apparently endless supply he kept in crates stacked in the kitchen, from which we never dared filch—good wine, too, rubious Cabernet and hearty Côtes du Rhône (I'm not sure what *hearty* means in relation to wine, but I like the way it sounds) and dry, green-apple-cheeked Chardonnay from somewhere Chardonnay is vinted. You knew the wine was good because the bottles were filmed with grit and the corks smelled mildewy on top but heavy and fruited and vaguely sweet when extracted. Kurt decanted the wine into a glass pitcher that was one of his few extravagant items, then poured it into whatever we had handy—I usually drank from a "Birthplace of Aviation" coffee cup that Kurt found funny. ("If man was meant to fly, God would have given him wings," he would scold, ironically, slopping the wine over the brim.) We gossiped and got into fights and told bad jokes and even worse stories, and eventually fell asleep in front of the fire. This was then repeated to infinity, or until repealed by fate.

Sometimes, when the weather allowed and the night was damp with stars, we climbed a spiral staircase with our cups of wine and cigarettes and sat on the roof looking over the city. Any city, no matter how small, has a skyline, and Dayton had one, too, and from Albion's roof you could see the whole thing, spread like the embers of our unattended fire, glowing warmly in the blackness. You could see the Mead Paper building, and National Cash Register, and the hunched shoulders of the giant Cúchulainn, trimmed with amber gems. Or you could lie on your back and guess at the names of the constellations. Kurt kept quiet while Amanda Early and Joe Smallman and Mary Valentine and the Rose Scholar and Daryl Hawes and Co-Daryl Hawes and even, occasionally, Magnetic Tom and Henry Radio and Violet McKnight and Jesus Of The World (there were others, unnecessary of mention) plied us with drunk stupidities, pointing out random stellar groupings and inventing or pretending to invent astrologies.

You could also see our two rivers, glittering darkly in the spaces between buildings or through notches in the low hills. The Great Miami River, which was not great and did not flow to Miami; and Mad River, about which much more much later, circumscribed Dayton like the arms of an enervated naiad. The satanic mills of Dayton included a corn oil processing plant and several car parts factories, all of which at some point had dumped waste of one sort or another into both rivers—although not anymore, I'm sure. As a result our waters were muddy, and usually gelid. I never knew anyone who tried to swim in either river. I don't believe you could fish fruitfully, either—anglers went north to one of the Great Lakes, or south to the Florida Keys. You didn't have to go all the way to the Keys, obviously, but many did. Key West was a popular Dayton getaway—straight shot by powerful automobile down the interstate to Florida, which you could make in ten hours, then another five or six down to Miami and across the long bridge to paradise. This is how it was explained to me one night by either Daryl Hawes or Co-Daryl, his twin brother, one of whom liked to fish.

You could see a lot of things from the roof. One thing we could not see was each other, and on occasion this sham anonymity led to drink-fueled fumblings of an erotic nature, involving most often Mary or Amanda and one or two of the boys. I did not see how anyone could prefer the crude thrill of sex to the spangled beauty of the night sky at Albion, but I've decided that I may be unusual in this regard.

In the late Cretaceous, just before the mass dinosaur extinction, Dayton was a much different place. According to the fossil record, we had for a while marsupials (possums and early versions of platypus and kangaroo and wombat) and some weird early placentals like the plageomenid, a gliding mammal that could spread a sail of fur. Flowers, in this period, first inclined their pretty heads toward the sun. Flowering plants are called angiosperms to distinguish them from the gymnosperms that preceded them (conifers, ginkoes, etc.—needled or broadleafed trees, in essence, or their forebears); the name refers to the type of seed produced. Gymnosperms made naked seeds, easily accessed by foraging vegetarians (not to mention insects, which started up a symbiotic relationship with the angiosperms, about this time, that continues, happily, to this day—120 million years, give or take a few). The angiosperms, by contrast, developed the familiar anther/stigma setup, which helped protect the seed (wrapped safely inside the ovary), and which brought about pollen, which in turn required the invention of bees.

The hills and plains of the Miami Valley were densely forested, and thick with animal life, some reptilian or even saurian in nature. The weather: subtropical, meaning hot and moist. I would have liked to live here then, not so much because of what existed as what didn't exist. I would have enjoyed perfect isolation, although I'd need my allergy medication. And

my books. The only form in which I can meet the
human mind without causing or being caused pain is
books, and I know exactly how awful and self-absorbed
and cowardly and immature that sounds. I know
because I'm a human being.

Le Vaillant, in his *Voyage de Monsieur Le Vaillant Dans
L'Intérieur de L'Afrique Par Le Cap de Bonne Espérance Dans les
Années 1780, 81, 82, 83, 84 & 85 Avec Figures* (1791), records
that "*L'intérieur de l'Afrique, pour cela seul, me paroissoit un
Pérou. Cétoit la terre encore vierge.*" "*La terre encore vierge,*"
virgin territory, is what I think I've been looking for
ever since I lay in bed one summer's night in the
renovated-by-dead-dad Lewisburg church, eight years
old and unable to sleep, the branches of a honey locust
scraping against my half-opened window, and decided
never to marry. The decision was purely practical: I did
not yet know what sex was, but I was well-acquainted
with loneliness, and did not see how that loneliness
could be relieved by another person. Certainly my
mother's love—unconditional, unearned—didn't seem
to help. How could anything? Even at that age I saw
solitude as a blessing, and little since then had
happened to change my tune (solo clarinet, sadly
tootling). The advent of puberty brought lust and self-
consciousness, neither of which I'd recommend to a
friend, although please don't think me reflexively
prudish, or unalterably opposed to the idea of romantic
love. But I can only speak from experience, and mine
has been meager and unrewarding in the area of human
relations.

And yet, when I first came to Albion, its strangely
intoxicating aura of decay, twined with a developing

sense of community I'd never before encountered in the bars or bedrooms of Dayton, held the allure of an unexplored land. I thought—and here I was very wrong, but also right, right, right—that a new and better world might open itself to me. That nothing came of my notion can be ascribed to the shortcomings of all human striving as much as to the particular failings we brought to the slumber party. We are not built to last, but we keep on trying to come in first. Hurray!

Kurt's money was a mystery we were not anxious to plumb. He seemed to have plenty, and yet lived in Albion with what's usually called monkish asceticism. Never once would he let us pay for a meal, or a drink, and the wine, as I mentioned, didn't look or taste cheap. He didn't drive, didn't spend a dime on creature comforts—to say nothing of furniture—and never appeared to work or have to deal with music business interests. I don't think I ever even saw him open a piece of mail. I don't think the postman ever rang once, as a matter of fact. I did one time come across a fax machine while wandering around upstairs, a plain-paper fax without a tray to catch its output. There was a small white hill of faxes scattered on the floor, and even as I peeked in, the machine was belching out another one, but no evidence that Kurt had ever so much as picked up one of these dead letters.

One night—emboldened by wine, and by the fact that Kurt and I were the only ones awake—I began, on an impulse, to tell him about my father's death, in a fatuous attempt at provoking pity. His response was gentle and forbearing. He told me he was sorry, and said that it must have been hard growing up without a father. He asked about my mother, too, which naturally led to a discussion of my religious upbringing, in which Kurt expressed unusual interest, although it's true he showed unusual interest in discussions of any religion. So he heard about my mom, and the mornings we spent before the school bus came reading passages from the Bible and their corresponding exegeses in *Science and Health*, all according to a weekly lesson plan distributed by the Mother Church, in Boston. The lesson was arranged according to now-archaic-sounding headings derived from Mrs. Eddy's text; so often did I listen to and recite these, groggy at the kitchen table, my cereal bowl pushed to one side, my orange juice leaving concentric circles on the oilcloth that competed for my attention with my mother's quiet voice, that most are burned into my memory: "Ancient and Modern Necromancy, Alias Animal Magnetism, Denounced"; "The Doctrine of At-one-ment"; "Are Sin, Disease, and Death Real?" Mrs. Eddy was an eloquent writer, and a persuasive spirit. I explained all this to Kurt, and he never once looked impatient or bored, though the whole discussion took hours, long into the night—two bottles of wine worth of talk. It's easier to measure wine than time.

I told him, too, what I had never told anyone, that when I was old enough to understand the tenets of my religion I went daily to the cemetery where my dad lay buried and sat cross-legged in front of his ugly rose granite gravestone and tried to raise him from the dead with the power of prayer and right thinking. This would have been third grade, because I remember we were learning the names of wildflowers in school at that time, and I was distracted in my prayer occasionally by the sight of an evening primrose (Oenothera *biennis*) or false foxglove (Gerardia *laevigata*). Jesus could heal the sick and raise the dead, and Christian Scientists were supposed to be able to recreate Jesus' feats, so it seemed reasonable to me that my father would rise wrapped in graveclothes and roll away the stone like Lazarus when called. I called a lot. I remembered from the Bible that it had taken Jesus—God's only child—three tries before succeeding, so I cut myself some slack, and tried and tried again. This went on for about six months. I would come home from school and head straight to the cemetery, which was only three blocks away from our house, on a sloping hill in back of Lewisburg's only (real) church. My father was buried under the shadow of rugged elms and one huge yew, alongside the rude forefathers of our hamlet. A little further off was a stand of pines in which nested doves, who would swoop, cooing, overhead and sometimes stop to rest on a stone, perched like the sail of a tiny sloop in the green-and-gray sea of graves. In winter, snow lay thickly drifted on the crooked crosses and headstones, on the spears of the little gate, on the barren thorns. I came anyway, every day. I came in every sort of weather, thinking that if God were paying attention to my prayers, He would likely notice if I stayed away because of snow or high wind or rain or failing will. But try as I might, with the purest mind I could muster (constantly berating myself for the self-ishness of my goal), my dad stayed dead, his tortoise-shadow soul still trapped like Zeno's arrow under the thousand and thousand idols of the sun, and I gradually lost faith in my abilities as a healer. The great thing about Christian Science is that failure on the part of the adherent is blamed on the adherent's imperfect faith, and no taint of imperfection adheres to the doctrine itself.

To my surprise Kurt did not mock my childish simplicity; he said instead that he shared Mrs. Eddy's distrust of doctors, and further that he'd had a baffling and very painful stomach condition for years, visited fourteen different specialists, received fourteen different diagnoses and fourteen different ineffective courses of treatment. I was glad to be talking about something other than my dead dad. Whenever I discussed my father I felt guilty, as if I'd somehow betrayed a confidence—because the secret of his dying should remain, like everything true, unnamed.

I never asked Kurt where he came up with the name for the house. No, that's not true. I did ask, once, late at night in The Pearl, but he just smiled in reply and turned a page in his notebook. I'm not entirely stupid, I know it's what the Romans called Britain, probably derived from *albus*, white, a reference to the White Cliffs of Dover (maybe—etymologists remain unsure, some claiming a cognate in Celtic of indeterminate meaning, and I wouldn't put it past Kurt to have uncovered that uncertain simile); I'm also aware of the neo-mythic uses to which William Blake among others put the name, but none of this makes any sense in Kurt's context. I can't help but feel I've missed something important, but there are limits to my intellect and my will, and this riddle overmasters both.

It's not true that when someone you love dies you gradually forget, that their memory fades and the pain of loss grows dull and unhurtful. At least, I think it's not true—I have evidence times three. Another thing: The word *repeat* and the word *repeal* are separated by one lousy letter. Anyone can make a mistake.

Notebook Eight

As autumn deferred to winter and the impact of Kurt's arrival slowly turned from green to dingy yellow and fell from the tree of our attention, we began at his invitation to turn Albion into something like our after-hours clubhouse. Where in the past we had argued and complained and worried about whose turn it was to allow the rest of us to trash his place, annoy his roommates, placate the cops, we now had a place which was already trashed, and whose owner did not care what we did to further the damage, who had no roommates, and who lived far enough from anyone else that no one ever called the cops, nor would the cops have come, because Kurt's house was in Oakwood, not Dayton. You could speed down Far Hills Avenue at fifty in a thirty-five zone, at half-past closing time, weaving from one side to the next, and if you happened to fall prey to one of the omnipresent cops stationed in the median to catch out-of-town drunks and/or speeders, all you had to do was flash your driver's license with an Oakwood address and his demeanor would change like a traffic light from stern to chiding and he would bid you drive with an increased eye for detail the shortest way possible home. Oakwood cops were charged with protecting Oakwood residents from outsiders, from people without enough money to pay Oakwood property taxes (rapacious), and were neither equipped nor inclined to deal with offenses committed within Oakwood by Oakwooders. So while we were at Albion, we were protected, not only from the law, but from ourselves. In this way Albion became our safe house, and for a while the atmosphere we created there held me in enchantment. Wine is strong, the king is strong, women are strong, but the truth overcomes all things. The spongy leaves of some sea-wracks, ficus, oaks, in their several kinds, found about the shore, with ejectments of the sea, are overwrought with network elegantly containing this order which plainly declares the naturality of this texture. And how the needle of nature delights to work, even in low and doubtful vegetations.

Albion seemed to develop a personality of its own. The pulse of the place was its hearth, the enormous stone fireplace in the main room. There was a time, not distant, a time I can just about reach out a finger and poke, when the flames would draw us like hell-bent moths to its crackling maw, and we would drink and talk in haphazard groups, squatting or standing or sprawled or otherwise arranged, bodies at rest, bodies in slow motion, bodies attracted to other bodies, bodies repelled, bodies with nothing in common but the darkness, and a continual craving for light.

Sky was the first who ruled over the whole world. And having wedded Earth, he begat the hundred-handed, as they are named, who were unsurpassed in size and might, each of them having a hundred hands and fifty heads. We created a community at Albion. We were able to create this community partly because we were not trying to create anything. I believe that environment exercises a powerful pull on human disposition, at least I believe that now. In a sense I think Albion created us, that its stately decay reflected or even magnified our inner decay, which was why we immediately felt at home there.

Or maybe I imagined everything. Maybe I was the only one who saw in Albion the ideal, the template of the possible. Here was no loud music, no chattering of drunk students, no neon brightness against which we shaded our lives with banalities and manufactured dramas and a slurry of lies and evasions. Here it was possible to be myself, because here my eccentricities were well known and accepted. I was a little crazy, but we were all a little crazy; craziness was the general condition at Albion, the done thing, the starting point. For the others this may have been a put-on. But not for me. For me Albion was freedom in a way that the bars could never be freedom, that an ordinary after-hours party at someone's house could never be freedom, because someone else's house entails abiding by someone else's proprieties, or notions of propriety, of not doing something embarrassing, whether to oneself or to another. At Albion you couldn't be embarrassing. Embarrassment didn't exist by firelight, in an absolutely neutral zone—neutral in the way I had always held myself neutral, apart from the intimate lives of my friends. Here I no longer needed to maintain that neutrality because the place maintained it for me, and I could speak my mind, and act my mind, and inhabit the space around me naturally, without constraint except insofar as I wished to impose upon myself, naturally, without regard for social norms or expectations. Maybe, as I say, the whole thing, the idea of Albion, was only a fantasy, an extension of my own silly dreams about how and why to live. But while it lasted it was a very beautiful fantasy.

The girl's grief was not at all soothed by this sort of blathering. How could it be? She kept her head down between her knees and wept uncontrollably. There never was a real Gorgon; there was only a prophylactic ugly face formalized into a mask. The ugly face at the mouth of the bag symbolizes that the secrets of the alphabet, which are the real contents of the bag, are not to be misused or divulged. How seductive that fantasy was to me, to Fiat Lux, to a girl who'd consigned herself to shadows and moreover loved her shadow-life, who loved ideas and words and the things beyond ideas and words that were only represented by ideas, and by words—which representation, or rather the long and strange history of the development of that representation, because I don't think of etymology as random, if you look at anything like Locke's *An Essay Concerning Human Understanding* or Müller's *Science of Language*, you can see that the process of assigning word to idea has been anything but random, has been a careful and constantly evolving process, one might even call it the common secret project of humanity—in the Platonic sense of the ideal, which is not dissimilar, I've always thought, to the Christian Science notion of

Divine Truth as opposed to Mortal Error, which is one reason I've always had an easy time accepting the existence of absolutes, and consequently of ideas beyond words. But here I was, at Albion, seeing ideas as more than words, as a sequence of little realities that might, I believed at the time and still believe, if certain things had happened or rather not happened, evolve into a bigger reality, a sustaining shadowless Real Life pregnant with possibility.

> "Much of the modern history of technology and science might be characterized as a continual increase in the amount of energy available through fire and brought under human control. Most of the increased available energy has come from ever greater amounts and kinds of fires.
> —Encyclopedia Britannica

The miraculous child set a riddle, based on a knowledge not only of British and Irish mythology, but the Greek New Testament and Septuagint, the Hebrew Scriptures and Apocrypha, and Latin and Greek mythology. The answer to the riddle is a list of names, claimed to be the original names of the Ogham alphabet, which is found in numerous inscriptions in Ireland, Scotland, Wales, England, and the Isle of Man, some of them pre-Christian. It may also have been current in Britain where, according to Julius Caesar, the Druids of Gaul went for their university training in secret doctrine. He is a mighty hunter and makes rain, when it is needed, by rattling an oak club thunderously in a hollow oak and stirring a pool with an oak branch, and so attracting thunderstorms by sympathetic magic.

That Vulcan gave arrows unto Apollo and Diana the fourth day after their Nativities, according to Gentile Theology, may paffe for no blinde apprehenfion of the Creation of the Sunne and the Moon, in the work of the fourth day; when the diffufed light contracted into Orbes, and fhooting rayes, of thofe Luminaries.

I have to lie down, below the level of the window sill, to smoke. I remember reading about de Gaulle during World War Two, that when he traveled by plane at night, and the plane's lights were blacked out to avoid being spotted by enemy aircraft, he refused not to smoke. So an eagle-eyed Luftwaffe pilot might have spotted him by the small orange glow from the tip of his cigarette. Obviously, no one ever did. But I don't have a general's guts. No matter what Kurt said.

I have been writing for almost three days straight. I state that merely as fact, as an objective observation. I'm not bragging. I wish that I had leisure to polish, correct, edit, rewrite. *All writing is rewriting.* So whatever I'm doing here, stands to reason, is not writing. I'm moving my pen over the page as fast as I can; my hand keeps cramping, and parts have gone numb, maybe for good, and there was a blister on my middle finger that popped and blood drooled down my arm but now it's nicely callused. I have not slept at all. I haven't eaten much—a couple of tins of tuna and some wheat crackers. I have drunk a fair amount of wine, because that is the only way I seem to be able to stay awake, which makes no sense but I believe it to be true and therefore it has become true.

I'm scared, all the time. Right now, I'm terrified. Because of what I have done, because of what I now have to do, and because if anyone finds out either of these two things before I'm ready I will end up in jail or dead. Worse than that, I will have failed. I'm prepared to accept jail or death, but not failure. That's over-dramatic and self-important and also true. Or it's neither over-dramatic nor self-important—because at stake is the future of the world, in the most mundane sense—and still true.

Oh, my sea-green incorruptible! Poor sallow Kurt. No longer orbiting our orbicle of jasp. By whose agency were you removed? By me. By Fiat Lux, who never before did anything of note, who never did anything, whose life was quiet and whose head was full of words and who would never have believed that she'd end up on the run, in hiding, a murderess, an accomplice.

Life is full of such surprises. The simplest turn in the smoothest road can be fraught with sudden danger, just as the most hazardous journey can pass without incident. It's safer to fly than drive, but most accidents happen in the bathroom. Timing is everything. There's never a right time for anything. Fortune doesn't exist, and the alignment of stars and moon has no bearing on the tides of individual affairs. Out of the routine rocks of day-to-day existence you can eventually hack, with great effort and a blunt tool, a shallow windbreak, but if you try it alone it won't last, trust me.

Notebook Nine

5.

- Though I'm unable to get down to the office much these days, doesn't mean I spend my days in idleness. Not long after the doctor's daily visit, and my daily injection to combat the sciatica that has troubled me ever since the Selfridge flight, I was back to work on the vacuum system that has never functioned properly owing to its many defects of construction. Basic principles: These are so much more apparent after the morphine takes effect, just as in early years our use of opium enabled us to visualize certain wind tunnel results even before we had constructed the wind tunnel! I should not say *our* use of opium. I should not lie to myself here in my own private journal. Will rarely smoked, and disapproved of my own use to the extent that I had to adopt a number of undignified subterfuges to keep him from suspecting the frequency, or more precisely volume, of my habit. Were it not for Charlie Taylor's faithful service—extending even to his regular bold excursions to the Negro section of town on my behalf. Not that these were entirely selfish trips; but I was more than happy to fund his harmless infatuation with reefer (and, for all I know, darker pleasures) in return for a ready supply of opium and Charlie's priceless discretion.

- To think of the time and energy I expended planning and devising hideaways for my opium here at Albion, only to have Will pass away before construction could begin. Still, these trompe l'oeil gimcracks served a useful purpose after K. moved in, though for a different reason. Again, the fault's mine, for introducing her to this pernicious habit: Though I do not regard as a vice something so evidently useful, and further cannot conceive of a Creator who would provide His offspring with a tool and then deny us its application. But with K. I think the tool (that is to say, the habit), over time, became an end in itself, and not an end toward good but one that perhaps changed her in some essential way, from a woman who understood and valued the virtue of family above all else to one in whom this virtue had become unhinged and replaced by fidelity to the brand of selfish individualism that I have always found abhorrent; to such an extent that I was driven to use the secrets of Albion, not to conceal my habit from my brothers and the bishop, but to conceal my opium from my sister. Was this the reason she

left? Was this why she abandoned me to the iso-
lationist hell of my house on the hill? Well, it
didn't help.

- There remains no earthly reason why a system of
built-in tubes, connected to a central vacuum
pump of sufficient power that wherever one
inserts the connecting device, in this case
simply a length of rubber hose with brush on
one end and a metal collar on the other,
activated by a simple electrical contact, should
not function as cleanly, forgive the pun, as the
cumbersome and inefficient machine Carrie now
must drag from room to room in this impossibly
large and ridiculously empty palace. In the ideal
mental state to which the morphine has now
enabled me—different in quality from the
opium in ways that only an experienced user
would understand—to see the larger problem,
which now seems clear as Mad River on a
summer's day: Albion simply does not produce
enough dirt for a vacuum cleaner to operate
with any degree of confidence in its own
abilities. All machines, I see now, have a personality not unlike the human soul, though of
course not the same thing at all, because man
creates machines, whereas God creates man. But
just as our souls are not visible or even readily
apparent, except in the refuge of faith, so the
personality of a machine is not apparent, to
itself at least. But I created this thing, and just
as God can peer into the deepest recess of the

human soul, so can I see and understand the personality of my machines. In this case, the vacuum system. Which suffers from insecurity, due to its perceived inadequacy, even though the problem's obviously not with the cleaner but with the cleaner's environment. Problem: How do I communicate to the vacuum system? Again, the parallels with human problems regarding God strike me; just as we are unable clearly to distinguish the voice of our Maker from among the babble that invades, even here, in the relative silence of Albion, both our waking and sleeping lives, how would my machine understand what I'm trying to tell it? I can hear its prayers as clearly were they my own: I can pity my machine for its lack of comprehension. But I have not yet figured out a way to make my language comprehensible to it. I may have to devise a language for my machines—not just the vacuum system but the furnaces, plumbing, and wiring, everything—so as to make my intentions known. So as to ease their suffering, for they do suffer, and it does pain me. The thought occurs to me, however: This may not be an easy task. If over the millennia God has not been able (or willing, I should concede, because that may be the reason, after all, and a great part of the teaching of our faith, of most faiths, concerns the reasons why the Lord may not wish to communicate directly with us—one of the main reasons, if I remember the Bishop's teaching rightly, is that we shall surely die) to develop a system of language suitable for two-way talking, as for instance English, or the telephone, then my attempts, should I decide as I now find myself inclined to do, to devise a Lingua Machina, so to speak, may not immediately bear fruit, may consume what few useful hours remain to me.

6.

• These halls echo with lead-footed memories. Especially now, late at night, when I'm unable to sleep and the fire in the main room has died to embers, and the swashbuckling romantic novel lies at my feet, its spine broken. I can remember being happy here. I can remember being happy. That happiness more often than not took the form of other people—the Bishop, K., even Loren before he died, and of course Ivonette and the children, all gone, swept away in the flood. Not literally, of course, the flood was thirty-five years ago and although we did lose a good deal of invaluable photographs and notes, drawings, ephemera, from our downtown office, we lost no people. I don't think—I'm not sure this is right but at my age I'm not sure it matters—too many people lost too many people in the Great Flood of 1913. Mostly a physical-damage phenomenon or Act of God. That God should act in such a destructive way: never understood. Man is destructive enough on his own, without help. We have destroyed enough in my lifetime alone to fill the graveyards of the world twice over. That's a witticism. I should not indulge in witticisms.

• I do still believe, I do, that the airplane will prove in time an instrument of peace. Seems clear to me that we are headed for a socialist society, because that arrangement's the only one that makes any sense, in fairness to all, in justice to all. Perhaps that's a pun: injustice to all? I don't believe in puns. I do not. Someone once asked me: But surely you are a capitalist, Mr. Wright? And my reply, which now I think of it, was a good reply, and which still holds true, was on the order of: Absolutely. Every penny I receive comes from capital. I have no paying job. But for a long time I've had grave doubts about the justice of getting interest for the use of money. Probably it's wrong to pay interest. The fellow then says: But without capitalism and the profit motive, whither inventions? I had to chuckle. Back then, in many instances when I was amused, I would chuckle. Nowadays it is rare that I do so. Most certainly if a profit motive were necessary for invention, I told this man, my brother and I would not have invented the airplane. Our chief concern was always to get money to put into it, not take money out of it. We were at it for the sport. Yes, well, that's fine, he replies, but here you are, the picture postcard of rugged individualism and hard work, two boys with no money, no influence, no advantage, you start at the bottom and you come up flying.

If that's not an argument for capitalism, he says, for what the French call laissez-faire, I don't know what is. Hah! I rejoindered. We did have advantages in youth. Great advantages. You mean to say your family was wealthy? he asked. No, wealth might have been a disadvantage, says I. The great thing for us was growing up in a family where there was much encouragement to intellectual curiosity. If not for that, we would never have gotten interested in the printing business, or the bicycle, or for that matter in the idea of flight.

- Another time I was asked: What was your greatest difficulty in solving the problem of machine-powered flight? Or something along those lines. And the answer? I can't remember the answer. No, I do remember the answer, but now that I think back it strikes me as something of a wisecrack, and not a proper answer. There was no greatest difficulty, only innumerable small ones, each interfering with the other, was along the line of what I replied. I will sit here on the couch in front of this fire, which casts a shimmer on the damask walls, and a red glimmer on the red stain of the floors and the doors. Took special pains to acquire that shade of red. The workmen were not at first interested in the exact right shade. I made them interested. I will sit here and smoke my pipe filled with a mixture of tobacco and opium leaf, or leaves, and I will consider the grandeur of this house, every detail of which I oversaw personally, because a house is a temple for the body in the way a body is a temple for the soul. The windows of a house are the windows through which the windows of the soul perceive or are shown or see the world, and the world, in my experience, looks back. The most frightening moments in a man's life are when he cannot see the world looking back, or when he imagines for an instant that there is no world at all to see or be seen. That the connections he has forged in the root cellar of his brain are phantasms, and not real, and further that nothing at all is real, not even the machine that he flew for twelve elongated seconds over the freezing sand at Kitty Hawk almost forty-five years ago. That event did not happen. That event could not have happened, because the idea of flight is ridiculous, because all ideas are ridiculous, and moreover unsanitary. What I have done with my reading glasses, I have removed one temple so that I may apply or withdraw them with facility. I do not believe in wasting time. That's exactly the answer I should have given. That, my good fellow, is the greatest difficulty with solving the problem of flight. The greatest difficulty with solving any problem: convincing yourself that the problem exists.

Notebook Ten

The night swarmed over Amanda Early stepping past the privet hedge and onto the sidewalk. A strong scent of azaleas, carried on the breeze, drew her attention to the sky, streaked with scudding clouds. Sum of the stars, and moon. Higher math. Wide white moon low in the dark sky, you can see the shine of its rim under a shank of backlit cloud. Not many stars: covered by clouds, or moonlight.

Amanda turned the corner from Morton west onto Oak Street. A starling swooped from maple to telephone pole, dark flying triangle, iridescing faintly in a buzzing white blare of streetlight. Sunset was iced-licorice melting, dusky red spread over the cross-hatched mesh of the porch screen, the lawn chair's broken webbing, laminated limbs brushed with ruddy twilight. Word he used: crepuscular. Shouldn't have let him. Just what part of no was giving him trouble? A car passed by slowly, its tires bouncing on the uneven cobblestones of the recently reconstructed street. Since they tore up the tar the road is hard to walk on; the bricks underneath are uneven, broken and scarred, stamped with the company name *Newtonville Brick* which seems more like a statement than a company name. But I don't know a statement of what. Down Oak to the small square of grass between the fire station and the corner of Wyoming and Brown. The grass was wet with unabsorbed rain from yesterday's storm, even in the dark she could see the wetness glistening around the ridges of her boots, just above the rim of the rubber soles. When I swing my arms like this it must look funny to other people. Marching, marching.

A group of people she didn't know came out of the bar on the opposite corner as Amanda stood waiting for the traffic light to change. Two of the boys in the group linked arms around one of the girls, who protested with sharp little shrieks of laughter. Amanda kept pressing the *Walk* button on the traffic signal post with her thumb. Then she rubbed her thumb in the palm of her other hand. He has nice shoulders, nice the way they slope sharply from his skinny neck to the bony points where the arms begin. But there's a twisty ridge of muscle so you know he's a little strong. I bet I'm stronger. I bet I could have cracked him in half like a lobster claw with my legs. Three months ago and the memory of that night still lingers.

Crossing the street, she hesitated in front of the door to the bar. A little early to go in. No one will be there yet and I don't have any money. I have three dollars which is one drink or maybe two beers. If Trip is there he'll buy me drinks. Amanda turned and headed south down Brown Street, aimlessly, gazing without intent at the darkened windows of the row of closed storefronts and old row houses lining the street. No one was on the streets, at least down here, and she hoped that she wouldn't run into anyone she knew. She walked as far up as the record store where Joe worked, looked in the window to see if he was still there. The store was closed, and she could discern nothing moving in the dimly lit interior. Wish I could see like bees, with the blue parts of things shimmering. The sky in daytime would vibrate, you could tell the time just from the intensity of blue, bending the sun. Fragments of light contain the whole truth of light, still. What is revealed? If you can see you can see.

She turned down a side street, even emptier and more desolate than Brown. Voices carried from a porch nearby, but she couldn't see anyone. Wonder if I really am nuts. Manic-depressive, the doctor said, after half a lousy hour of talking. How can you tell anything in half an hour?

Her feet carried her automatically back to Wyoming, opposite the bright façade of the hospital, alongside the bar. When she came around front, a car full of kids she didn't recognize sped through the intersection and one of the kids yelled something rude through the backseat window. Amanda looked up, unsure whether the rude comment had been directed at her.

Through bee's eyes, would even stuff that's invisible to us appear visible? Emotions have auras. Heartbreak has an aura. If you could see that, what would it look like say in ultraviolet? Sometimes I think I can see things but as fractured designs. Are there patterns or is it all incomprehensible jumble. Chaos that doesn't resolve in wider perspective, only wider chaos. Maybe move closer, like with those 3D gimmicks. No matter how I blur my vision, focus, squint, unhook my head, or grimace: I can never get those things to work. I can never find the angle that springs the gimmick's secret.

Amanda Early tugged at the brass knob, her slightly crossed brown eyes with ochre flecks squinching in the late winter cold. Stepping into the bar, she smelled the beer smell and the smell from the stale pretzels lying in a stainless steel pan under a heat lamp at the edge of the bar. Ice crystals sat clumped on top of the salt chunks on top of the pretzels, thawing. She quickly scanned the front room for signs of anyone she knew, then saw Joe and Trip sitting opposite each other in a booth in the back room, and headed past the bar, waving at Billy the bartender as she went.

"Hey, Billy. Quiet night," said Amanda.

"So far," responded Billy gloomily. Although Billy's living was dependent on the largesse of the largely college crowd that patronized the Hive, he regarded customers as an unwelcome intrusion into his routine of gathering empties and loading them into racks to be carted to the dishwasher downstairs, through a narrow trapdoor and down wobbly wooden stairs to the basement.

Amanda greeted her friends and sat down. Trip was occupied with a sheaf of typewritten pages, as usual—his book proposal, he took great pains to tell anyone who asked—leafing slowly through the pages from back to front, stopping to make a pencil mark. Joe bent low over his empty drink, sucking the last few drops of yellowish liquid through a red plastic straw, noisily, by way of returning Amanda's greeting.

Trip looked up and his face contorted into a version of a faint smile.

"To the bar I betake myself," he announced, noticing Joe's empty drink and Amanda's arrival in the same moment. "Who would like what to drink, specifically?"

Amanda made a vague gesture of demurral.

"I insist," insisted Trip. "I will buy a round of drinks with the money I am due upon completion of this beastly book proposal."

"Greyhound," said Joe, without looking up from his glass.

"Greyhound for Joe," said Trip. "And for Amanda?"

"Well, if you're going, I guess a whiskey and soda." She reached into her pockets, pulled out a couple of crumpled dollars and some change.

"No, no," said Trip, seeing Amanda separating her change into little piles. "I'll pay. That's the point of buying a round of drinks."

Amanda shrugged, and Trip walked toward the front room. She heard the front door swing open, the low whoosh of air as it swung back on its heels, and involuntarily turned around. A girl with blond hair and a small nose, wearing a robin's-egg-blue scarf, walked smiling into the bar.

Mary Valentine breathed a sigh of decision. She knew it was too early, there was no way he would be there, and so no rational fear of an uncomfortable encounter. But the ghosts of awkward moments past conspired to produce in her stomach a churning fear that only alcohol could soothe, and she walked through the

144 ❋ Artificial Light

warm air straight to Billy at the bar and ordered a whiskey and water. She saw in the back a group of friends, Amanda Early and some others, but didn't feel ready to socialize, and instead pulled up a stool at the bar. She sat next to Fred, a gentle-featured guy with a heavy West Dayton accent whose attendance at the Hive bordered on the devotional—to the point where he was eventually hired to work the door, checking IDs of the University of Dayton kids, which was what he was supposed to be doing now, but you can't be everywhere at once, he explained to Mary. There was a baseball game almost over on the TV and it was more or less dead in the bar: Fred bet Mary he could name every person in the Hive right at that moment, but Mary never bet unless she was sure to win, she told Fred, which Fred explained you're gonna have to wait an awful long time between bets if that's the case.

"You're telling me," said Mary, sipping her drink and giggling. She'd decided after all to wear the green skirt because of the colors of the tile in her bathroom, even though her knee was scraped and now cut shaving. My legs, she thought, still look good and sometimes if I wear pants with this top I look like a tater-tot.

Mary giggled, again, at the thought of herself as a tater-tot, which would have been a better costume than the pumpkin-lady one with the big orange boa she'd tried last Halloween, where no one had come to her party because everything was still too awkward.

No use trying to make anyone understand, thought Mary. Everything important needs to be left unspoken or it gets ruined. Let them think I'm a flirt or boy-crazy or whatever, it's partially true, but a partial truth is hopeless and frustrating, like a partial orgasm. It's fine if everyone hates me, I can't wait to get out of this town. If I had even a little money, or a car . . . I'm twenty-three. I'm twenty-three with a degree in English and I work at a novelty store and if I could grow wings right now I would never look back at this tired, dingy place.

She swallowed angrily the dregs of her drink and ordered another. Mary had hoped, possibly even expected, that love might give her the sense of freedom she craved, the lightness of limb and strength of purpose to make a life anywhere, even here. Instead, what she got was a more complete sense of futility, and the worst parts of passion: The ground had fallen away beneath her, replaced by a vortex of quickly shifting currents of feeling, from jealousy to rage to bliss to despair to emptiness, the void of detachment that can feel like peace but nobody's fooled, even for a second. She was inflicted with an ache of unremitting need, and Mary, who had always prized her self-sufficiency, found this unwonted neediness galling in the extreme. Above all, the twisty feeling in the stomach that never leaves, the hard knot of incomprehension that makes even the thought of food ridiculous and nauseating. She'd lost ten pounds and taken to drinking heavily and alone. At one point she'd torn the phone cord from its wall jack and not gone out of her single-room apartment for five days, calling in sick for three shifts of work at The Magic Hat.

But all that was almost a year ago, both a century and an instant in terms of human emotion, and in that time Mary had made an incremental recovery from the disease of love. Only once had she broken down, prompted by some inner spasm of sudden fury to drive by his house and unload a carton of eggs in rapid succession at the unlit windows on the second floor. Maybe half of the eggs, five or six, had come anywhere near their target, the rest splattered on dusty red bricks or lost in the bushes, their broken yolks dripping from the fragrant white blossoms of the row of azaleas lining the front of the house. She still felt a rush of shame recalling the lapse into drama queendom, a thing she hated in other girls but especially in herself, to be so affected by a stupid boy.

So things remained awkward, and their inevitable encounters were fraught but usually uneventful, as neither Michael nor Mary was a fan of confrontation. Worst was the sinking feeling whenever he threatened her sense of no-problem viability by entering her peripheral vision. As if his mere presence punctured the sagging balloon of her personality, and whatever hope she'd managed to salvage from their collapsed romance hissed into the room, joining the smoke on the ceiling, the chatter of her friends, and the low hum of general despair that subtexted every such gathering. This was usually how she ended up making out with someone she didn't even like.

Mary Valentine finished her second drink and moved toward the back of the bar. The same people, she thought, every night and part of every day, in my eyes and hair and nose and throat. I'm sick of their stink. I'm sick of the sinking in my stomach every time I see them gathered here or in another bar, the fake smiles, the stupid jokes, the general lack of anything resembling an idea. And that's just me, tee hee.

Useless to complain, though, thought Mary, moving with a parodic wiggle in her hips, deliberately, toward her friends grouped in little clumps, twos and threes, around the booth where Trip and Joe and Amanda sat, the center of the social circle. I complain but I'm here, and I'm here because I'm attracted to the idea of here, which is never the same as the dull tangible thing itself. You'd think I'd have figured that out by now.

"You know that thing where you can't figure out whether you're looking at the front of a building or the side?"

Joe was looking expectantly at Trip as Mary slid in next to Joe, wordlessly, smiling.

"I think that's déjà vu," replied Trip, his eyes on Mary.

"No, no," insisted Joe, "I'm pretty sure that's not correct."

"Check again," said Trip, eyes still on Mary, blindly stirring the ice in his drink.

Mary giggled involuntarily. The table was covered in empty glasses opaque with smeared fingerprints, beer bottles with torn labels, a raft of discarded red straws, and waterlogged napkins. An abstract series of canals connected the various objects, and in the map of intersecting rivulets you could see mirrored at crazy angles the speckled ceiling tiles and the hanging plants like leafy spiders and the warmly orange ends of cigarettes.

"How's the ankle, Joe?" asked Mary, the shadow of a smirk flitting across her face.

"Thank you for asking," muttered Joe darkly.

"Do you mean in a picture?" asked Trip.

"Yes, of course, in a picture or a painting," said Joe impatiently. "How're you gonna get confused if you're in the true presence of something and all you have to do is walk around and around until you figure it out?"

Trip sat silent for a moment, fingering Mary's lips with his eyes. "That could either be *trompe l'oeil* or perspective, I'm not sure where you're going here."

"This is an important discussion," deadpanned Mary. "Important boys are having an important talk about important things. I am so turned on."

"Isn't it enough that you've crippled me for life?" bleated Joe.

"The only way to placate the goddess of boredom is with alcohol," said Trip. "Who's drinking what?"

Strange how he keeps looking at me, thought Mary, as Trip got up from the booth to buy drinks. Not strange, because I cultivate the looks from him and every other, but strange because he seems to get the joke but not care, like there might be some actual feeling behind the kneejerk hormonal response to my flirty façade. A year ago there was some life in me that might have responded.

"Does anybody have a cigarette?" she asked.

Joe reached wearily into his shirt pocket and tossed a crumpled pack onto the table. The weariness, Mary considered, was an affectation to deflect his awkwardness at Amanda's presence. I have some experience in that area, she thought, I know how it feels to have every heartbeat and the slightest gesture magnified a thousand times in your own eyes and ears. Where you wish you would just explode or disappear or instantly become much smarter and better-looking.

She extracted a cigarette from the pack and pulled it smooth between two fingers. Amanda reached across and clumsily tried to light a match for her, the sulfurous head of the match smoking but no flame appearing, probably because the matches had been sitting in a puddle of drink sweat. Joe took a lighter from the same shirt pocket and held it out for Mary's use without looking at her. Token of his non-playing status, she thought, taking the lighter and applying it to the end of her smoothed-out cigarette. He thinks any gesture of kindness toward women implies interest, so he signals he has none. Which usually to me represents a challenge, except I don't think so, pal. I'm all challenged out, at the moment, especially where Joe is concerned. Maybe it's the stupid puppy love aspect of his Amanda crush that makes him pathetically unappealing, or maybe I'm just jealous, which I doubt. Most likely, and most depressing, is that I can see the hopelessness. Either she never responds, and he's heartsick for a while but recovers and acquires a sheen of bitterness, or worse, she does respond, and they become a couple for a while, until the inertia of this place works on the centrifuge of love and the gravity of ego, or something, I'm not a math brain, and things fall apart and people get hurt, and never heal. These are the two available options, set in feldspar the day Joe decided some combination of physical beauty (and not to be catty, but please) and probably invented-by-Joe or otherwise mythological personality traits was the recipe for his own personal opiate of the masses.

Mary took a deep drag of hot smoke from her cigarette, exhaling noisily through her nostrils so that a focused light gray fume spread quickly across the table to envelop Joe, who pretended not to notice. She listened to the chatter of people around her, thinking she could distinguish simply by the pitch and speed of their voices the emotional content of the mostly super-ficial conversations. It's never the things people say that carry the meaning of their words, anyway, she thought. Someone could compile a phrasebook with just the gestures people use in bars to express fear and desire, which are the root feelings of every normal exchange. I want you, say the eyes of one, darting from feature to feature of another's available topography, while their mouth moves ceaselessly, like an insect eating. I fear death or intimacy or loneliness or the emptiness of existence, say the frantic hands of someone else, picking compulsively at the frayed label of a beer bottle. It's an easy language to learn, I'm already pretty fluent, but I don't have the energy to do the necessary catalog work. That might be something Trip could do, it's not far from what he spends all his time doing anyway.

She reached under the table and fingered the scar on her knee, smooth and glassy compared with the rest of her skin. Nothing ever pans out the way you think it will, thought Mary. But then it becomes something else and you forget how much you wanted it to be the first thing. You get caught up in the nextness, the back flip of expectation over reality's head, the nearing new day, all that totally insignificant loss. I should have clipped my toenails, for instance. What happens when you get distracted.

* * *

"And how are you this dark, cold, and lovelorn evening, Amanda?" asked Mary. Amanda suddenly found a pattern of great interest in the water that had dripped from the glasses onto the dark-brown varnish of the tabletop.

"I don't know," replied Amanda. "Good." She drew a connecting bridge from one small roundlet of water to its neighbor with her straw. Wonder why I'm not scared of death, thought Amanda. I'm afraid of many things, including but not limited to large, creeping insects, severe thunderstorms, being made to look like a fool, being a fool, and rats, but I'm not scared of dying. I know that I will die, because death is the bargain we make with life, but the question that seems to obsess people about whether consciousness continues, or at least individual consciousness, and what form that might take, doesn't bother me. Not because I don't care, but because the answer either way is not very interesting. At least the answers I have heard. Most of us, around here, spend a good part of our conscious lives trying to become unconscious. What kind of consciousness is that? If individual consciousness does survive after death, I hope it will be better formatted than the present type. Or I hope you will be able to make better use of it. I hope you will have the chance, at least.

Before I die, though, I want to see these stones—megaliths, as they're called. I want to go to England and see the megaliths, still in place thousands of years later, worship at these sites, in person, instead of through the color plates in books that Fiat finds for me

in the library. I'm reading one now which is supposed
to be the best. *The Stones of Britain.* Apparently the famous
megalithic site, Stonehenge, is not even nearly the best
or most authentic site. Or oldest, either. The guy who
put together the book, which is mostly pictures and
maps of how to get to the places, took three years
traveling around to get everything right. I wouldn't
need three years and also I'd probably be bored by the
end of three months, but I want, I need, to connect to
the Earth Spirit or *Gaia*, as the author of *The Stones of
Britain* calls Her. The culture that built or arranged the
stones has long vanished, but not everything connected
to that culture is gone. You can supposedly still feel the
power of what they knew, and what they knew was
connected intimately to real knowledge of the Earth
and of Nature. Eventually the knowledge these people
had got corrupted by other forms of worship, not even
Christian but other pagan ideas.

The system of belief most closely resembling my
own notions would be, I think, the one followed by
what used to be called Druids. If I had to say I was
anything, then, I would say I'm a Druid. But not out
loud, not to anyone I know, not unless Kurt's there to
prevent everyone laughing. Hard to be a Druid in Ohio.
No other Druids, for one thing. A secret unshared's no
fun. No one to decipher the tattoo on my ankle, or the
one on the small of my back, not that anyone ever sees
that anyway. Not even that one time, because he was
too quick, too rough, and I think had his eyes closed the
whole time. Navigating by touch, or some approximation of touch, like someone who'd only recently
regained the use of his hands after a bad accident. Why

did he not want to look at me, at my face, even when he kissed me? I always keep my eyes open. It's the closest you get to another person, in terms of seeing them, and I like to see them. But he wouldn't look. That was because he did not want to see me. Because I have a moonlike face which some find unappealing. Other parts of my body boys are not as fussy about.

Also even though there are places with trees, and the Miami Valley is a fairly green (or *verdant* is a word I like, too) area, especially in spring and summer, there's no place you'd consider natural, in the sense of Nature. Any magic in this place, tree-spirits or such, would long ago have fled in despair, I think. You wouldn't want to stick around all these bricks and dead wood and cars and people. Mostly people.

Fiat gave me a book about the White Goddess which was written by a poet and I could not understand even the first thing about it because, maybe, I don't like poetry. The guy in the book was going on about secret tree languages and the magic power of words and even letters of words when used with the proper magic understanding. I don't know if he's right but I do believe that there's a power in trees, in Nature generally, that makes me feel hope in things, generally, that I don't often feel when I'm around people. It's not that I understand Nature any better than I do people, or relate to it, or however you would say that—just the opposite is true. I don't understand anything about Nature. It is beyond my compre-hendibility, if that's a word. Because of that, I like or respond to that power. People I sometimes think I understand too well, in the very specific meaning of

they do not surprise me. Almost never anything
someone does will cause me to say, "That's surprising.
I would not have expected that of him or her." I am as
predictable as the next person. Even if I say, "I am
absolutely not going to do X," I probably will do X if
that's what I really meant, and it's easy to see what I or
anyone else really means. All you have to do is look at
them, which is why I like to keep my eyes open during
sex.

Light from the fake Tiffany lamps nearby flecked the
honey-colored ice in Amanda's glass with gold
highlights as she tipped it to and fro on the tabletop. If
you could see like a bee you might be able to know the
meaning of color. Because now, when you look at a color,
you have a feeling that the meaning of the color is just
past the actual color—if you could see a little further in
the visible spectrum, maybe a line of code would appear,
like on magnetic tape that carries more information than
your stereo can decipher. That's not a helpful example.
Sometimes when you see a painting where the painter
understands color as best as anyone can without bee's
eyes, you get a faint smell of meaning; but it's just the
painter's explanation or idea of meaning rather than
actual meaning. The way I know this: Different colors
seem to have different meanings in different kinds of
light. Under direct sunlight versus twilight or electric
light in its multihued forms, for instance. Meaning of
color in these instances strikes me as fake. Might as well
talk about the angle of perception, or individual realities,
or any of that nonsense. I'm looking for the real thing.

Outside the Hive, the moon was swallowed in a

purplish thunderhead. The wind had increased in intensity, to the point where the row of anemic maples strapped into their squares of dirt at regular intervals along the stretch of sidewalk leading away from the bar, up the quarter-mile toward the convenience store on the corner of Stewart, was bent northwards, in the direction of downtown, in a synchronized gesture of submission. Whenever someone hurried into the Hive from the street, overcoats flapping in the pre-storm breeze, there was a burst of brassy noise from the oblong of yellow light revealed when the door was pulled open. The door swinging heavily back into its casement caused the noise to cease abruptly, and you could hear then only the whoosh of wind through the trembling maples. A crushed paper cup skittered through the gutter and into the intersection of Wyoming and Brown. Crossing against the light, the jaywalking litter was swallowed by the mud-encrusted maw of a sewer drain on the opposite corner, near the gas station whose pumps gleamed in the halogen light like glossy headstones.

The stretch from the Hive to the Gulp-N-Save, from Wyoming to Stewart along Brown, was the length of a gunshot, to crib from Gloomy Gus. Because of the cold, few figures populated the sidewalks along either side of the street, and few cars rolled bumpily over the cracked and pitted asphalt in either direction. One, a robin's-egg-blue station wagon ornamented with terra-cotta rust near its rear bumper and along the edges of its undercarriage, pulled into the parking lot across from the Hive, and sat nestled in its slot for some minutes, engine idling roughly. Inside the car, silhouetted by street light, a slim figure smoked a slim cigarette, smoke curling from the rolled-down window and upwards, through the complicated shadow of a nearby sycamore tree, disappearing by degrees (the way everything good disappears) into the leafy murk.

Michael Goodlife sat in his robin's-egg-blue station wagon, smoking one after another cigarette. The smoke from the cigarettes continued to climb up the sycamore shadows, occasionally backlit by a lemony gleam when the wind brushed back the tree branches to admit the streetlight's shine. The moon passed in and out of the turbulent clouds, and whenever in its course the fullness of moonlight dusted the parking lot, the shadows would deepen, shift into focus, and Michael felt himself recede into them, becoming less a visible integer and more a part of the pattern.

There's not a spot where God is not, he thought, smiling ironically. He reached over and turned off the engine, stubbing out with his other hand a half-smoked cigarette on the outside of the driver's-side door. A constellation of black smudges dotted the dull paint where other cigarettes had met similar ends, and the pavement below was strewn with butts like dead white worms. If I go in now, he thought, there's a good chance she'll be there, but enough other people will be there, too, so the chances of an awkward meeting are less. I can't believe that almost a year later things are still like this. Every other girl I've ever gone out with or even slept with is no problem, and even this is no problem, except for the way it somehow makes me feel, still. Maybe a sense of incompleteness because she never answered my letter. All it does is make me cold-hearted and mean. I'm not an angry person by nature, not at all, but she's like a magnet for my iron-rich bile. Not her but the memory itch, the irritation, of our former thing. Like a diamond ground to dust, chafing under my sleeves. Not that we were very gemlike, together.

Michael opened the door and got out. Stretching his arms under the arms of the sycamore, he smelled the rain on the sky's breath and smiled. Two reminders in the space of five minutes, he thought. Two examples of the immensity of divine intelligence. But the hugeness of the evidence at hand was more than canceled by the hugeness of Michael's doubt. If it's true that a thing contains its opposite, he considered, I wonder does it lay inside me as potential energy. I have the potential for great faith, buried in my heart like a maggot, feeding off the trickle of misplaced hope that still somehow runs alongside the torrent of despair. He shivered in the open air. There's no way I'm going inside that bar, he thought.

Michael opened the door and got back in his car. He turned the key in the ignition so that the radio would play. Music is a powerful friend, a friend with connections in high places, he thought. You stick with music and you'll end up at all the right parties.

He closed his eyes and listened. The music playing was an old song from maybe the '60s, a lightweight pop song with a girl singer. He remembered hearing the song many years ago, as a small boy, lying in the backseat of his mother's car. At that time, he believed that the songs on the radio were played and sung live, down at the radio station, which for some reason Michael envisioned as a fancy-dress bowling alley. It was late spring or early summer, he recalled, and maple tree shadows webbed the hot vinyl of the car's backseat. The engine was running but his mother had gone into the Green Stamp store to redeem an armload of booklets for a lamp, or a toaster, or a magic wand that properly operated could bring her back, now, in the ridiculous and lonely present.

What make of car was that? he wondered. I remember an emerald-green color, inside and out, deeply and thoroughly green like wet leaves in spring rain, and the smell of her cigarette smoke wafting back, as we drove to the supermarket. Not much help in brand identification. I think the cigarettes were menthol, though. Who smokes menthol anymore? I do. Maybe there's a gene for what type of cigarettes you smoke.

He sighed and switched the music off. There's never a chance that I'll do something unexpected, he thought. I could drive right now wherever I want and never look back at this town. But he knew there was no way of that happening, because there was no way of not looking back in his mind. Too much of Dayton was knitted into too much of Michael—if you tried to remove one you would end up unraveling big swatches of the other. You could argue that people here give undue attention to unimportant things, but what's an important thing? As far as he was concerned, everything vital to life and love was easily obtained, and at a cheaper price, in Dayton. And even if that were not true, even if he were delusional and blind to the stifling cultural isolation of this provincial backwater, just like in an old Russian novel, did any of that matter as long as he was happy?

Okay, maybe not happy, but at least content. It's not the way things were in old times, where no one ever traveled and the whole world was contained within the county borders. You don't have to leave to see things anymore, things come to you now. The idea of flight is the real delusion, the idea that you go from one place to another and leave the one place behind until you return. People everywhere are strange; I have the hardest time relating to other human beings. You get used to them, but you get used to anything after a while, including the sweet kick of love, loneliness, habitual disappointment, patterns of seeming coincidence that contain the imprint of fate, loss of innocence, and the constant and comforting presence of death.

Once again he got out of the car. A gust of wind swept across the parking lot, causing innumerable particles of sand and discarded paper and cigarette ends and even the sawtoothed fragment of a red plastic cup to tumble along the tar in a way that looked choreographed. The lot had been recently resurfaced, so little specks of quartz imbedded in the new tar glittered like broken glass in the streetlight. Michael cracked the knuckles of each hand, lit another cigarette, and started across the glittering tar toward the Hive.

"Almost a full moon tonight," said Amanda suddenly and for no reason to Mary Valentine, who looked at her strangely but made no reply. The door swished open; when Mary saw that it was Michael, she looked away quickly, her whole body rigid with emotion, then quickly, as if guided by some invisible strong-arm, headed for the back, to the girls' bathroom. Thus pre-occupied, she missed the rest of Michael's entrance, particularly the part where he slipped on a wet spot of melted ice from someone's spilled drink, lost his balance, and in trying to right himself, legs flailing, grabbed the edge of a nearby table, arms windmilling, which happened to be filled with an unusual number of empty and half-empty glasses, nearly all of which came tumbling with impressive speed and force down on Michael's now-prone body. The clatter of glasses, only a few of which broke because most of them bounced off his chest, attracted the attention of a number of patrons in the front part of the bar, who broke into a spontaneous and sustained round of applause as Michael unsteadily stood, dripping with the dregs of several different types of alcohol, but mostly beer, and acknowledged with an ironic grin the crowd's ovation.

Michael Goodlife was upset more for the loss of a good entrance than for the damage to his clothes. Around him on the floor lay the debris of his accident, more than a dozen capsized beer glasses, frothy dregs pooling around his shoes and the baseboard of the bar and the upended table. He shook himself, a dog shaking off rainwater, and splattered a group of nearby girls, who shrieked but didn't mind. Billy the bartender went down through the trapdoor to the cellar to get a mop, leaving a line of thirsty customers waiting impatiently by the unattended taps.

I am wet, like the sea, thought Michael. I am sticky as pine sap. I'm ridiculous, and everyone knows. I am.

"I better go clean up," said Michael, to no one and

everyone, gesturing to his soaked shirt. He turned and began to make his way through the drinkers crowded around the bar.

When he got to the men's room, there was a line, three people. He knew one of the three, Trip Ryvvers, and the two nodded to each other.

"Raining out?" asked Trip, who was listing slightly.

"Got in a fight. Bunch of beer glasses ganged up on me, must have been like twenty of 'em."

"You shouldn't tease beer. Beer's touchy."

"Apparently." The men's room door opened and a boy wearing a tie-dyed T-shirt, nascent dreadlocks jutting from his ellipsoidal head, walked out. Trip and Michael exchanged looks.

"You still driving that old rust bucket?" asked Trip.

"Still."

"You've got money, now, right? The big record deal. You should be buying a house, a car, a machine gun."

"That's theoretical money, not real money. No one in the music business gets paid except lawyers and more lawyers. And the record company. Unless you strike the motherlode like Kurt."

"You complain an awful lot for someone with a boatload of theoretical money." The door to the men's room opened and two more tie-dyed teenagers walked out, laughing, the soundtrack to Trip's joke. "How many of them do you suppose are in there?"

"As many as it takes," answered Michael with a wry grin, or what he hoped looked like a wry grin.

Following the collegiate fellow in front of him, Trip opened the door and peeked in. "All right," he sighed, "I'm going in. Wish me luck."

162 * Artificial Light

"Good luck," Michael called politely after Trip as he ducked into the men's room. By now there were three or four more collegiate-looking young men lined up behind Michael, and he decided that it might be a better idea to go to the back of the bar, to one of the two girls' bathrooms, to the one in particular that locked, which might afford him the time and privacy necessary to perform a cursory cleanup.

His anxiety level had risen, in any case, the moment he saw there was a line, as there was little Michael despised so much as the rituals of the crowded public bathroom. He would have turned then and headed to the back, but seeing Trip did not want to seem rude. Group activities in general he found noxious, but mass micturition in particular held a taint of unmitigated masculinity that made Michael physically sick. Until he'd had four or five drinks and was desensitized to the process, he could not bear the thought much less the sight of entering the fluorescent-scrubbed cubicle, ribbed with sweating pipes, across the warped linoleum wet with beer, water, and piss, to the lone stinking urinal, or worse, to the lone stall whose width barely permitted turning around, and whose badly hinged door would not stay shut. At peak hours, it was not unusual to find both stall and urinal occupied and another backwards-baseball-cap-clad fratboy or pony-tailed hippie poised on tiptoe over the sink, one arm casually extended against the dingy wall, whistling or talking to a friend who wasn't listening or farting unconcernedly, the bang of the fart punctuating the desperately ridiculous nature of the activity, which is more or less why everyone laughs.

Why are males in general so crass and unself-conscious about their bodily functions? thought Michael. In the interval between sixth grade and the start of junior high, he would fantasize about burning down the school just so he wouldn't have to take showers with the other boys after gym class. The prospect of group-undressing filled Michael with a horror he could neither explain nor describe, an instinctive reaction to the display of so much juvenile nudity, or so much scrutiny of his own—either way, the options were too gross to coexist with Michael's still-developing notions of his own self and sexuality. Even years later, after he managed to overcome his instinctual fear and disrobe in locker rooms with the sort of studied casualness that the very shy often adopt (the key is to change pants first, then shirt), he was still uncomfortable, even in situations of extreme intimacy involving girls. After sex, he almost always pulled his pants back on, unless the girl complained, which she sometimes did, feeling that Michael's gesture was meant to force apart (however slightly) the closeness between them. When really he was just uncomfortable being naked, completely naked, always had been since puberty, and pulling on his pants reflected in no way his feelings toward whatever the name of the girl lying in his bed was.

Joe Smallman turned in his seat and looked to the front of the bar just in time to see Michael come around the corner from the men's room and begin threading his way through the crowd. He turned back around to face Amanda, who looked down, at her drink, at her hand stirring her drink, at the straw making frantic circuits in her glass.

"If you stir fast enough, time will go backwards," observed Joe.

"That's what I'm hoping. Backwards to the time when you weren't sitting here, maybe."

"What's up with you, anyway?"

"I could say the same thing back."

"I'm miserable."

"Then you know what's up with me. We could maybe start a secret society: handshakes, tree house."

"We tried that already. Too hard to remember the password."

"I guess you're right." Amanda scratched the side of her face with the straw from her drink. She stood up. "I'm going to the rest room. See if Mary's all right."

"Why wouldn't Mary be all right?" asked Joe as Amanda left.

Tried and true, thought Joe, what does that mean? Everything in Dayton is tried and true, or false, and tried again till true enough. In the lack of education, because half of us are high school dropouts and the other half college dropouts, you can see compensatory self-taught erudition everywhere, too much almost. Maybe there's no such thing as too much, though. What's most surprising is the secret ambition of everyone to do something real, despite the outward show of null and void. Even if something real means only to fall in love.

Tear-stained Mary Valentine stood over the sink in the Snafu Hive bathroom, the taps turned on full to cover her sobbing. She watched herself in the mirror, or rather that part of herself not engaged in sobbing regarded her sobbing self with detachment, curiously, only a little worried.

"Hi," she said to the mirror, and giggled, and started crying again. The sadness is never very far below the surface, she thought, and requires only a keyword to break the skin of composure I stretch across my face, every day. Every day. Silly, stupid girl. Brought to tears by a word, well, not actually by the word but by the memory evoked by the word. Why is it memories hurt more than when the thing originally happens to you?

Mary walked over to the stall and tore off several squares of toilet paper. Dabbing her face, she returned to the mirror. She shut her eyes and tried to imagine the scene where Michael had broken up with her, except he hadn't even broken up, it was more like he shut down, or shut off, or retreated. That was the feeling, thought Mary, it was like he retreated to the part of yourself that you keep from everyone, except the one person you love, and so in retreating you're declaring your lack of love. Watching that retreat happen, feeling him withdraw right in front of you, is the scariest feeling there is, I think, like in that dream where everyone and everything looks familiar but up close they're strange and sinister. All of a sudden Michael was just not there. In his place was some curly haired ghost babbling about phases of the moon, while we sat in the wet grass in Carillon Park drinking very bad wine.

The part that will drive you crazy is trying to figure out why, thought Mary. That and the sudden absence of safety, the vacuum of no protection from the painful and hate-filled world. In space no one can hear you scream, but on planet Earth, let me tell you, sometimes that's all you can hear, if you're near my room. But the screaming is just a way of trying to breathe, because when he left he took all the air, too, and nothing worked, especially lungs.

Everybody now thinks I'm overreacting or faking it, probably. Too many times I run crying to the bathroom. This is complicated by the fact that most of the time I *am* faking, she considered. I'm using the pity ploy to draw the attention of some boy or other whose attention I don't want except reflexively. Like everyone I have tried, not to be crude, but I have tried to plug the leak with sex. Nothing, nothing, nothing, nothing, nothing.

The bathroom door opened and Amanda came in. Mary reached for the taps and turned them off, then gathered some toilet paper and blew her nose exaggeratedly.

Amanda gave a sort of snort, still holding the door open. "You all right?" she asked.

"I'm fine," replied Mary, through a veil of tissue. "Allergies. How." She balled up the tissue in her hand. "Are." She aimed the balled-up tissue at the trash can in the corner by the door, next to Amanda. "Yo-u-u," she singsonged, letting the ball of tissue fly. It bounced off the rim and landed at Amanda's feet.

"I'm good," grinned Amanda, closing the bathroom door and walking toward the stall.

"Uh-huh." Mary examined her face in the mirror. The letter he sent me from Europe when he was on tour with his band. That's one of those things: If he'd bothered to check the address, make sure it was right, and I got the letter in a few days instead of a few months later, would *everything be different*, the way it works out in drippy romantic movies? I hate that movie more than anything.

She listened to the sound of Amanda peeing in the stall behind her. "Hey, Amanda?" she called. "You think maybe the red one tonight?"

From the stall came a sound of clothing being adjusted. "You mean wig? I don't know. What's wrong with your real hair?"

"First of all, it's not my real hair color anyway, it's from a box. And second, people are getting bored with me. I can sense it."

The toilet flush echoed across the bathroom tiles, and Amanda came out of the stall and moved to the sink. Mary turned the taps for her so she wouldn't have to touch them.

"That's ridiculous," said Amanda, "no one's bored of you." She rinsed her hands and shook them dry before pulling a paper towel from the dispenser.

"Well, then, I'm bored of me." Mary reached into her bag and pulled out a wig, cranberry red. She held it up next to her face.

"You're bored of here, probably. Who isn't?" Amanda sighed and went to throw away the paper towel. Mary reached over and turned off the taps. "If I had any money, know where I'd go?"

Mary put the cranberry wig on her head, tucking wisps of bright blond real hair under the elastic. "I went to Paris once," Mary said. "For three weeks. I stayed near the Notre Dame." She pronounced the last sentence in an affected briar drawl.

Amanda pulled open the bathroom door, looked out into the bar. Then she looked back at Mary, who was pivoting back and forth in front of the mirror, examining her bewigged figure. "I'd go to England, to see the sacred stones. You look great." She started to leave. "Oh, Michael's here," she said in a casual voice as the door closed behind her.

Standing at the sink, Mary continued to adjust her wig. She stared at herself for a while, then reached again into her bag and pulled out a slim tube of lipstick, which she began to apply with slow care to her slightly trembling lips. I think maybe the problem with Michael, thought Mary, was that he wanted to know the answer to the question "Who are you exactly?" instead of "Who are you supposed to be?" which is all most boys want to know. And I couldn't answer that question. I was hoping he could answer it for me. Or maybe he did, and that's why he left.

Notebook Eleven

Record 3 (8:49)
Protestant Desire
The Cuff of Our Sleeve
A Yellow Coincidence

We have been told in ancient tales many marvels of famous heroes, of mighty toil, joys, and high festivities, of weeping and wailing, and the fighting of bold warriors—of such things you can now hear wonders unending!

For ten years, swear! we have, alas, philosophy, medicine, and jurisprudence, too, and to our cost theology with ardent labor studied through and thorough, for all of which we remain foolish still, no wiser than before. Scruple nor doubt comes near to enthrall us, hence also our heart must forego all pleasure. Speculum. Spem. Spes. *Laissez toot ses deséspoir, vous qui entrez!*

Explicit sentiment never serves any purpose—or rather serves only its own ends, which is validation-by-announcement, which always (at least in others, it's often hard to see what's going on in your own life) seems a little desperate, and dubious, as if an emphatic statement of one's love can will that love into being. Even when it works, it's not the best basis for long-term success. It's easy from the perspective of *here* to see the flaws in our thinking and behavior *there*, but in our defense we were all a little guilty of wishful thinking at the time.

Spirits are of all substances the most capable of perfection, and their perfections are different in that they interfere with each other the least, or rather they aid each other the most, for only the most virtuous can be the most perfect friends. In the strictly metaphysical sense, no external cause acts upon us excepting God, alone, but we can't expect people whose business doesn't rise or fall in metaphysical tides to understand or react in the way such a truth would dictate.

These were heady days for us, for people who in any way cared about music or music's future. A lot of very great rock bands had been signed to major labels after years of underground accolades. The traveling rock festival referenced earlier gave birth to itself with a minimum of labor and a maximum of media cooing. We had a sense of tectonic shifts in the underlying makeup of the industry, of which became more sensible when Whiskey Ships also signed to a major label, because we were in a better position to pay attention to these things—and we had a reason, too, since anything that affected the business affected the band, and by extension us.

There is another aspect, too, under which this epoch has its importance—in it for the first time abstract truths sought to intervene in the world of facts. The meaning of a truth always differs greatly from its tendency. In the world of facts, truths are simply means, and we felt ourself, as a truth-in-itself, somewhat at sea. Which, coming from an extremely landlocked state (meaning State), was disorienting, and then things got, for a while, even weirder.

Because then N—'s famous record N— was released *[though there's a way of looking at things that suggests the release of N— was actually a signal of the end of any future for what we then thought of as indie rock, which was shorthand for independent rock, which had no real meaning (except literally it was supposed to mean that the record was released by a small "independent" label instead of an enormous corporate or "major" label, but many independents were actually owned by or at least funded through major labels, so even the literal definition grew, over time, fuzzy at the edges), but could maybe be generally defined as an uncodified but mutual adherence to a set of values with regard to the production and distribution of music, rather than by an aesthetic manifesto. These values were all in a rigorously* ars gratia artis *vein, meaning any commercial aspirations, or the elevation of commercial aims above artistic ones, were viewed with great suspicion by the (elusive, shifting) community, which consisted of mainly devotees (you could even call them consumers) of the music produced according to these principles. Naturally, there were exceptions. Naturally, there was a lot of nail-biting about selling out, but the economics of being in a band have never been straightforward or pure or anything but hopelessly compromised. Until the Collapse, of course. Now that we've taken economics out of the equation, what were formerly moral dilemmas are no longer available, and seem quaint and old-fashioned]* and an irrational exuberance, to misuse a phrase in currency some years ago, took hold of many of us, who wrongly extrapolated the success of one record to an entire feeding trough of fame-hungry bands, most of which, we earnestly reasoned, had labored in obscurity for too long, and deserved the success that N— had, it seemed to us, achieved on the shoulders of other, better music.

The nameless loneliness of chance, yes, it was that which we saw before us as, ready for the fall and already falling, we stood there at our window. Unconquered and unconquerable in its abandonment, the estranged night lay open, unchanged, immobile but strange, brushed by the gently ungently unyielding yielding of the moon, of the new moon, full, immobile, and flooded by the ungentle flow of stars, submerged in the silent unsilent song, submerged emerged from the beauty and the magical unmagical unity. So remittingly unremitting gray and so low as no sky we have seen before. They fought so fiercely that the whole castle echoed and reechoed *halloo! halloo!* and the din was heard in the dinner hall of the din-din-nabulated Nibelungs.

Après N— *le déluge*, as you may know. And even as we watched in horror while monstrous fabrications based largely on the templates we had forged in the smithy of our souls took the stage, we could not help but be tickled by the ascent of many of our former underground heroes. Not for long, of course. The whole thing collapsed under its own weight alarmingly fast, and most of those heroes were either destroyed or slunk back to their caves even more bitter than when they had emerged, blinking, into the harsh glare of the limelight. We could give you names, but these names would likely mean nothing to you anyway, which is the way, we've come to think, things should have stayed. Timelessness might be an outdated and romantic and inapplicable notion, or it may be the key to the whole thing, but the way of survival for any art form, for any love affair, for anything that you or anyone you know holds dear, is to shut the hell up about it. To avoid hype at all costs and let the thing speak for the thing's self. Promotion, advertising, marketing: These really are tools of the devil, it turns out, even after everyone already knew this and then moved past that knowledge in a frenzy of postmodern, ironic knowingness. You cannot co-opt what you don't know about, however, and even though it's increasingly difficult to do something that nobody knows about, we're told, it's still worth the effort.

If there's ever a next time, we'd do better to keep everything to ourself. But at the time it felt like we were being offered the world. And even though we always knew that we would turn the world down, it was nice to be asked. Why was the phenomenon of the world passed over at the beginning of the ontological tradition which has been decisive for us (explicitly, in the case of Parmenides), and why has this passing-over kept constantly recurring?

We arrived in Münster yesterday in the afternoon, after flying for what seemed like forever from Dayton to Chicago, from Chicago to Newark, from Newark to London, from London to Münster, a smallish town in the district of Upper Alsace, 16 m. from Colmar by rail, and at the foot of the Vosges Mountains. Its principal industries circa 1905 were spinning, weaving, and

174 ✳ Artificial Light

bleaching. The town owes its origin to a Benedictine abbey, which was founded in the 7th century, and at one time it was a free city of the empire. In its neighborhood is the ruin of Schwarzenberg. The Mlinstertal, or Gregoriental, which is watered by the river Fecht, is famous for its cheese. Münster was founded as a bishopric by Liudger, a missionary of Charlemagne; town grew around the monastery; was strong member of Hanseatic League from 13th cen.; was badly damaged in WWII.

We're in a German private-label motel, or an inn of some kind. The rooms are very small, which we know is standard for European hotels, having traveled here after college for a few months. The bathroom's down the hall. This can be a problem if you have a propensity to drink a lot of red wine and pass out. In Germany, red wine is called *rotwein*. It's the first and pretty much the only German we bothered to learn (other essentials: *Was koste?* and *Bitte eine bier*) on the plane on the way over, from a small traveler's phrasebook that Stanley, the drummer, had brought. This was Stanley's first trip to Europe and he was hopeful to have a continental experience, even if that experience was mostly defined by movies he'd seen that featured European locations.

Wenn er das bezweifelt—was immer hier "bezweifeln" heisst—dann wird er dieses Spiel nie erlernen. Imagine that someone were to say, "I don't know if I have ever been to the moon; I don't remember ever having been there." In the first place—how would he know that he is on the moon? How does he imagine it? Stanley's experience had somehow reversed Ludwig's proposition: He had never been to Germany, yet he remembered being there.

Even though for almost the first time in the band's history we have a professional tour manager, nice kid from Sheffield, England who can drive and do sound as well—his name's Sammy Sparks—we feel still a certain familial responsibility for the rest of the band. Especially Henry, our singer. We've never met anyone more deeply, honestly xenophobic than Henry Radio. Even our grandfather, who wouldn't eat spaghetti because it was Italian. It's not that Henry's wiring is intolerant of strangers, because he's an extremely friendly person, willing to talk for hours to anyone who wants to listen, as long as the conversation is about rock music, or even better, specifically the rock music of Whiskey Ships. But having spent the first twenty-seven years of his life without ever once leaving Dayton, Ohio, which is only a slight exaggeration, Henry only feels comfortable in his own backyard, drinking light beer and playing basketball on the half-court he put in upon graduating college, marrying his high school girlfriend, and moving into the house in Northridge he's occupied ever since. His xenophobia has a specific perimeter, actually, which starts at the border of Vandalia, the slightly-tonier-than-Northridge suburb just to the north, where most residents of Northridge moved if they ever got any money, and which is thus despised by longtime Northridgians as pretentious and fake. Evil Vandalia, Henry calls it, laughing. But his laugh has an edge of real bitterness, we think. We remember him once saying that when he first went to Wright State University, and saw for the first time in his life college kids wearing backpacks and eating bagels, he nearly threw up.

We're somewhat surprised, then, to shower and dress and walk downstairs to the breakfast room of the Münster Inn (name has been changed) to see Henry and Stanley and Trinket, the other guitarist, sitting at a table peaceably, and from appearances happily, eating eggs and sausage and orange juice and muesli and even coffee. Sammy the tour manager's on the phone and motions us to the buffet table on the other side of the room where all this stuff is spread out in serve-yourself fashion. We don't usually eat breakfast, which makes sense since we're not usually awake until lunchtime, and were surprised to find that others of our age still made a regular habit of doing so. On tour, we're always the last one out of bed, which would have made our tour nickname Sir Sleeps-A-Lot or something along those lines, except: Magnetic Tom, our T-shirt guy, who's Henry's friend from high school, and who travels with us always and who sleeps, we swear, seventy percent of the time. He's a very sweet-natured guy. His great ambition on tour is, when we get to Amsterdam, to disappear into a coffeehouse and for the first time in his life get legally stoned. We're absolutely certain he will realize this ambition. Our tour nickname is Kool-Aid Lips because of all the red wine we drink, which tends to leave a purple residue on our lips.

Hidden in his magic cloak, Siegfried left by the gate that opened onto the shore. There he found a bark, and, boarding it unseen, sculled it swiftly away as though the wind were blowing it. It's smaller than usual rock band tour buses, more of a glorified van than a proper bus. No bunks, just seats, but the seats are comfortable and the windows large and there's a TV with VCR. Sammy brought some tapes of a British TV show, too, some apparently very popular comedy that may well be funny but we don't know, since the accents are so thick you can only catch every third word or so in a sentence, and even that imperfectly. But Sammy keeps trying to indoctrinate us into the club of people who adore British television comedies, with which he's not having much luck, even with Henry, who's an Anglophile when it comes to rock music but not much else.

A band spends a great deal of time on tour in its bus, so the bus assumes a supersized importance in the band's touring life. Ours is blue and metallic gray, like the sky in Dayton before a thunderstorm, of which there are many, noisy and spectacular. The yellow license plate reads *K6 STA*, registered in Sheffield, and we spend a lot of time trying to decipher the license number for omens, but find none. Sammy, in addition to tour managing and sound engineering, is also our driver. He's a good driver, possessing the necessary qualities of abundant stamina and not drinking much. Back in the States, our bass player, Tub, does most of the driving, because we used to use his van until it fell apart and we started renting, and he just got in the habit. Tub's usually okay on the way to the show, but afterwards, on the way back to the hotel or on to the next primary market, he was almost always catastrophically drunk, and we got usually lost. One time a cop pulled us over and we thought we were done for, especially Tub, who already had somewhere around seven DUIs and didn't even have a license, but Tub somehow pulled it together, played it cool, asked the cop for directions, and the cop was taken aback by Tub's totally cool demeanor, didn't even glance in the back at the rest of us frantically stubbing out joints and pouring our open beers down the rusthole near the rear axle, and gave Tub the directions. With Sammy we don't have to worry.

We arrived at the soundcheck: Then the soldier pulled out his pipe and lighted it at the blue-light, and as soon as a few wreaths of smoke had ascended, the mannikin was there with a small cudgel in his hand. But to please the maternal Earth and honor the God of the waters now the city revives: a glorious artifice, firmly founded as galaxies, wrought by genius that readily thus will make himself fetters of love. Love fetters. Love. Check one two. Check.

Soundcheck is probably the most painfully boring and/or annoying two hours you can imagine. The worst part is the drummer's part of the soundcheck, which is exactly the same (if you'd like to reproduce this at home) as someone bouncing a heavy rubber hammer off your skull for extended minutes. Slowly. Adding to our aggravation in Münster: severe non-drunkenness at an hour when we should be drinking, but the club manager hasn't delivered the pre-show beer yet, which is part of our rider, which is what the beer and wine and deli meats and cheese and so forth that you see backstage in movies about rock bands is called. We're nervous about our first shows overseas, and confused about the rented European equipment, which works on a different voltage system than American stuff and may blow up at any minute (and later, at a show in Köln, does, but thankfully when the opening band has borrowed it for their set). Most importantly, we're anxious about appearing to worry about any of the above stuff, except maybe the beer, the lack of which incurs in the rock band Whiskey Ships a universal emotion best expressed by the famous pop song "Pain."

Playing a show in a foreign country is inevitably more exciting than playing a show back home, partly from the exotic quality of even everyday things, from the brand of beer they give you to more complicated matters like currency conversion. We're endlessly explaining to Henry how many dollars equals how many marks, and we foresee this happening in every country for the next three weeks, even though we're only guessing and half-making up the conversion amounts. Henry's obsessed with money, a side effect of his not ever having had any for most of his life, and now that he does he's convinced everybody is trying to rip him off. Not trying: actually doing it, ripping him off. Once when we were in the office of the president of a very large record label that wanted to sign us, the president—who was an old-school music-biz type—said, "You should enjoy this time, when everyone's [crude phrase for oral sex]." It's not true that Henry then replied, "I'm tired of [crude phrase for oral sex]. I'm ready to get [crude term that can apply both to passive, not necessarily consensual sex, and to active, n.n.c. sex, past tense]." That's the way we always tell the story, but that's what Henry afterwards said he should have said. It's a fine example of staircase wit: what he actually did was laugh. But the point is, the sentiment in the mythical comeback to the president of Ocean Pacific Records remains Henry's idea of the music business. It's a not-unhealthy attitude.

Beyond the inherent excitement of the first show by Whiskey Ships on foreign soil, there's some attendant anxiety on our part, in re first of all, do we have any fans over here? In each EC country, we're signed to a different label. In Germany it's Geist, which is one of the larger German independents. We have no way of knowing how well we're doing, sales-wise, in any particular country, because the representatives of the different companies who come to the shows and give us posters and ask us to sign them are professionally vague about sales figures and moreover don't always speak very fluent English.

We will say about Germans that they are comically blunt in their opinions. We first encountered this during the morning interviews, when we were asked at one point, "Your new album is not very good. The songs we think are terrible compared to the last record. Why is this?" Our response was wild, inappropriate laughter, which we think is the only response possible under the circumstances. But Germans, we're beginning to understand, don't see their invective as in any way an insult. It's just a statement of their opinion, to be refuted by a statement of your opinion, in a spiraling dialectic that leads nowhere since it's a discussion of aesthetics as regards rock music; if there was ever a dead end or wrong turn on the way to the land of relevance, follow us here. Germans can't help taking everything seriously, even stuff we would never have thought of taking seriously, because they have no other way to take things. We know it's a received notion, this lack of a sense of German humor, but it is wholly borne out by our experience so far in Münster. Unless, again, it's just a language thing, which leads to additional anxiety with regard to the shows here, as to how that might affect the reaction to certain lyric-dependent songs or Henry's stage patter, which is always drunken and funny and spontaneous; but will anyone understand what he's rambling about over here?

His vision, from the constantly passing bars, has grown so weary that it cannot hold anything else. It seems to him that there are a thousand bars; and behind the bars, no world. So that once on stage, you understand, no other place exists; he performs his ritual dance around a center in which a mighty will stands paralyzed. He's not aware of the audience; he barely recognizes his own band; so in the brief pauses between songs when Henry stops to acknowledge that which is External to his Being, he will spout one of two things: brilliant nonsense; rote nonsense. The crowd, which naturally understands his speech as directed toward them, also understands and responds on a different level, or perhaps two different levels: the one at which they have been trained or otherwise learned to mimic the rituals of rock show participation; the one at which Henry's music has elevated their senses, thus understanding, in whatever country, to whatever degree of incoherence he's been reduced by drunken-ness, whatever he says. As for us, unless he addresses one of the band members specifically, which is rare— we have received a number of high-spirited kicks to various parts of our bodies caused by unwise proximity to his flailing presence, and one time he unwittingly smashed our guitar's pickup to bits—we don't listen. The experience of playing in Whiskey Ships is wholly other than the experience of watching and listening to the band; because we have done both, we can attest to this truth. Playing, we are focused on necessarily mundane matters—not losing place in the song, staying on tempo, tuning, tone, volume—and it's the exception rather than the rule that the song's supernatural qualities sweep these matters from our mind and we can participate in a wholly engaged way in the spiritual uplift that Henry creates. As an audience member, on the other hand, engagement is normative, in a way denied even Henry, who exists on a private plane, connected to the audience only in the sense that he's connected to every soul in the universe, or more properly to the universal soul. As a player, you can see only parts; as a listener, you see the whole. You are also afforded the luxury of bathroom breaks whenever you choose, a thing not to be discounted.

Geist, who despite assurances apparently have little faith in our ability to headline clubs on our own, have paired us up with a popular German rock group called Kokotek. These guys speak *very* little English, which we think may be an ideological statement, because the Geist guy at the club in Münster tells us that Kokotek belong to something called the Hamburg School, which from what we can tell means they come from Hamburg and espouse a rigorous rock dogma the tenets of which are obscure but the main one seems to be a refusal to sing songs in English like any other rock band that wants to become internationally famous. You have to admire their determined nationalism, but at the same time it's a little scary when any group of Germans, even just a rock group, expresses determined nationalism.

Other than that, though, the Kokotek guys seem friendly and nonthreatening, and whenever they catch us sneaking into their dressing room to steal beers because we drank all of ours already, they're pretty cool about it, which may be a trick to guilt us into not doing it anymore, but if so, nice try.

Our one special request upon joining Whiskey Ships was that two bottles of red wine be put on the rider for our own personal consumption. We picked wine over whiskey because we're a more pleasant person at the bottom of a bottle of wine, and because it was generally cheaper, which appealed to Henry's frugal nature. We start on the first bottle on arriving at the club, and most times it will be gone before we play. We open the second bottle, take it on stage, drink about half while playing, then finish the rest after the show. Often we finish the second bottle before we go offstage, or at least by the second encore, which means we have to switch to beer, or try to find some whiskey. Our worst nights are probably when we manage to find some whiskey. Luckily, in Germany a bottle of whiskey seems to be as rare and precious as a sense of humor, so we mostly stick to the wine and beer. There's a number of shows we don't remember clearly, or at all, which goes for the rest of the band as well, maybe even more so in the case of Henry, who often has to be reminded that we played at all the night before, and where, though never why, because he was born to rock, end of sentence.

We're infamous for our drinking, at least among the certain small group of music enthusiasts who number our fans. Before every show, Magnetic Tom carries a large cooler of beers (in the States, always Light Beer, never Heavy Beer, as you can drink more and not get incapacitated) onstage and sets it down lovingly in front of the drum riser, within equidistant grasp of everyone except Stanley, who doesn't drink. There's usually about a case in the cooler, and Henry goes through most of that himself. He doesn't play an instrument, just sings, so he's got a free hand to swig beers while the other swings the microphone or grasps it tightly while he sings. Many people, watching Henry down almost an entire case of beer almost single-handed (remember, we're drinking red wine and playing guitar, Stanley doesn't drink, and most of the time Trinket and Tub have their hands full of stringed instrument), are moved to express concern at his self-abuse, but there are two things these people don't know: 1) [expletive], and 2) there's a secret to Henry's rapid-fire consumption, which we will now divulge. He uses a technique of his own device wherein the beer bottle is tipped completely upside down and held against the drinker's lips, the lips forming the usual seal around the rim of the bottle's mouth, which gives the impression of shotgun drinking, where actually there is none because his tongue blocks the flow of the beer down his throat. The beer foams up and most of it pours harmlessly down his chest, and the whole thing is a very convincing simulacrum of chuggery, but like the rest of our show, is mostly a performance.

Which means what, exactly: that Henry's a phony, that his apparently prodigious capacity for alcohol is an elaborately staged sham? Not hardly. Henry, when he comes onstage, is already severely drunk, with very rare exceptions. He could not function otherwise, because he suffers from a nervous condition called "stage fright" that can only be remedied by application of what he sometimes calls "Liquid Backbone," and other times "Uncle Henry's Nerve Tonic."

Let us put this in mathematical terms: Our rider includes five cases of beer total. Two to be delivered before the set, one for the stage, and two to be delivered after the set. There has never been a beer left over from our rider at the end of any show; in fact, usually we run out early and have to steal beers from the other band(s) on the bill, or somehow wrangle another case out of the club, which sometimes when the club's in a good mood is not a problem. Thus, granting that there are three other drinking members of Whiskey Ships, plus Magnetic Tom, who despite a pre-ulcerous stomach puts away his share, minus us because we're drinking our *rotwein*, means that on any given show night Henry puts away somewhere near two cases of beer, which is forty-eight beers, which we think is probably enough. Even if he only dumps half of those down his clothes, or spills them on the stage making a dangerously slick pool of beer scum, the cause of many disastrous-looking but rarely harmful falls and extended balletic slides, that still leaves a case of beer each night personally consumed, which is twenty-four, which now, in Germany, is equivalent to much more than that on account of the superior strength and quality of the German beer. We have been lectured at great length on this superiority, both by friends of ours who have traveled, prior to our departure, and by new acquaintances, here, like Sammy the tour manager and Ute, the concierge back at the Münster Inn. "You're in for a treat," Sammy and Ute and our Bund-friendly U.S. friends assure us. "German beer is unlike anything you've ever had." We are collectively unimpressed, however. German beer is viscous and massy, *like drinking a loaf of bread*, italics ours, and worst of all, you cannot do with German beer the thing we call *pound*. You cannot pound German beer, you cannot nail a six- or twelve-pack like you would on the playing fields of North Dayton without thinking twice. We reject German beer wholeheartedly, settling for a brand of Czech-brewed lager, which is a heavier version of our favorite watery domestic, but acceptable.

We ambled onstage at 10 p.m., or thereabouts. The gallant Minstrel stood there fully armed. His battle-dress was of a magnificent hue; he laced his helmet on and affixed a red pennant to his lance. Later he was to come to dire straits, along with his men. How could warriors ever test each other more keenly? From a powerful joust by Gelpfrat, bold Hagen flew over the cruppers and took a seat on the ground—his horse's poitrel had broken, and the woes of the battle were brought home to him! We played almost fifty songs, as usual, including encores, of which there were three. We were done by midnight. We couldn't hear anything but the squall of our own badly tuned guitar for the first half of the set, as the monitor in front of us wasn't working until we kicked it enough times. The crowd was enthusiastic and attentive, as the crowd almost always is for us, because we don't tour that often and we put on a good show, jumping around like idiots and smoking and drinking to excess. We don't smoke except onstage, except Tub and Stanley, who now smoke for real after fake-smoking only onstage for years. The club was packed and overheated; we almost passed out twice from the heat and the smoke and the jet lag and the *rotwein*. The first time we almost passed out was onstage right in the middle of a song called "Nectarine Machine." The second time was backstage after the show, when everyone crowded around Henry like he's the savior of rock, which may be true, but we need our space.

After the show we take the short bus back to the Münster Inn. We had to leave the next morning early for Köln, which used to be called Cologne if you're keeping track of our movements on an old-fashioned map. Our purposeful plan to go straight up to our room is easily derailed by the unavoidable fact of the still-open hotel bar.

The bar is cool and quiet. Only Ute, a near-six-foot statuesque woman with dark hair and brick-red lipstick wearing a dark blue dress, remains to serve customers, of which there are none until we get there. The Münster Inn is a frequent rock band waystation, so Ute knows to keep the bar open later than usual. We're not sure there's anything on earth we love more than a cool, quiet bar late at night, preferably in a foreign country. Henry, Trinket, and we sit at the bar while Ute pours whiskey drinks. It's safe to drink whiskey now, because it's very late and we're all long past exhausted, so the effect of the liquor is mellow, like the soft lemony light from lamps with fake Tiffany shades.

"Show was good, I thought," Trinket says, thoughtfully, sipping from a glass of maybe whiskey and soda.

This is what we talk about late at night after playing.

Henry slumps over the bar rail, grunts. He looks at his shot glass, now empty, and at his full pint of pilsner, but doesn't seem to have the energy to pick up his head and drink.

"Did you see Tub cockblocking on that German chick, the one with the silver miniskirt?" asks Henry. "Did you see that?" He laughs, full-throated, his body still slumped but his mind now alert.

"Thought he was gonna get his ass kicked by her boyfriend," we offer.

"He will someday. He's begging for trouble. What's he thinking?" The question is obviously rhetorical, less obviously pointed. One of the things our band does on tour most often is talk behind each other's backs. It's not serious, most of the time, and then eventually it is, when Henry reaches a certain ambiguous fed up point. He goes through band members with astonishing frequency, which is how we got the job in the first place. In Whiskey Ships, the songs are the stars. And Henry, too, by extension, because he writes the songs and sings them. Everyone else is expendable, even interchangeable, to a certain extent. So Henry's nitpicking serves a purpose, clarifying his attitude toward this or that member. His attitude right now toward Tub's relentless womanizing is mixed: admiration and disgust. But because he's more amused than anything by Tub's incorrigibility, Tub's in no immediate danger. You're pretty safe on tour, anyway. Henry's not likely to work up the bad mood to fire someone until he gets back home and faces a lengthy stretch of domesticity.

Before long we are as drunk as we are capable of getting without actually passing out. We've seen Henry in this condition many times; it's one of the miraculous things about his alcohol consumption—that he never gets sick or (usually) rowdy or blacks out in any conventional way. He usually just falls asleep, often in a sitting position, his head drooping closer and closer to his chest until you can hear him softly snoring. Even then, though, he's not always done. We've made the mistake once or twice of talking about Henry in the third person when he was in the room in an apparently unconscious state, only to have him rouse himself and gruffly mutter a response or rebuttal to whatever observation we had made.

We say goodnight and head to our room. Trinket's already gone up. We're rooming with him for this tour because, to be honest, we can't take the constant strain of serving as audience to Henry's nonstop performance. Trinket hardly ever says anything; at age thirty-one he's the oldest of us and the least-invested in the rock myths we all, to a certain extent, treasure. He's got a wife and two kids and paints, very well, could maybe even make a living off selling portraits of rich Daytonians, but he's also a fine guitarist and songwriter with a distinctive high tenor, and if he weren't in a band with Henry he might be famous on his own. But the very qualities that prevent the limelight from settling on his thinning hair make Trinket an ideal roommate on tour.

As we lie in our safe European bed and wait to pass out, we start obsessing about our creeping anxiety, and the unbanishable depression that has seized us upon arriving in Germany. We have an unsettled feeling in our stomach that has nothing to do with the quantity of alcohol we've sluiced through our kidneys tonight. We worry that the unease we feel is purely selfish: in other words, that our slow-growing dissatisfaction with the practice of playing in Whiskey Ships versus the *theory* of playing in Whiskey Ships betrays an unbecoming ungratefulness, and our willingness to let minor annoyances grow into major justifications which are, at the far end of the longest day, a den of chimera hiding the fact that we are lazy, and proud, and greedy, and envious.

Our bed is right below a window cut at an angle in the angled roof that looms low above our head. Through the window, we can see the moon and stars in a clear night sky and a branch of a plane tree waving in the summer wind. The patterns of light caused by the moon shining weakly through the tree's leaves cast moving shadows on the wall. Objects in the room—dresser, suitcase, clock—acquire a hollowness in the dark we fill with bright worry, until the hollows glow, until they blaze with moonlight. The window is loose in its frame and rattles with every gust of wind. We feel the frayed edges of our personality unraveling. Outside the angle of another person's perception, we're afraid we have no real being. We're an accretion of foreign fluids—the sweat and saliva we've sucked out of everyone else. That equals us. That's our sum.

In the morning we'll remember what we're doing here. Sea-sperm and driftwoody, heaped up on the sand and sore. Whoreshoe crabs. Our flat life in the ebb, erasing.

The distant air arrives in waves. A mingled junk of

stars and winking trawlers warps before us, controlled in its slow fall and rise by God's easy breath.

We sit on a bench, looking out at the whole empty thing. Imitation of cerebral effort: one cumbrous claw scratched at thinning, greasy hair. It's true a liar can be an artist, but only to the extent that he can distinguish his creations from those of nature. But the line between illusion and deception is often imperceptible. Why is it a lie can be the most exalted of things (when it is called a fiction) *and* the most debased? A metaphor is a ladder to the truth, and yet is not of itself true.

Red wine has been no friend to us. Swinging in the porches of our ears, insipid vocabulary of the sweet tipple-o. Head's unhooked. Heart stuck, caught between rush of love and stooped and seething fear. A great shadow passed suddenly behind, like the impenetrable evil of the whole world. Nothing in the night sky could have produced such a shadow.

Falling into the ether/or, no life clung to no thick bones. Draw the curtains on the artificial starlight outside and light a cigarette by feel in the close and inky blackness. Smoke spirals and gathers on the ceiling, up in the pitch.

We sleep the sleep of the just. The just sleeping.

Rock will not kill you or make you stronger, it will simply drain every life-affirming instinct from your soul and spew from its ulcerous mouth the resulting brew of misplaced ideals and ideologies all over the future. You are the future. We can't stand the mere thought of you.

Here now began the combat which Adam should have undergone in paradise; for on one side God's love-desire, which had manifested itself in the soul, did eagerly attempt the soulish and bodily property, and introduced its desire into the soul's property; and on the other side the devil in God's wrathful property did assault on the soul's property, and brought his imagination into the property of the first principle, viz. Into the center of the dark world, which is the soul's fire-life.

Journal entry from around the same period: We just grow older with very little to show. Need to take more pictures.

Rock is not meant to be part of pop culture; in its purest form it is a reaction against that culture, not a happy participant. You don't use rock music as a soundtrack to peppy teen comedies or dramadies or maladies. You use rock music to sandblast that dreck from your mind, at least for a moment. (Moments are the building blocks of community, and rock is community, however limited.) Rock is a rhythmically religious experience. It is a motion of the spirit toward its essential nature. It does not sell anything except itself, which does not mean you can't sell it to someone else. Paying money for rock in a consumable form (record, concert) has nothing to do with the purity of the thing being conveyed or experienced. Commerce dilutes nothing on its own—it's simply a method of transmission. Rock is not supposed to be a mass medium, it was never designed to carry the weight pop culture would like to impose upon it. If you want rock bad enough, you will find a way to get it.

On the other hand, looking at this in the subjective aspect: Just as music alone awakens in man the sense of music, and just as the most beautiful music has no sense for the unmusical ear—is no object for it, because an object can only be the confirmation of one of the essential powers and therefore can only exist insofar as the essential power is present as a subjective capacity, because the sense of an object goes only so far as a particular person's senses go (has only a sense for a sense corresponding to that object)—for this reason, the senses of the social man are other senses than those for the nonsocial man. The forming of the five senses, he goes on to say, is the labor of the entire history of the world down to the present.

We will not be upbeat to soothe you. Remember that.

Don't be misled by Great Minds who mutter that ability "to rock" is as important as ability "to tie your shoelaces." These talentless mediocrities are descended from the same Great Minds who once insisted that "Pushpins [thumbtacks] are more important than Pushkin [poet]." In other words, don't listen to anyone: especially us, because we're up against deadline and have to fill a certain number of pages with a certain number of words, so who knows what we'll say next, and how devoid of meaning, although as we should have pointed out several times before, but never got around to doing, meaning is in the end meaningless.

What we like about Whiskey Ships' music, for instance (picking our band as an example because we consider ourselves pretty much an expert on that and only that subject), is that despite its absolute denial of meaning (resolute refusal to make sense), we get more "meaning" out of a song like "Hinterlanding" than out of any N— or [*insert favorite band name here*] song ever written. But the lyrics make no sense, you say. Now, we'd have a hard time proving it to you, but Henry never wrote a syllabilly of nonsense. Where there is no obvious meaning, the mind sifts through the rubble of sense to create an entirely new edifice, and one that resounds all the more for the effort put into its construction. Talk about audience participation!

Let it be told, and related, and sung, that we know our interpretation of any particular Whiskey Ships song is most often completely different from Henry's, because we talk about his lyrics a lot, but the great thing is he allows for both ours and his interpretation, and a host, if you will (you won't), of others as well. This freewheelin' Henry Radio is made possible mainly because the lyrics, while crucial to the sound and sense of the song, are not the main argument—only a part. The argument of a Whiskey Ships song is the melody/rock mix crossed with those sense fragments that evoke a response in the listener. The way these three elements work together in the context of a song like "Infra Dig," for instance, is to produce a reaction (dependent, as always, on the individual listener) of pure melancholic joy capable of restoring everything Kurt took away with his suicide. The song's lyrics "mean" nothing in any conventional sense, but when paired with the chord structure, the melody, the singer's emotional delivery, and the band's performance, your heart cannot help but leap from its constraining cage. There's an infinity of probabilities, and the gracelessness with which we clodhope through the murk of the possible and impossible cannot help disincline even the bold, even the beautiful. Things have meaning or thingness only in relation to other things, and sometimes a rock song is at the center of that web.

We will not be upbeat to soothe you.

We will not be upbeat to soothe you. Most of rock is drudgery and tedium, relieved at rare intervals by very short-lived sparks of actual Quiddity. Most of rock is Not Rock. Most of Not Rock is Not Good. Consider the possibilities.

(Skepticism alone is a cheap and barren affair. Skepticism in a man who has come nearer the truth than any man before, and yet clearly recognizes the limits of his own mental construction, is great and fruitful.)

Notebook Twelve

The boys, under Kurt's direction, had hauled a giant spruce into Albion's ballroom late one night in mid-December and decorated it with things Mary stole from her job at The Magic Hat, a novelty store on Brown Street near Stewart. So there were twists of crepe ribbon in black and orange, left over from Halloween, and trick rings with paste rubies and emeralds that opened when pressed in the back to reveal a secret compartment, strung together on fishing line from the hardware store where Co-Daryl Hawes worked. We stood the tree just behind the chairs and the piebald rug facing the fireplace. At night, with the fire stoked, the reflected light in the fake jewels, threaded through the sweet-smelling branches of our tree, gleamed religiously. We drank our sacred wine from holy cups and toasted the blaspheming town.

Kurt suggested we get together on Christmas Eve after midnight. Not many of us had places we had to be, so most everyone showed. Kurt insisted that we not exchange presents, but since we knew that he was planning on getting us all things we pooled our resources and bought him an ugly mustard-colored sweater, chosen by Amanda, which Kurt dutifully tried on and wore almost every day thereafter. He seemed embarrassed by our gift, and overcompensated by plying us with more than the usual complement of bottles from his kitchen stash. Then he handed out his presents.

He had clearly put some thought into his choices. For Mary he got a cashmere scarf of delicate robin's-egg blue, which she would not remove from around her neck for weeks afterwards (even during sex, it was rumored). For Joe Smallman, Kurt got an antique silver cigarette case. For Amanda, he found a rare recording of her favorite jazz singer, a Harlem woman from the '40s called Gilda Lily who had made only three albums before dying of a heroin overdose. The others were similarly gifted (the Rose Scholar, for instance, received a book called *The Rose Encyclopedia* by T. Geoffrey W. Henslow, M.A., F.R.H.S., Arthur Pearson, Ltd., London, 1912), with the exception of me. Poor Fiat. I said nothing, but my disappointment must have been obvious, because Kurt came over on the pretext of filling my cup of wine and whispered, "Yours will come later." If any of the boys from the Southern Belle had said that I would have thought something vulgar, but Kurt was never vulgar, except for effect, and I detected no such effect here.

Later came, and later went, and then people started to leave, and then everyone left except me, and of course Kurt. Through the tall windows on the north side of the ballroom shone pale Christmas light, making irreligious shadows of our high-backed chairs. We said nothing but watched the fire die. I think I may have pretended to read a book by dying firelight, but Kurt seemed content to stare into the embers, his unnaturally long fingers tented together, his elbows propped on the chair's worn arms.

Eventually Kurt stirred and walked or swam out of the room at the far end that led to the front door. I assumed he had gone to bed, because by habit he never said goodnight, just disappeared. I had slipped into a cozy dream, peopled by characters from the book I'd been pretending to read, when Kurt returned carrying a package wrapped in plain brown paper with a ribbon of twine. I sat up, rubbing my eyes, and reached for my cup of wine. Kurt handed me the package and sat down in his chair.

"I was dreaming," I said irrelevantly.

"I never remember my dreams," replied Kurt.

I swished the wine around my gums and swallowed. "Is this my Christmas present?"

"You talk sometimes about an Irish writer, O'Hanlon."

"Only when I'm drunk. I know you don't like to talk about books, and he's someone I try to keep to myself, anyway."

"I would have no pleasure giving you something only I liked."

I attempted to untie the knotted twine but soon gave up and tugged until it snapped. My expectations at this point were deliberately low. I expected at best a cheap hardcover edition of *Miserogeny*, or even one of O'Hanlon's earlier books, like *Hunting Accidents*. The bulk of the wrapped package suggested more than one volume. I tore the wrapping and threw it on the floor next to my chair. The heat from the fire cause the discarded paper to skid across the floor toward Kurt's chair. He bent over and crumpled the paper into a ball, then tossed the ball into the fire, where it ignited instantly. Black flakes of burnt paper floated lazily up the flue.

"It's a book!" I said with affected irony. I found Kurt's intense interest in my reaction unsettling. It was three books, in fact, or rather three volumes of the same book. As I examined the volumes closer, real excitement took hold of me.

"This can't be what I think it is," I said, looking at Kurt, who returned my look warmly, almost impishly.

I examined the first volume carefully. The title page bore the name of the original publisher, Odeon Press, and the original date of publication, 1948. At the bottom of the title page was stamped the number "73." I knew then that I was in the presence of a very precious thing, and my hands began to tremble.

I could hardly stand to hold the book in my hands— it felt warm to the touch, vibrating with the force of the words held captive in ink impressed on yellowing, brittle paper. I closed the first volume and put it down, in my lap, dizzy from the intensity of feeling. The set I was holding was the very first edition of *Miserogeny*, one of only 250 printed in large format, and bound in midnight-blue with gold lettering. It was not out of the question that it had been handled by O'Hanlon himself. There was no *ex libris* stamp or dedication or other sign of ownership—the lack of which increases a book's value among collectors but for me only increased the mystery, and the admittedly remote but still-real possibility that the volumes came from O'Hanlon's own library, in other words that it was a set he'd reserved for himself. Kurt would give no explanation of how he'd come by such a treasure. I had only seen pictures in rare book catalogues, and the prices attached to these pictures were usually a multiple of my yearly salary. I said as much to Kurt, who only shrugged and said that I should not consider such things.

My first impulse was to refuse the gift, but here again Kurt warned that such a refusal would not only be rude but pointless—he had no use for the books himself and the circumstances were such that he could not return them. I argued halfheartedly, but was hamstrung by the realization that here, for the first time in my life, was a book I actually wanted to own. So I shut up and began flipping through the pages, while Kurt watched, and smiled.

I had flipped through these same pages countless times, so many that my borrowed paperbacks (the paperback edition was in two volumes, as opposed to the three-volume hardcover) had come unleaved in several spots—one entire chapter had fallen out of the first volume, still glued together and discrete, but freed from its mooring. For a few weeks I carried around just the separate chapter, which was 22 of Volume One in the paperback set, which corresponds to Chapter 1 of Volume Two in the hardcover edition. O'Hanlon did not title the chapters of this book, so those few who still read him had developed a shorthand method of making sure we were on the same page, which was simply a form of notation: *HC V. 1, 14*, for instance, or *PB V. 2, 6*.

PB V. 1, 22 was the chapter that started, "*In sweller days, on taller nights, Farrell conceded that his life had uneclipsed its genesis . . .*" and because so much of it dealt with things I knew or felt I knew firsthand—rites of adolescent passage, but writ huge, on mythic scale—it became for a while my favorite chapter. Rarely did O'Hanlon's chapters follow coherent themes through to anything like completion, but *PB V. 1, 22* came as close as he or I could ever come (because he was dead, and I was dumb) to dialogue.

O'Hanlon's deal, in brief: He was born in Galway in 1893, third son in a family with four sons and two daughters, both younger. He studied biology at University College Dublin, then went off to America in 1913 to seek his fortune, at the insistence of his mother. His father had vanished two years earlier down a crevasse in Norway. He published a book of short stories, *Hunting Accidents*, in 1920, which did not sell well. His first novel, *Reverse Chronological Order*, came out in 1927, sold even worse, and in addition was attacked by the Council for Decency and the American Family as being generally opposed to both, although to modern minds (as with most controversial novels of the time, *Chatterly* and *Ulysses* et al.), the subject matter—a cross-country trip by railroad with an unnamed narrator and a department-store mannequin he calls Lailah, or at other times Dalailah, and which comes to life toward the end of the trip (or maybe it's a delusion of the narrator—we never know for sure)—seems tame. The two are married in San Francisco at the end of their journey by an eccentric pastor who may or may not be Mark Twain. With any O'Hanlon book, though, the plot's just a peg from which he hangs his versicolored sentences. Disappointed with the commercial and critical reception of his two books, O'Hanlon returned to Ireland just before the Second World War, in 1938. His timing was fortuitous, as of course Ireland remained neutral during that conflict and he was able to write unhindered. The result, his second novel, published in 1948, is widely regarded by those few who remember him today as his *chef-d'oeuvre*. *Miserogeny* purportedly records the Atlantic crossing O'Hanlon made (or rather his fictive alter-ego, Thomas Farrell) on the steamer *Erato* back to Ireland from New York City, but there's little of the diarist's accretion of mundane details in this soaring, hymnic novel. Actually, I take that back—there's an insane accumulation of detail, and among these you'll find copious references to weather patterns and tidal flow, but these might as well be weather patterns on Venus and tidal flow at the center of the earth. The narrative thrust of *Miserogeny* is in the oceanic rhythm of the prose itself—its "inhuman music," to quote a contemporary reviewer—rather than the threads of sense that intertwine and tangle over the course of the two (or three) volumes. It's not impenetrable in the sense that *Finnegans Wake* or later Beckett is impenetrable—in other words, the language is recognizably English, and there are spiraling stories within stories within stories, but all recognizable, *enfin*, as stories. Nor is it curlicued and immense in the way Proust can be; O'Hanlon's muse (signified, possibly, by the name he gives to the steamer in his book, which I have not been able to find in any shipping registry, ancient or modern, available to me) was lyric and concise, and worked, by repetition of themes and phrases, a fugal magic.

That this magic seems to affect only a select few does not, for me, lessen its impact. I first found *Miserogeny* while plowing through middle-of-the-last-century Irish literature (Flann O'Brien, Donleavy). I came across a footnote in A.B. Marconi's admirable overview, *The Uncreated Conscience*, referring to *"the eccentric autodidact Sean O'Hanlon, whose* Miserogeny, *a diffusely prolix meditation on death and dying, is too little read these days,"* which quoted the passage from the first chapter that begins, *"High above the piling waves . . ."* and something gave way inside me. I tracked down the two-volume paperback in a library in Columbus, after first exhausting the "resources" of the Dayton area, as well as the libraries of Cincinnati and Yellow Springs. My reaction—such a limp word for such a profound event—to the first read-through was immediate and permanent. I have never been so deeply affected by anyone or anything in my life. The books seemed to contain everything I had ever thought but lacked the skill to express, filtered through the perceptions of a mind so subtle, and so finely pitched, that the resultant prose seemed as close as I would ever get in mortal guise to the Divine.

After publishing *Miserogeny* (which again failed to find the audience it deserved, or maybe found exactly the audience it deserved, depending which side of the elitist razor you choose to straddle), O'Hanlon himself turned silent. He lived until his death in the mid-'60s in a stone cottage on the northern coast of Ireland, refusing visitors, much less interviews, and producing nothing. Some said he was still writing, some said he had renounced writing and had turned his full attention to a study of the Eleusinian mysteries, some said simply that he had gone mad. I don't think any of these options are unlikely, nor do I think any cancels any other out.

No, that's not true. It's true that I don't think that any of these options cancels any other out, but it's not true that he turned silent after retreating to the northern coast of Ireland. In fact, he did simply go insane: He began first by trying to reissue his previous writing under the pen name James Joyb, on the theory that a careless browser might be tricked into buying what he thought was a book by Joyce, whose work would be shelved right next to his. The ruse didn't work, naturally, as no respectable publisher was willing to serve as accomplice. After that, his descent into madness quickened: He began self-publishing crudely anti-Semitic and racist tracts with titles like: *Let's Go Fly a Kike!* and *To Hell with the Negro*, and others even more depressing, if possible. At the end of his life, he took to wandering the streets of his rural village, muttering dark curses to anyone careless enough to pause for a moment in his vicinity, until one night a gang of drunk kids leaving the local pub beat him to death with rocks.

As I turned the books over in my hand and examined the title pages and flipped through the prose I had nearly memorized, resisting the urge to quote one or another of my favorite passages to Kurt, my initial shock at his generosity transformed itself into a growing excitement, which in turn morphed into a feeling of the deepest, purest affection I had ever experienced. In that instant, I was possessed by a sense of true love. Which is what led directly to my blunder—because unharnessed true love requires, I've come to believe, an analogous and mitigating mistake; otherwise the world might blow apart from the stress of a billion overflowing hearts.

I'll allow that the flavor of the hurried present may color the memory of that slow moment, but I imagine—I see, as if it were happening right now, as if that precise piece of time had been woven forever on some minutely detailed tapestry that I could examine at leisure—that I jumped out of my chair with possibly frightening speed, though Kurt did not look scared. I bent or sprawled over him, and hugged him for the first and only time. His body went rigid, and he did not move his arms, but I was too drunk and flush with gratitude to notice. I hung on too long, as a result, and breathed wine-flavored endearments into Kurt's ear. When I let go and stumbled back to my seat, he looked pale and seemed to be making an effort to control his emotions. I didn't say anything for a while. I guessed that Kurt was embarrassed by my effusiveness, but that his usual equilibrium would soon reassert itself. Honestly, I didn't care either way. I had never received so perfect, so precious a gift, and would have reacted the same no matter the giver. The fact—unexpected yet impossible to imagine otherwise—that Kurt was the one to do such a thing, was particularly pleasant. For such a man to recognize the worth not just of books in general but this specific book to me, and to go to Lord knows what lengths to find such a rare and valuable copy (valuable not in monetary terms, though certainly there's that, but in the sense of its lineage, and its direct connection to the author), was all the more touching.

But Kurt's reaction troubled me. He got up from his chair, walked out of the room without saying anything, went straight up to I presume his bedroom. I was left with my expansive emotions and no one with whom to share them. I picked up my gift, cradling the volumes together under my arm, put on my coat, and went out into the silent, snowy streets. The mile-or-so walk to my apartment seemed to take five minutes, and I cannot tell you now if the weather was bitterly cold or merely cold, because I didn't notice anything. I walked automatically, as one does when thoroughly preoccupied, the way certain mathematicians are said to become when obsessed with an unsolvable proof. I remember sitting down on my bed and setting Kurt's present next to the pillow. I remember turning the pages of *Miserogeny* reverently, the way you should never turn pages in a book. I wasn't reading: I was caressing. And the thought did occur to me, as I dropped off by degrees into uneasy sleep, that I was not caressing the book.

Of the brown bubble of time surrounding Christmas I remember little else. For the past couple of years, I'd tried not to notice the holiday season because I was reminded that I had no close friends and no lovers except the ones I summoned when I read. Also for another, more definite reason.

My mother's unexpectedly swift death by cancer two years ago, when I was a sophomore at Antioch, had drained the surrounding days of color and light, until everything had the hue of Joyce's *Dubliners*—a paralytic yellow, clotted with dun-colored leaves in the gray slush on the side our gray street. She died on Christmas Day. I had gone to bed after midnight, having read her to sleep with *A Child's Christmas in Wales*, which was a favorite of ours both, which was rare. When I went to her room to wake her the next morning, she had acquired a delicate jacaranda-flower color, and her skin was unresponsive and cold like close friends or lovers in books. *Birth of Christ, death of Mom*, was the unreal first thought to plop unwanted into my brainpan, where it rattled around uneventfully for a while. I did not fall apart. I did the opposite of fall apart. I drew together very, very tight. Every strand of my being twisted itself around a central core of rigid awareness. I would not break; I would not even bend. I pulled aside the curtains, light green with a spiraling pattern of blackbirds, to admit the sun. I remember puzzling over the cerulean sky and dazzling light—Mom's bedroom window was oriented eastward, if that's not redundant—before walking carefully, so's not to wake her, down to the kitchen where I put on some coffee and started making the necessary calls.

She had not allowed herself the fallacy of medical treatment. She had refused even medication to lessen the pain, and so she died in pain, as she had lived in pain for many months. For a long time she would not let on that anything was wrong, but during one of my infrequent weekend visits that fall, her uncharacteristic languor and evident difficulty with basic tasks— walking, talking—disclosed what I had already begun to suspect, but had not wanted to believe, from our phone conversations. I knew better than to suggest a visit to the doctor, and I knew, further, that her mother had died in a similar way, refusing any treatment except that of the Christian Science practitioner, or nurse-practitioner, as these brave unmedical souls variously billed themselves. You cannot intervene in matters of faith, even when your one living connection to the world is threatened. Even when the deep and abiding love you hold, on some subsumed level, for all people and all life is focused and directed onto one human body, and that body is dying. My mother's faith never wavered. Where I saw passive suicide, she saw righteous affirmation of her lifelong principles. Death was a test she was determined to pass, and in the end she did pass.

Was I being selfish? Of course. Is selfishness a defining characteristic of human beings? Okay, sure. Everything fades, fails, falls. Everyone leaves. I've always known that—everyone has always known that, every infant even, who experiences a tiny death when his father leaves the house, when his mother leaves the room. The periodic reminders fate had conspired to present me of this central fact served the useful purpose of detaching me from myself, so that I might at least survive, so that I could live. This detachment, in turn, inspires selfishness—requires it, even. So I am selfish, and sad, and cut off from the people I love by an impermeable wall of mortal flesh. Just like you.

Around this time Kurt started to vanish. Literally: We wouldn't see him for a while, and then he would reappear and act as if nothing had happened. Someone would see him shuffling down Brown toward the grocery store or the laundry or the coffee shop, or, more often, he'd simply show up at his usual table at the Hive or The Pearl, or both, and without preamble, as usual, pick up the thread of some dismembered conversation. He would not discuss where he'd been nor even acknowledge that he'd been anywhere at all, so that if we were drunk enough, we would start to unbelieve our former conviction that he hadn't been around. I think most of us knew the truth, but it took a number of these disappearances before we were convinced that a pattern was forming. Not that his whereabouts were any of our business, but his refusal even to admit that he'd been gone split the regulars into two distinct camps: one who believed that Kurt was simply vacationing, pursuing one or another of his imagined-by-us hobbies, although the various theories advanced regarding these ranged from the ridiculous ("He's a closet bird watcher") to the even more ridiculous ("He's moonlighting as a train conductor"); and the other, who assumed he was off on music-related business, possibly touring some far-flung patch of earth in support of some record his band had released, despite the fact that we never saw or heard from any other members of his band, and despite the fact that Kurt himself never made reference to any kind of music-related activity. I only once saw him with a guitar at Albion, though I'm sure that somewhere in its recesses he must have had one, or a hundred. There were also quite a few of us who simply didn't care. Some of my friends asked me in a knowing tone, assuming that I was privy to Kurt secrets; even if I had been, I would not have vouch-safed them, and they took my shrugging silence as a complicit yes to whatever guess they'd made.

Kurt would leave for days at a time—the longest stretch I remember was five days, the average was probably three—and when he came back he was tired and disheveled and didn't come out at night and refused all visitors. Or at least me—he refused to see me, even when I came by at 3 or 4 in the morning, drunk with the gift of a bottle of Sangre del Toro, a very cheap Spanish wine you could buy at closing time from the Hive for eight dollars. I usually bought two. He would not answer the door, though. I shouted up to the dark windows of Albion that it was me, Fiat, and that I had brought red wine, and that I knew he didn't drink much but I certainly did. I was trying my best to be charming. My best was not well-received by shamming Kurt. Or maybe he really was asleep, impenetrably asleep, maybe he slept more deeply than I ever have in my life, no matter what quantity of alcohol I have drunk, no matter what combination of prescription medications I have swallowed. On my gravestone it will read, *Here Lies Fiat Lux, Asleep at Last.*

When dawn comes, and I shut my eyes in anticipation of a few sweet verses of semi-slumber, I experience the only real moments of happiness and peace I've ever been able to count on. The half-life of my prolonged drowse seems to last a good few hours, but probably's considerably shorter. Time stretches as you fall asleep. Fragments of thought expand to hallucinatory size, assuming sometimes the shape of inspiration, and since

I've never had any purpose to which to put inspiration, it serves me instead as an effective soporific—infusing my subsequent dreams with a hopeful tinge, so that I'm almost always disappointed on waking up and seeping back to real life. The shapes outside my bedroom windows, usually dendriform, shed meaning and acquire form in daylight, much in the way most writing seems to do.

Now that my former life's forever gone, I miss my thin mattress wrapped in flannel sheets, creaking on its uneasy frame. I miss the ragged shank of carpet covering up the badly stained and warped floorboards of my apartment. I miss the insulating properties of the bricks outside, and the heat vent close to my bed that buffets me with super-dry hot air no matter where I set the thermostat. I miss the small, scarred desk with its ancient lamp at which I would sit, in a chair too solid to be real, and read books I had brought home from the library. No more reading for me. What I do is hide, and write. When I'm done writing, I'll be done hiding.

What words are: cancellation marks on the stamp of infinite space. Proof, I think, for those who lack faith. When I leave here, if I manage to leave, I'm gone for good. You will never find me. I do not want to be found. All that's left to signify my existence will be words.

Notebook Thirteen

What crimes we have committed in whose name? I excoriate us, humanity, and our numb thumbwrestling, left hand versus right, pointless and pointlessly harmful. What is the world coming to, and when? When! I haven't lost my mind, but I haven't come up with anything in the way of a plan yet, and so all this writing is stalling, and though I suppose you could say that all writing is stalling, this is graduate-level stalling. Stalling grad. O Jack Christ.

By the end of winter, just before the time of no reply, we no longer used Albion with any frequency, mainly because Kurt was so often gone on his walkabouts. And when he was there, and we did go, the atmosphere was different. A new seriousness had replaced our formerly carefree attitude, a darkness had descended—gloom supplanting gloam, if you like—and I did not then and I do not now understand why.

At the time I thought the difference was in my imagining. Certainly on the surface nothing seemed different, in fact the relative scarcity of our Albion nights only served to highlight and set them apart from

214 ✳ Artificial Light

the normal run of bar-going and after-hours party-making, and in so doing make them special. We learned in those days, I think, to appreciate what we'd formerly taken for granted at Albion, but as with most appreciated things, our learning came too late. A thing is gone; you miss the thing; but what you miss about the thing is precisely what cannot ever be recaptured, which is why you miss it. So it's not fair to say, as some did, that Albion was never again as good as in its vogue. Some nights it was better. But even on those better nights the original spirit was missing; a simulacrum decanted from desperation and longing took the place of that original spirit, and if you drank enough, and tried, you could convince yourself that nothing had changed.

Nothing *had* changed: instead, we had changed. Amanda Early confided to me late one night that she was pregnant, though she would not say who the father was. Unplanned pregnancy is a fairly common event in Dayton. It's responsible for most of the weddings and subsequent divorces in our circle of friends. But Amanda assured me that she had no intention of marrying the father, that the conception was a more or less one-time thing (as most things in Dayton are more or less one-time things, meaning infrequent rather than unique), and that she was sure that the unnamed father, who by the way she had not bothered to notify yet, would be relieved that Amanda did not plan to make demands, financial or emotional, on him, in the event she decided to keep the baby.

She wanted advice on what to do, she said, though as with most people who ask my advice, she wanted mostly to explain her reasons for making whatever choice she would, in the end, make. And, I suppose, she wanted my assurance or approval that her choice was the right one. A person likes to have such assurances or grants of approval in times of great stress or when hard decisions must be made, even if from someone he or she doesn't know well, or respect, or understand. I'm happy to provide this service, although I can't imagine asking anyone's advice about anything important to me. But my lack of imagination is not anyone else's problem, and so, as I say, I'll issue advice like the Roman emperor who used to fling pots of white-hot coins to the rabble from the roof, in other words for fun. And because I love everyone.

With Amanda I was hard-pressed. I don't know what I think about abortion. I haven't formulated a position. Most people in our circle are fairly pragmatic on the issue: against, until it happens to them. I have been lucky, or prudent, or possibly just pathetic, but I've never missed a period. My punctuation's punctual, I used to joke, back when we told jokes, and understood them. I've never known the panic of delay, or had to undergo the private humiliation of the home pregnancy test. I did once take a pregnancy test, as a gag, late one night at Albion in the bathroom with Joe Smallman. We each took one. I had as much chance of being pregnant as he did, so I thought—if the process that led to the two of us peeing on plastic sticks in a mold-encrusted john can be dignified with that word— that his false negative (because Joe was neither pregnant nor unpregnant, he was, as all men are, the opposite of pregnant—barren, uncreative, infertile, destructive) would be the funny complement to what I fervently hoped would be my false positive. My hope was of course unfulfilled.

The value of life seems to me a constant: unquestionably sacred, for reasons that escape me. In other words, irrationally sacred, but sacred nonetheless, whether invested in a splitting ovum, or branching tree, or weed, stone, seed, foal, gull, wisp of wave, field of sun-blanched wheat, green-eyed lady frowning, brown cloud, dream or sneeze or bleating heart. But we don't always honor what's sacred, we often kill what's sacred, we sometimes murder what's sacred, in the name of a principle or higher law or out of carelessness, ignorance, or brutal glee. Or as a favor. When I say *we*, I mean me.

So the value of life is a constant, but our treatment of that constant, especially our perspective as regards its purpose, shifts uneasily under our stomping feet. At least from where I sit. My instinct to regard its sanctity as absolute clashes with my recognition of the relative value of absolutes in practical terms. That's to say, as life applies to life. What my mother would call the Divine Principle governs a realm removed from here by our inability, or unwillingness, to see. I don't know whether it's inability or unwillingness, but I do know that no one living can see what many intelligent people have told us, speaking from seeming authority, is plainly there but not-there. That's the Religious Nut. The core of the God-apple.

When my mother died, I did not feel immediately sad. I did not feel sad for some time. Her funeral was sparsely attended, mostly by people from church who I recognized but did not know well, if at all. A few of my friends came, too. I'd invited them less to blunt the pain of my mother's death than to blunt the pain of dealing with her relatives and friends trying to console me. I did not need consoling—actually, the opposite. The man who read from the Bible and *Science and Health with Key to the Scriptures* at the funeral, whose name I remember but would prefer not to commit to paper, had been my Sunday School teacher for three years when I was on the verge of adolescence, which as *we all know* can be a difficult time for a fatherless child. There's a thrill to be had at that age from profaning the sacred, as there's a thrill to be had at any age from discounting the things of real value to oneself. My Sunday School teacher was telling us, the four or five in his class—none of whom I can now name, none of whom may remember what I'm recounting here, but that doesn't mean, does it? that what I'm recounting didn't happen—the story of Mary Baker Eddy's sunburst revelation, her Saul/Paul moment, when she first entered the region of thought that became Christian Science. She was laid up in bed after an ice-skating accident, I think my Sunday School teacher said, an apparently very serious accident that even threatened her life, maybe (the details are frangible—not the details themselves but my remembering), when she had a sudden inspiration, the sky opening like a heavy blue door (with a golden knob, I'm tempted to add) to admit the presence of Love. I suggested to my Sunday School teacher, at this point in his story, actually I *rudely interrupted*, as he told my mother later, and pretended to wonder aloud if maybe the crack on the ice hadn't scrambled Mrs. Eddy's brains, and if the resultant religion we were forced, week after week, to learn and revere, wasn't erected on an edifice of insanity. Of course I didn't say edifice of insanity at the time, I was only twelve years old, not nearly smart enough to see how insanity might be the soundest basis for a religion.

The other kids giggled. My Sunday School teacher looked at me with an expression of great sadness. This exact same expression of great sadness he wore as he read passages from the Bible and from *Science and Health with Key to the Scriptures* intended to mark the passing of my mother and to comfort those left behind. This expression of great sadness, along with my Sunday School teacher's balding head, bulbous nose, and high, reedy voice intoning with unbearable solemnity words upon words from these important books, moved me to a fit of uncontrollable nervous laughter that proved infectious with my friends and drew angry looks from the audience that only spurred my laughing.

I didn't mean anything by my laughing. I didn't mean any disrespect, as I hope my mom realized, looking down as we like to think the dead look down on the living, watching me sweat in my dark green dress as I struggled to contain the laughter that flowered evilly in my throat with every sentence my Sunday School teacher read. I had worn the dark green dress because it was the closest thing I could find to black. Now I have a lot of black in my wardrobe. Black and other morbid colors clot my closet like a stack of photograph negatives, torn or curled at the edges and smelling of chemicals. Last year my Sunday School teacher was diagnosed with a rare brain disease that's not fatal, but reduces the victim to a near-vegetable state in a short period of time. I heard about his condition but I did not go visit him. I was afraid I might laugh.

After the funeral, my mother's second cousin, who I'd met maybe once before and have never spoken to again, organized a reception for the mourners, where a number of people informed me that my mom had passed on to a higher plane of existence, like waking from an extended dream, which is how Christian Science treats the idea of death in very general terms. I did not argue, then, as I would not choose to argue, now, with their consolations. I have no genius to disputes in religion and I have often thought it wisdom to decline them, especially upon a disadvantage, or when the cause of truth might suffer in the weakness of my patronage. That these difficulties might prevent us from expressing in true words the desert in our heart we understand, and forgive. But we cannot, whatever the cause, watch without judgment the cold trajectory of lies issuing like arrows from our mouth, to pierce the fragile envelope of our only relations' empty heads. No weapon scores more deeply than untruth.

I accepted their acceptance, as graciously as my throbbing temples would allow, with silent nods and a half-smile of beatific ambiguity, permanently since that day etched on my face in any awkward situation. I believe the world grows near its end, yet is neither old nor decayed, nor will ever perish on the ruin of its principles. By end he means end and not a kind of change, is quite clear: as the work of creation was above nature, so its anniversary, annihilation; without which the world has not its end, but its mutation. Much more pessimistic than me. I conclude, therefore, and say, there is no happiness under the sun. All is vanity and vexation of the spirit (the preacher, again—these gloomy men always turn to him, misunderstanding the hope he taught). Whatsoever else the world terms happiness is to me a story out of Pliny, an apparition or neat delusion, wherein there is no more of happiness than the name.

We have thus by reverse-engineering the image of Christian Science, which would agree with Sir Tom in respect to apparitions and neat delusions, though he was a much better writer than Mrs. Eddy, sorry to say. My mom would tell me that she spent a great deal of time trying to separate the evil from the person, because the person was a perfect child of God, just like she was. Only it was a struggle sometimes to see that perfection through the corrupt eyes of mortal sense. For my own part I'm not always sure it's worth the effort.

The things I have had to do in order to preserve what used to be called my sanity these past few days I would not do again, nor do I choose to relate. In the same room with me, though at the far end and thankfully not yet begun to decompose (the reason I have not tried to figure out how to turn on the heat, or light a fire), lies Kurt's corpse. Blood everywhere. Bits of brain stuck to the wall, his face unrecognizable in an instant and now pale purple from either the cold or the rigors of death or both. Is it grotesque for me to say that the color is lovely?

I don't look over there much. The sight reminds me of the last few minutes of his life, which were the last few minutes of mine, too, in a sense. I have spent too much time in the company of dying souls. In one sense

I know that's ridiculous, because either souls don't die, you tell me, or every soul dies, you add. But until you, and you, have faced one of these poor human beings in the brutal bloom of his misery, you will never know what you would have done in my place. I suspect you would have quailed. I suspect this because I quailed. I suspect you would have broken down in tears and pleaded to be relieved of so awesome a responsibility. That is what I did. And I suspect you would, in the end, have pulled the trigger, because that's what I did.

I'm afraid of falling asleep because either his avenging ghost will gut me or the cops will come, or someone at least, the meter reader or the plumber on some long-delayed appointment, and I will be caught. I will be caught and arrested because there was no note. I have in my defense only Kurt's word, and his words are no longer available. Now you tell me: If you were sitting in that jury, dear peer, would you believe a scrawny young woman with matted hair that one of the most famous, rich, successful human beings on the planet had begged you to put a bullet in his brain? Because even though he wanted to commit suicide, even though every atom in his body cried out to the setting sun in mine, who among you, ladies and gentlemen of Humbert's jury, would believe that a person as fortunate as Kurt, who had attained the summit of celebrity mountain, a place I'm told every normal boy or girl aspires to climb, would volunteer to end his Perfect Life, and further would recruit someone like me, to whom no rumor of fame (forgive the very small Latin pun) had ever attached itself, even in the confines of my provincial prison, to implement his end?

Don't kid yourselves. You'd do what I would do: You'd say *guilty*, you'd judge before you'd even settled into the juror's box, before you heard the prosecutor's opening statement, before the weakness of my own defense was laid bare in the first few moments of the trial. Reason: I *am* guilty. I murdered Kurt. Whether by his request or by my own free will, or both, I did the thing that I am accused of doing. It's not guns that kill people. It's me.

On the last night we were all together at Albion, which turned out to be the last night, forever, or else the beginning of one very long night, Amanda confided in me that she had asked the still-anonymous father for money for an abortion. But now, she said, she'd decided to take the money instead and buy a plane ticket to England and visit the sacred stones and plinths and mounds and so on, and then maybe disappear into the forest and give birth to a woodland creature and eat off the land and dwell among the trees forever. I didn't tell her what I thought—which was that I wasn't sure much of England was any longer forested—because the first words to Wordsworth's *Prelude* went through my head at that moment and I agreed, absolutely, with Amanda's plan. I told her she was doing the right thing, and that I would never tell anyone, because she wanted to keep her trip a secret not just from the father, but from everyone else. She told me because she knew I would keep her secret.

I told Amanda, too, what I think to be true: Whatever her choice, ending anything is difficult, and sometimes necessary. All endings are a bore.

Notebook Fourteen

7.

- My name is Orville Wright. My name is Orville Wright. My name is Orville Wright. My name is Orville Wright. My name is Orville Wright. My name is Orville Wright. My name is Orville Wright. My name is Orville Wright.

- No matter how many times I write my name, I am still Orville Wright. I am still the man who invented the airplane: That is who I am, that is how I will be remembered, some forty-five years after the fact, some thousand years after the event. I understand that my complaint is small, and that I should be thankful for having contributed to such an evidently important piece of human progress, but good Christ, how I have been bored these many long years since! When your life's work has been achieved at age twenty-seven, even if you don't know that, even if you remain blissfully ignorant of the fulfillment of your purpose on earth for decades hence (because you have an almost limitless capacity for illusion), nothing that you can imagine will fill the hours and days. The hours and days will pass; but they will pass as husks, empty, formless, and you will remember nothing of their passing except their passing. No hedge against the numb parade avails itself, except the sick refuge of pipe and leaf. The pipe! And visions therewith produced—enjoyed—which are not visions Heaven-sent, or maybe are, but cannot salve the open wound of time. Had K. remained, had K. not broken her vow, the more pronounced for never having been uttered, I might have lived usefully. Or had I forgiven— had I been granted the capacity to forgive, as the bishop would insist, when we were boys, that we forgive each other some small slight—but this! Her leaving was no mere childhood prank. It's an awful thing to leave a man alone, and one by one I have been left alone, by (over time) everyone I have ever loved, which number is not great. My sister bore the best part of my love, the majority; bore it far away, though not so far that I couldn't have visited if I'd wanted. I didn't want. Oh, there is no word for what I sought— want, need, require: These are pale emblems of the fierce palliative I should have applied, if possible, to the profound thirst in my deepest recess (I dare not call it soul).

• And so the pipe my last best friend, whose chief merit lies in its capacious appetite for time. In the reveries provoked by its use, I surrender myself to a current of air that is not air, yet behaves the way I understand air to behave. But is rather a current of time, and by entering at the proper angle of incidence (the key, as I have outlined in countless interviews and speeches and articles, to proper adjustment of an airplane's wings so to achieve optimum loft), I can travel anywhere, by which I mean any *when*. I can return to the days of my youth, to the excitement and anticipation with which I greeted every day, the sense of satisfied exhaustion with which my cheek greeted the pillow at night.

• Often I wake the next morning and read what I have scribbled in my journal the previous night without understanding a single word. I am no writer. I have never claimed to be; though long ago Will and I did publish a newspaper for which I wrote a fair amount of copy. I can spell, I do know that. I understand the principles of grammar well enough to ignore them when I want; but I can't make a hell of a lot of sense, without a great deal of effort. No man should expend such effort on something as worthless as the written word, doubly worthless when the subject is himself, when the subject has no object.

• The fact remains, staring like an insolent child at my long gray pipe-smoking face, that I have out-lived my purpose. Out-lived for many empty years my only purpose on earth; no tinkering or puttering or what-have-you in my laboratory or at Albion can obscure the pointlessness of any such experiments, or better, distractions. That I have managed to fill my days, with or without the aid of opium (with): entirely secondary to the point of living. I can be, I am sometimes, I have often in the past been, content. You will note that Jefferson did not write "pursuit of contentment" and that true happiness belongs to those who serve, without cease, not just mankind but the Creator. That I once helped, that I joined in the devising of a good machine toward whose uses I continue to keep a hopeful outlook, provides solace and a warm pit of pride in the hollow of my heart, but that same pride, that same warm pitfall, will take me to Hell if I do not let go before death plucks me from my habits and my habitat. Named Albion, for reasons I do not choose to share. I would prefer not to!

- *Imprimis:* I am a man who, from his youth upwards, has been filled with a profound conviction that everything revolves, in other words that there are cycles, and that these cycles are limitless and not necessarily inter-secting (in other words bi-cycles). When I was a child I caught a fleeting glimpse, out of the corner of my eye, of a woman walking on water—impossibly, because I was at home in bed, sick with fever then, and cannot trust the memory of my senses. She was bathed in light not from the sun but that somehow she herself provided, proceeding from inside her but not herself glowing. And not so much walking as gliding, on a cushion of air, a visible inch or two above the shimmering surface of what looked exactly like Mad River where we sometimes fished, down south. In that instant—which I have always regarded as the defining moment of my life, though I did not confide my vision (if that's what you want to call it) to anyone, except K., who promised never to tell anyone, and may have kept that promise, as she kept all but the most important one—my duty, my purpose, my destiny unfolded like one of the Moorish carpets now spread on Albion's floors. That part of the vision I did not share with K., I was afraid she would think the fever had diseased my brain, and that I would end up confined in some dreadful ward for the insane. But I was not insane, then, and I am not insane now. I know the reason I have kept myself alive the long and dreary years since we invented flight, since we helped invent flight and freed man from the shackles of gravity. But that reason, that secret, I must bring with me into the grave. I dare not speak aloud, nor write down, even here, the words the skimming woman spoke, in the brief second her path bisected mine.

• I am an engineer, not a scientist. The new

theories that led to the development of the atomic bomb I have struggled not to understand but to comprehend, and I hope that I have made some progress in that regard, but remain far from expert. Splitting atoms, the relationship between mass and time approaching the speed of light—all of this makes solving the problems of manned flight seem as complex as a game of cards. To split an atom: why? Unleash the fearsome power of the sun, by force creating exponentially greater force. I see the applications for good, I see that we can harness these limitless forces as a source of energy, and that the sun's process becomes our process. Again: why? We are told that the atomic bomb was invented by us to prevent our enemies from acquiring the technology first. This implies an inevitability to the development of the technology that I am inclined to believe; just as the discovery of the means of flight was inevitable, so the discovery of the means of nuclear fission was most likely inevitable, despite the well-intentioned efforts of some of the scientists. I bought a book recently, intended for laymen or perhaps children (I'm not sure on which count I qualify, possibly both), called *The Einstein Theory of Relativity*, in which the authors use a method of emphasizing their points by placing certain stress words in ALL CAPITALS. It's a VERY distracting method, and FURTHER has the opposite effect of the ONE intended: It ENCOURAGES speed-reading and skimming by MAKING you think that only the words and phrases so capitalized ARE important ENOUGH to read. Nevertheless, the authors' explanations are relatively clear, relatively concise, and relatively informative. The included algebraic and mathematical formulations even a school boy could follow. The most interesting part of the book, for me, was the last chapter, which—after exhausting the various implications of relativity—treats of the atomic bomb. It was written recently, very soon after the conclusion of the Second World War (published in 1945), and as such seems awfully full of self-righteous justification for the bomb's use, which, as coauthor of the invention which delivered the atom bomb to its destination in Japan, I understand but find silly. The bomb was made to be used. The bomb was used. What other purpose has a bomb than its use? Here the authors come to my aid: *The MORAL is obvious: "We MUST realize that it has become too dangerous to fool around with scientific GADGETS, WITHOUT UNDERSTANDING the MORALITY which is in Science, Art, Mathematics—SAM, for short."* That's my favorite part; suddenly there are only three branches of human endeavor, and they are a boy named Sam. As for religion: *"Religion has offered us a Morality, but many 'wise guys' have refused to take it seriously, and have distorted its meaning! And now, we are getting ANOTHER CHANCE—SAM is now also warning us that we MUST UNDERSTAND the MORALITY which HE is now offering us."* I have forgotten to mention that these urgent strictures are accompanied by whimsical illustrations that rival the visions produced by my pipe, though never my childhood. Never that. I'm not convinced that Einstein's theory and its practical applications (if you call blowing up cities a practical use, and I suppose under limited conditions I would) has produced any great change in the world, the way the authors of this book seem to think. Certainly we are too close to the subject to judge. The distance of time, which makes all things, even the airplane, commonplace, is required. And I am afraid I have very little time to give anymore.

Notebook Fifteen

Record 4 (3:42)
Simplicity
Watcher of the Night
A Plea for Common Courtesy

When a man allows music to play upon him and to pour into his soul through the funnel of his ears those sweet and soft and melancholy airs, and his whole life is passed in warbling and the delights of the song; in the first stage of the process, the passion or spirit which is in him is tempered like iron, and made useful. But, if he carries on the softening and soothing process, in the next stage he begins to melt and waste, until he has wasted away his spirit and cut out the sinews of his soul.

Within the space of one sad week we learned that Kurt C— had committed suicide and Michael Goodlife had died in a car accident. To further an already unbearably dreadful irony, since Kurt's body was not discovered for several days after he shot himself in the head, and Michael's accident took place as he was driving home from Albion, it's possible—and therefore, in our minds, terrible and true—that Michael and Kurt died at almost exactly the same time.

Of the two deaths, Michael's was more immediately and deeply felt, for two reasons: that we knew him better and for longer, and that we found out sooner. Had our consciousness been less fully dissolved by drink, we would perhaps have been woken by the early-morning phone calls from various friends whose whispery, somber messages gave no details but, when we eventually pulled ourself groggily from the depths of alcohol-related shut-eye, communicated by tone the morbid news. We did not yet know who, but we knew what, because we had received this type of message before.

So we returned calls, and though we like to think we are perpetually prepared for bad news—that bad news will be greeted by an attitude of weary surprise but not shock, not anymore—our reaction to Michael's death was just that: shock. Because he was not one of the ones who figured in any reckoning of likely too-young-to-die candidates. We would have been less surprised to find that we ourself were dead.

That we quite think.

And the result of the whole discussion has been that we know nothing at all.

We felt Michael's loss keenly not just out of affection, but out of the inaptitude of his passing. His band had only a week earlier signed a deal with a major record company, and was preparing to leave town for New York to make a record, which would be financed and produced and distributed on a worldwide scale, with everything such an endeavor implies or entails. He might have flopped, he might have risen to the top of the pop firmament, he might (most likely would) have fallen somewhere in between, but we were happy, by extension, for him and his bandmates, but mostly for him, because we knew him best, and because we knew that he wrote all the songs and sang and that the band's success was his success.

During the week before his death, whenever we gathered in the Hive or The Pearl or at Albion, we were excited, there was a real thrill in our conversations about and with Michael. Something had actually happened, something good, or something that seemed good—someone with aspirations had seen those aspirations met. That he had managed to meet this aspiration while remaining a citizen of Dayton—anyone with genuine ambition along this line, like Kurt, usually plied their luck in a far-off city on one of the coasts—only enlarged our estimation of his accomplishment, because not since Henry Radio had anyone stayed here while succeeding there, and Whiskey Ships were elder statesmen by now, happily so, and Michael's potential accession to the World Stage was confirmation that Henry and Kurt were not a fluke, that Dayton had begun (as we always pretended to think) to invent America again, just as in the old days of Kettering and National Cash Register and Wright Bros.

None of this matters, of course. It didn't matter then, and after the accident it mattered even less. Guilt's a strange thing: We were one of the last to speak to Michael before he left Albion. We were on the front steps, smoking a cigarette as pretext for a moment alone with thoughts. He asked if we wanted a ride home. We said no, that we had driven ourself, which was the truth. We could have said yes. There was absolutely no harm in saying yes. We could have said we were too drunk to drive, and left our car there, to be retrieved the next day or several days later, which we had often done in the past. It's just always been a difficult word for us to say. Had we said yes, Michael might still be alive.

Michael hopped into his aging station wagon for the downhill drive north through the city center, across Monument Bridge, to the house he shared with Joe Smallman on North Main. Joe had left earlier, slipping away without saying goodbye. Michael crashed his car five blocks from his front door, directly across from McCabe's. No one else was involved in the crash. No one else saw the accident happen. Two theories presented themselves in the aftermath. The first: that a known and very small leak in the exhaust pipe had somehow found a route into the car's cabin via its rust-ridden body, and that because Michael was driving through a freak late-spring thunderstorm, he'd rolled the windows up. Thus, even in the short trip from Albion to his house, he absorbed enough carbon monoxide from the exhaust to cause him to pass out, lose control of the car, spin around and around, smash into a utility pole, and sprout a penumbra of devouring flames.

The other: that he was drunk.

Of course he was drunk. We were all drunk. We were always all drunk. But we'd seen Michael drive drunk before, we'd been in the car while he was driving drunk, and we can say without hesitation that he was an excellent drunk driver. Such a thing exists, despite government propaganda to the contrary. We've been in the car with excellent drunk drivers and terrible drunk drivers; the difference is related less to their actual driving skills than to their respective abilities to handle liquor. Michael could handle liquor as well as anyone we've ever met, and we'd ask you to consider the source.

So we're inclined to believe the first theory, with the amendment that perhaps his alcohol intake diminished his sensitivity to the presence of the poison gas. There remain, of course, alternative theories, but these exist in alternative universes and as such are as infinite as possibility itself. In the months ensuing Michael's death, we examined many of these anyway (aliens, jealous rival bands, terrorists, some unspecified emotional distress that clouded his eyes or his judgment), and rejected them each by turns. It was something to do. A form of grieving, you might even say, but we don't think so. If you follow that line of thinking everything becomes a form of grieving, and we worry that might be true. Certainly in our case there's limitless potential for morbidity, and we're afraid of morbidity and morbid people. "Morbidity" reminds us of "sobriety," produces in us the same repulsed shudder. The medical examiner said he probably never regained consciousness, so therefore didn't feel any pain, at least, which for some reason always comforts those left behind, as if any death is painless, or painful, or can be measured in terms of pain.

The image we have had trouble erasing concerns

McCabe's, which broadcasts at all hours and at unreasonable volume a tape loop of barnyard chickens clucking frantically, which is supposed to stir the appetites of passersby. We don't know anyone who's been brave enough to sample the chicken there, though, at any hour, no matter how drunk, with the exception of our former bandmate Tub, who used to tell a story about going on a crystal meth binge that culminated in a visit to the talking chicken place, but even if true he could not remember any details about the visit, although he claimed to have been overcome with a serious case of the shits for days afterwards. The idea of Michael's burning car careened to a stop right out front, with the sound of clucking chickens easily audible above the flames, and the sirens of approaching firetrucks in the distance, and the rain hissing on the crushed car frame, Michael dead or dying inside, trapped, burning: We don't know how many more *saisons* we need to spend *en enfer* with that vision engraved in our mind.

Not long after, the news of Kurt's death spread among us, and was confirmed by a sprawling invasion of media trucks and reporters and camera crews with long, dangling microphones that no one had any problem shoving in our faces at any time or in any place, despite that we had nothing to say and would not have said anything anyway. The only comments the news people were able to gather came from those who did not know Kurt, and whose insights would have made us laugh if we had not temporarily lost the capacity for laughter. The reporters were reduced after a day or so of aimless milling to interviewing each other on the significance of Kurt's life and career and the innumerable warning signs, missed by everyone, of his suicidal bent: warning signs which, we might add, everyone of us has exhibited regularly, and which have proved unreliable in the extreme as a yardstick for guessing who's going next.

The presence of the media made our grief both less personal and more trivial, and further complicated the process by which we would normally have excised that grief—which is to say, by drinking; we could not go to the Hive, we could not go to The Pearl, because that's where the news people lay in wait, and after the news people, the swarms of fans, for which we were wholly unprepared, not having any real notion of celebrity except on a local level—for instance, Whiskey Ships was not a well-known band except to a devoted few across the country; we were more likely to be recognized and treated with anything approaching fanlike veneration in New York City than in Dayton, where most citizens outside our group of friends and acquaintances did not know what we did for a living, nor care—who thronged any spot Kurt was rumored to have hallowed with his shabby shoes—and so through circumstance and because we didn't know where else to go, we ended up mostly at Michael Goodlife's house on Main, drinking John Glenn cocktails, a modified screwdriver which Joe insisted Michael had invented. The atmosphere was both dreamlike and wakelike, and strange ideas were embraced without reserve; the unexplained absence of both Fiat Lux and Amanda Early was regarded an ill omen, and the behavior of

Mary Valentine regarded unduly giddy, even though that's the best word to describe all of us, at that time: giddy.

When we went up to the Hunt Club to meet Henry and the rest of the band, we were more reserved, especially Henry, who had nursed a secret bitterness toward Kurt, or rather toward Kurt's success, mollified somewhat by Kurt's worshipful attitude toward Henry. We had all seen a good deal more death than the younger crowd, and were somewhat inured to its effects, though Henry could not stop saying, "Can you believe he did that?" and pointing out the coincidence of Kurt and Michael's twinned passing, as if we had not noticed, or could not without his help. In general, Henry Radio was the kindest human being we have ever known, but the obverse of his kindness, most often to be found in private among intimates and when well-hungover, was a misanthropy you did not want to find yourself in the way of, ever. In rough times, though, there was no one better suited to provide perspective, because few have survived rougher times than Henry.

Eventually we realized we could not stay drunk and with other people forever, and besides, we don't like other people all that much, and we went back to Hickory and our apartment to sleep, which is when the trouble started.

Now, he said, every art has an interest?

Certainly.

For which the art has to consider and provide?

Yes, that is the aim of art.

And the interest of the art is the perfection of it— this and nothing else?

The whole point of shooting himself, of making his death an act of will, was to reinforce the purposefulness of his actions. Kurt C— wanted us to know that he meant it, man, and he didn't want to take the junkie's easy way out, even though he was undeniably a junkie and it would have been undeniably easy. But that way would have absolved him of responsibility, to a certain extent, and he wanted, with horrifying clarity, to take responsibility for his death. What scares us about Kurt's death is our underlying suspicion that he was right, and that his suicide was a pure, noble, and even brave act. What we've been fighting against in the ensuing days is the idea that rock is worth dying for, which is something we would have unhesitatingly affirmed as an immature, unformed, ridiculous teenager, but have long since rejected, as we all do. We don't think Kurt ever got past that part. He was unable to come to terms with the ridiculousness of his passion for and belief in rock as a force for redemption. That's a part of the reason why he killed himself—the only non-chemical reason—and while that makes him immature, unformed, ridiculous, it does not make him wrong.

The extent of the wreckage from Kurt's death has yet to be measured across the span of the rock continuum, but the plain fact is, nothing will ever be the same again. In no way is Kurt's death anything other than a "senseless tragedy" (these words themselves are senseless); rather, his gesture was the inevitable tragic result, in one form or another, of our relentless insistence on larding random manifestations of individual genius with more sociocultural weight than they can bear. That said, genetic predisposition and physical frailty probably had more to do with Kurt's decision than any cultural factors, all burbling about the burdens of fame notwithstanding.

In the end, though, even Kurt bought into the lie of his own importance. His death contradicts every song he ever wrote, every note, and that contradiction is the exact point we are trying to focus on, even though it keeps slipping out from under our fingers, even though no matter how many words we spill onto the perfect white sheet of his funeral shroud, nothing will keep him from dissolving, over time, into an imperfect assemblage of fading memories. His music, we're told, is the enduring, important part of the man, but that consolation is so utterly, ineffably weak. No cliché can encompass the full measure of Kurt's death. A tragedy this tall eats clichés and belches them like cinders from its fiery heart. However noble or pure, Kurt's suicide was a devastatingly pointless act. We cannot make sense of it. Things are different now. Things will always be different. Despite that most of the blather about Kurt's music completely misses the point, both dehumanizing the tragedy of his suicide and inflating the sociological import of his art: Something has changed.

We woke the next morning and went to meet Henry, who doesn't drive, and drove our car out to Albion, about twenty minutes from Henry's place in Northridge. It was a beautiful day, a cloudless spring day, the sun was almost warm and a number of the guests gathered outside on the lawn, behind the long hedgerow that separated us from the crowd of photographers, reporters, and mourning fans just on the other side, thronging the street. We heard there were special high-sensitivity microphones planted in the hedges, so we were careful what we said, but what we said wouldn't have been very interesting—we mostly talked about trivial stuff so as to keep our minds off the reason we were there. There were a lot of bad jokes, as we recall. We made most of them. The most notable thing, maybe, was walking out onto the back lawn and seeing someone who looked exactly like Kurt—so much so that you involuntarily did a double take, thought you were seeing a ghost. On closer inspection, the ghost turned out be . . .

. . . a ghost. We know how that sounds, and lacking the expertise necessary for accurate extranatural classification, maybe we should just call what we witnessed an Unidentifiable Phenomenon and leave others the job of definition. But whatever the thing was, it looked just like Kurt, even down to the cigarette burning in his/its fingers, from which he/it would take short frequent nervous puffs. We sat down, cross-legged, in imitation of the way the U.P. was sitting, and didn't say anything for a while. The U.P. didn't even look at us for several long moments.

"Trip," sighed the U.P. in acknowledgment of our presence, after some time, exhaling a thin cloud of smoke. We looked closer. You could see right through the vaporous stuff comprising the U.P.'s form. The hedge, for instance, was visible through his shirt sleeve, the blue sky through his head.

"Kurt?" we managed.

"How you been?"

"Fine. Kurt?"

"I'm not really Kurt, of course. I'm not *not* Kurt, either. I'm *a* Kurt. One of a number of possible Kurts, is a good way to put it."

"But you're still dead."

He nodded wanly, made a trigger of his finger and thumb. "Bang."

"Mind if we ask a question?"

"That's why I'm here, Trip. Fire away," said Kurt.

"Why did you do it?"

"Do what?" He considered for a moment. "That's a ridiculous question."

"Sorry."

"No, don't be. I overreacted. I'm not used to dealing with finite intellects."

"You mean because humans aren't capable of grasping all the stuff available instantly to the immortal mind?"

He looked at us like we'd gone insane. "What are you talking about?"

"Nothing. So. Why'd you do it?"

"You've been working for a long time on a book, right? We talked about this once. About Orville Wright."

"Yes."

"Well, the reason you're working on that book is related to the reason I killed myself."

"Okay. What? Because the act of writing about something destroys it or freezes it and prevents it from becoming?"

"No."

"No?"

"The problem is liminal, basically. The limits of everything: the world, our perception of the world, everything. The book you're writing?"

We nodded.

"Don't write it. Seriously. Stop. Burn what you've got, or otherwise dispose of it so that no one ever sees. If you write that book, you become visible, like me. Which is exactly the opposite of the point."

"You don't look all that visible to me." We pointed at a robin pecking around the lawn, easily seen through the fabric of Kurt's jeans.

"The proper aim of living is disappearing by degrees. Everyone has to find his own way to disappear. For me, in my circumstances, I took the only available route."

"No regrets?"

"Infinite regrets. But that's not any of your business. You better go now. The wind's picked up and it's getting cold."

He was right, too. About the weather, anyway. We decided the circumspect thing was to keep our encounter under wraps, not even tell Henry, who would have thought we were joking, and would not have appreciated the joke.

But: no joke. Everything we described here actually happened, and exactly the way we described. Were that not true, were we making this incident up or embellishing an actual incident or anything in between, there would be no point in writing anything, ever.

Suddenly we're just really, really tired.

If you could see us right now, maybe you'd

understand. Our place is littered with empty Coke cans and cigarette butts. We started smoking when we quit drinking, mainly because we couldn't stand the idea of being completely vice-free. We smoke Camel non-filters after a brief flirtation with Pall Malls. Also there's a bunch of candy wrappers, mostly Rice Krispie bars with a few Hershey's white chocolate. The shucked husks of pretty much everything we've ingested to sustain ourself through the writing of these pages thus far lie on the carpet around us. We don't have the energy to do anything but write until exhausted, climb into bed, get back up, start writing again. We think we're afraid that if we stop we won't start again, because that's a pattern in our life. Our follow-through is not great. We're running out of supplies, but going to the store in any organized way is out of the question, and none of the girls who occasionally stop by to see us at 3:30 in the morning drunk out of their minds have shown any inclination to shop for us. There's one sleeping in our bed right now. She has cranberry hair and the dress sense of an autistic. On the plus side, she doesn't seem to mind when we pace from living room to bedroom and back, muttering, "I hate myself and I want to die," which was a rejected N— album title for the follow-up to N—, but that's not why we say it over and over like a mantra without meaning either end of the sentence.

Right now we just want to know why Gail has not called. We're trying not to fear the worst, but fearing the worst is our specialty, and when we have a bad feeling we're about fifty-fifty on being proved wrong. Which is not very comforting when we're in the middle of the feeling. The only thing to do is keep working to the point where we're too exhausted to worry. Unfortunately, when you're exhausted pretty much the only thing you can do is worry. Or listen to music. Or both. Right now the song playing is "The Falling Down Show" by Droplet, at very low volume so as not to wake neighbors or the girl in our bed. It's an okay song, but has little effect on our emotional state, which is probably for the best. Do you know that feeling where you're simultaneously uplifted and depressed by something, usually a song? You'd think such a thing was impossible, or ought to be impossible because it's not fair. Say you hear something undeniably, ecstatically great, like Samuel Granta's "In Time," probably the most romantic pop song ever committed to vinyl, back when people used to commit things in general, and to vinyl specifically, which never happens anymore. At first you sit rooted, immobile, the adrenaline from the aroused emotion paralyzing your limbs and speeding your breathing and heart rate. Doesn't it seem like the world for that moment has potential, that everything isn't necessarily going to hell via handbasket, and all you need is love, etc.? Then the song ends and you're left with a hopeless aftertaste, which we think has two causes: 1) you're worried that your reaction to the song was overblown, unrealistic—in other words, that you were duped by the skill of the song's writer/performer into believing in the viability of something (i.e., the possibility of perfection on earth) that you don't or at least shouldn't, for sanity's sake, believe; and 2) the song, if your reaction isn't overblown but appropriate, raises expectations so high for what ought to be true

246 ✸ Artificial Light

that the clash with the inevitably imperfect real, confronted at the song's conclusion, immediately destroys the thing the song sought to foment. Then, what's worse, you listen to the song too many times in a row, hoping to revive that initial moment of connection and inspiring spirit, but all that happens is you wear out the song's welcome, and it loses its power of effect.

These are the perils of a life lived through music, though. We know that the majority of the world is not like us, and live their lives tone deaf and soundless and perfectly happy. We further realize that the non-listening portion of the world considers the listening minority immature and childish and we agree completely. We are not a full participant in the human conversation because part of us is always distracted, always listening for the perfect note, the one maybe contained in the next song, or the next, or overheard in our dreams. We don't ever expect to hear the note, and we don't know what would happen if we did, because (you'll have seen this coming) it's the hunger for the note that's important rather than the note itself. But the wonderful thing about an imperfect world is that as long as you can find a way to sustain your hope (a matter of being able to recognize hopeful things, which is not as easy as you'd think), you will keep looking for perfection even in the face of undeniable, and often tragic, evidence to the contrary.

The sexiest sound in the world to us is the sound of a woman breathing. "Edicule" is a song by The Grin that features the sound of a woman breathing over the final few seconds of music. This is therefore the sexiest pop song we can think of right now. We're reminded because it's very late at night, or very early in the morning, and we can hear the sleeping girl in our bed in the next room breathing. The morning has lightened to the color of grime, and the sparrows who inhabit the middle-aged ash tree outside our bedroom window are awake, and singing. We have written all night, again, and very soon we will stop and crawl into bed next to the girl. She won't wake up because we don't want her to, because, like a perfect song whose conclusion both contains and betrays the secret of life, her breathing holds the rhythm of our secret life.

Notebook Sixteen

Mary, after some time adjusting her wig in the bathroom mirror, and finally removing it altogether, decided she could no longer remain in hiding. He might be there, he might have moved on, but the obviously prudent assumption, she thought: still there. You put a face on, you compose a face, like an artist composes a picture, to convey a feeling to the viewer. Is that right, the viewer? The watcher. Watchman, what of the night?

Trace of crying jag remained around the eyes, but only if you were looking, and who would be looking for that? Not when I've got the unkempt promise of sex.

She pulled open the bathroom door and stepped into the tumult and visions of the bar. Of course he was there, but much to her relief, Mary saw that Michael was deep in conversation with Trip Ryvvers, and Kurt C—, and Henry Radio. She was able to pass that table without more than a tiny smirk directed at Kurt, who looked up and smiled briefly in response. No one else did. That's deliberate, thought Mary. I'm a distraction, a frivolous girl whose only possible use is entertainment. Michael has an excuse, but the others are older and wiser and wary of powers of manipulation in my hips. And I'm supposed to feel how? Never consider that, because you don't consider feelings of an object, like a lamp or a table.

She made her way to the next booth where Joe and Amanda had been joined by Fiat Lux. She smiled and slid in next to Joe, who was still preoccupied with his drink.

"Hey," said Fiat. "You okay?"

"Just powdering my nose," said Mary.

Joe Smallman sneered into his drink. "I wish," he said.

Fiat looked at Joe, bemused. "That doesn't mean anything."

"You wish," countered Joe.

If I was plain like Fiat, thought Mary, would I be happier. She moves freely from group to group, doesn't have to hide her brains to avoid scaring boys. But at the end of the day, or more accurately, at the end of the night, nowhere to go but home, alone. Too scary.

"Kurt says we should all come to Albion," said Fiat.

"Well, since he says it."

"Joe, you don't have to go. You can go home and you and your bad attitude can have nice game of—"

"I'm going," interrupted Joe. "Nobody said anything about me not going. I was making a sarcastic comment, which is not against the law."

"When I rule the world, it will be. You'll have to pay a fine of three sincere compliments."

I fear the names of things, thought Mary. Afraid if you put a name to the thing you somehow reduce its power. Or yours. Nothing more moving than discretion. Desperation bores me. Dayton reeks of desperation.

Everyone tells everyone everything, different every time. Secrets fly through the ether, piled ironies topple under the weight of disclosure.

"Anyone know what time it is?" asked Mary. "Is it near closing?"

"I think maybe around midnight," said Amanda.

No one in this town wears a watch. Don't need to know what time, might as well be like farmers in fields judging by the sun. Sun goes down, go to bar. Sun comes up, go home.

Jacket Michael was wearing. Must be new. Midnight-blue and shiny, matches his nail polish, matches his personality. I see everything that's important about a person in a glance. The way his body tensed in response to my approach, very slightly. Trip in his over-large T-shirt and sweater, Henry Radio in his untucked work shirt. Older guys who think it's a trick to hide their bellies. As if we're as superficial as them. Only sometimes.

Then Kurt in plaid shirt hunched over, the trailing ends of his brown pea coat draped from the back of the chair he's pulled up alongside the booth. Blond hair in lank strands pushed back behind his ears, dimpled square jaw badly shaved, weirdly out of proportion. His smile is so kind.

The Hive had grown progressively more crowded as midnight approached, a phenomenon known as "college creep" among the regulars. Behind the bar, Billy had been joined by his late-shift partner, Rob Roy, an amiable bear-sized man with wire-rimmed glasses that gave his fleshy face a focal point, and further softened his potentially intimidating features. In contrast to Billy, Rob Roy's disposition was unflaggingly pleasant, no matter how crowded the bar area grew. He and Billy performed an intricate dance behind the counter, their shoes protected against the slick floor by rubber mats perforated in geometric segments to allow beer froth to flow freely underfoot while they worked.

Fiat knew, which means that either Joe or Amanda told her, thought Mary. Most exciting thing to happen here all night, probably. An electrifying performance! I was on the edge of my seat! This one will run and run! And why was Amanda so nice to me, and why is she so fidgety, like there's a dragon crawling up her throat to breathe fire on us all. Welcome, dragon. Welcome to the berthplace of aviation. Due to whether conditions, we have been grounded indefinitely.

Would a dragon, a little one that could fit in your throat, emerge glistening and wings folded with little claws that can only tickle, and sneeze fire, be too much to ask on a dreary winter night? In a bar that blazes with color, that's on fire with sexual tension and stupid boy aggression and drunken fury that evaporates in sunlight and colors of clothes worn by people who don't know how to wear clothes with color and the piping of neon and the noises that have colors, too, the bright violet of girlish laughter and the dark green of shouting back by the pool tables, the stripes and solids of the clacking balls: Who would even notice a grayish little dragon sneezing fire if she crawled out of someone's throat and unfolded her veiny wings and lapped at a puddle of spilled beer on the table? If I were not medicinally barren, chemically incapable of conception, that would be a thing I could imagine squeezing from inside me, and you would feed her insects and fronds of leafy plants, and you would keep her in a shoebox with holes for breathing, and maybe you would find a piece of string and carefully tie around her scaly neck and promenade, is the exact word I would use, down the cracked and frozen sidewalk. You would be riven with concern for your dragon all day, which would delete the long hours at work in a keystroke of concern, and you would rush home to see your precious offspring, you would play light-the-cigarette and light-the-stove all night and not even want to go out and see anyone, and any time someone called or came over or you saw them running errands, all you would talk about is what your dragon did that day until people would leave you alone, but you wouldn't care because the bond between a mother and her dragon replaces every connection on earth with something that transcends every connection on earth. And then you would be happy.

Trip came up to the table, pulling on his coat. He stuffed the papers he'd been writing on into his coat pocket. "We're getting out of here," he said, with a vague wave at the table where Henry and Michael and Kurt were slowly gathering their things. "Heading up."

No one moved. "You guys coming?"

Fiat shifted in her seat. "I'm ready." The others slowly stirred and began the process of finding coats, scarves, bags.

"I need a ride," said Joe. "Too cold to walk."

"I don't mind walking," said Amanda. "It's good for you."

"Rule of thumb: Nothing's either good or bad.

254 ✺ Artificial Light

Drinking makes it so," quipped Joe, who then laughed noiselessly at his own weak joke, made funny through alcohol.

Mary wrapped a light blue scarf around her neck. Everyone I know is different. Different people all thinking one same thought, which is the only thought. If I had my dragon to consider, maybe I would pay more attention.

Rethread the reel, thought Joe, tonguing drops of yellowy liquid from the tips of his mustache. Rewind. What hurts is the gradual shadow of her fading smile when I say something funny. I nearly faint from the effort of renewing that smile, only to see it fade again. If I could keep it there, could I keep her? The song says everybody hurts, but I can only feel my own individual pain, thought Joe. Light from the fake Tiffany lamps flecked the honey-colored ice in Joe's glass with gold highlights as he tipped it to and fro on the tabletop. Joe watched the movements of the glass, then closed his eyes and let the negative image flicker on his eyelids.

This is impossible, thought Joe, scratching the side of his mouth. I can't, I cannot breathe when she's around, can't focus when she's not. O hell. I am a fool, and I think I'm going nuts. I need life support: her breath, her lips, her heart. I don't ask for much. I want to drink coffee in strange places with the morning sun in my face and her across the table, smiling. I'm no stranger to the rapture of attraction, but this is different. This is a matter of tides, of gravity. Of ineluctable force. I'm a fool.

Joe groaned involuntarily and put his hand quickly

over his mouth to stop his heart from flopping out.

"I'll walk with you," he said to Amanda, who shrugged okay.

As many times as that, thought Joe, as many times as she wants. She can open the door without thinking and as easily slam it shut. I'll walk through, too, I'll follow wherever, every time. Now she's here and I'm here, and whenever that happens it's like life switches on, there's an electric charge to the most insignificant action or word someone says, anyone, until she leaves. Mostly it's potential energy: the possibility that she'll say something to me that will carry the meaning I need to see me through the night. Some nights are more endless than others, but they're all pretty long. And they're all dark, lit up from inside by stray sparks of her presence, or the memory of her presence.

No one laughed, but that doesn't mean it wasn't funny. Not everything that's funny you laugh at. Sometimes you just smile, or not even that. Sometimes you have this inner chuckle that produces no outward manifestation of getting the joke, but there's a slight thrill in the spine, and a warmth of satisfaction with yourself and your relation to the world, an incremental orientation toward okayness which, despite your pervasive feeling of being separate on account of the alienating intensity of emotion directed at one person or one thing, lends you an illusory sense of strength and purpose. Despite the foreboding of darkness behind the momentary pinprick of hope, though, maybe the sense of strength is not the illusion but the whole point, and the overwhelming passion—I'm just saying *what if*, thought Joe—is a transitory phase, as brief and powerful as early spring rain, and just as ruinous, and just as cleansing.

The assignment of riders to available cars was efficiently if thoughtlessly sorted by Trip Ryvvers. "I can take Henry and Kurt and Fiat," he told the small group huddled in the parking lot. "That's all I've got room for. Michael, you can handle the rest of the car-free?"

"We're walking," said Amanda, nodding at Joe, who did not look pleased. "We want to walk."

Michael Goodlife, momentarily fazed, glanced briefly at Mary, who giggled, realizing that she was the only one of the group left. He gave Trip a brief grimace of acknowledgement. "Sure," he said, thinking what can five minutes hurt.

He walked to the passenger side of the robin's-egg-blue station wagon and unlocked the door. Scarf matches my car, he noted in passing, as Mary opened the door and got in.

"Could I possibly trouble you for a cigarette?" asked Mary, as Michael slid behind the driver's seat and started the engine. He reached into the inside pocket of his coat and without looking at her offered his pack. For all her premature dissolution, thought Michael, she remains uncorrupted, the image of the thing she imagines herself discarding; a chrysalis dreaming its metamorphosis.

"Ugh. Menthol. I forgot," said Mary, sliding a cigarette anyway out of the pack. She pushed in the lighter and sat back as he turned out of the parking lot south onto Brown Street. Her innocence is compounded by self-absorption, which in turn deflects the abundant opportunities for real learning that present themselves to anyone with eyes to see and a heart to break. Everyone knows this about her; no one is made happier or wiser by the knowledge. She is untouchable because she refuses to be touched in any other than a purely physical sense.

Things Henry and Kurt said about loneliness of touring. Kurt claims that's his favorite part. Nice to hear I'm not the only one. Really starting to hate that bar. Clutter is not a new idea in bar decor, but the aesthetic at the Hive escapes me. Each new layer of decoration obscures the last—horrible beer-stained red-and-white wallpaper in the pool room distracting from awful pseudo-surrealist mural above entrance, stylized tortoise plodding across a stylized desert—overload of sense-impressions. You're drunk with color and light before you've had your first drink. Are we drawn to the Hive in pursuit of noisy familiarity, or are we there for another reason, and drink to avoid it? The bar drives me to drink. Low-grade sophistry. Another thing Kurt said: The man who discovered the secret of life is dead.

Stewart Street. Longest red light in the history of red lights.

"Is there any way you would consider a truce?" Michael blurted, out of sheer impulse, waiting at the light as the engine idled noisily.

Mary rolled down the window despite the cold. "I feel sick. Menthol," she said, tossing the unfinished cigarette out the window. She turned and looked at Michael, who was staring straight ahead.

"I'm not the one at war," she said softly.

"I know. Okay. I'm offering a truce. I'm. I'm apologizing."

"You don't have anything—"

"I do. I'm sorry. It's difficult sometimes for me to act like a human being."

"It's difficult for everybody, Michael. Don't be precious."

"I didn't mean—"

"Thank you. For apologizing. Believe it or not, that means something."

"It's just, so much time goes by, and—"

Mary lifted a finger in the direction of the traffic light. "Ain't gonna get no greener," she said.

Second law of thermodynamics, thought Michael as he depressed the accelerator, dictates that in a closed system, disorder or entropy inevitably accompanies progress of time. Time's arrow moves in only one direction, inevitably. Is there a thing that transcends that unidirectional flight? Is it too squishy to say love? On even a pragmatic level I think that's right, though, because time is relative to each person's perception, and perception of time tends to suspend in moments of heightened emotional connection. So the only real problem is there's no such thing as love.

There is a way to connect that goes beyond sexually, doubtless, but even that for me would be a step up. Kiss me, please. Erogeny recapitulates physiognomy, right? My heart against your heart. Slowpokes unite: The race is to the swift, but we're all on the wrong track.

"You missed the turn," said Mary, languid with relief.

* * *

Amanda Early, though taller and more fit than Joe Smallman, struggled to keep pace with him up the slope of Brown Street just south of Far Hills near the crest where a sharp left turn and two hundred yards brought you to the front door of Albion. I am paralyzed, she thought. What's the word, quadriplegic. I am walking but still. Standing still but walk. There's a force field humming from my brain that renders me immobile, plus my voice doesn't work either. Isn't it romantic? It is exactly as romantic as the biggest pile of garbage in Huffman Prairie, i.e., the dump. Stinks of romance. The strongest soap could not clean the stench wafting from every pore of my moonlike face. The feeling is a feeling of every available drop of adrenaline in the body rushing through arms and legs at double normal blood-speed because the heart, which is the only non-paralyzed body feature, is working twice normal rate, pumping not just the blood but this unordinary amount of adrenaline, or some other chemical, but I call it adrenaline because it's the same effect as when I was younger and played soccer and the ball came toward me on the field, down out of the multifaceted blue sky, spinning black-and-whitely in a corkscrew motion because of the slice from the left-footed kicker, high enough in the air to do a header, which I'd been practicing but still wasn't very good at. The moment before the ball hit me full in the face instead of high on the forehead and the blood spurted almost immediately from my busted nose down my chin to the formerly yellow with blue arm stripes of the soccer jersey was, from what I remember, very exciting.

Amanda tried without success to swing her arms so as to pick up her walking pace. Exactly the same chemical-induced paralysis, which is adrenaline, which is just one of the many imbalances my body provides me at no extra charge. The excitement provoked by her secret decision had ironically frozen her typically overly-keen responses to external stimuli: In other words, Amanda did not notice that Joe was walking fast on purpose, trying to stay ahead of her so that he wouldn't have to talk, because he was beside himself with anger at having agreed to walk with her, and then, after making what he considered but did not make clear was a chivalrous gesture, she had spoken for him in the parking lot as if walking to Albion was something he had embraced, as if it was his idea. He had hoped by erecting a wall of silence to prod some challenge to his surly silence—a reasonable hope, as that was exactly how Amanda would usually react, but not now, not tonight; she had not even noticed that Joe hadn't spoken, was only vaguely aware of her surroundings, had even forgotten, at least in an immediate sense, where they were going.

In two days I will touch earth I have never touched. Many other people have touched that earth but I make it new, because I have never. Cannot believe I'm going to do this. Cannot believe I've managed to keep the secret of my going. No one knows, no one will probably even guess for a while at least. No one—here's the real truth—will probably even notice. For a while. At least.

"Slow down, can't you, Joe?" said Amanda to Joe's dwindling figure.

"Too cold. I need to get inside," Joe shouted back

down to her. "We're almost there anyway."

We're almost there, thought Amanda. All my life I've been almost there. All my life I've needed to get inside. All my life with my nose pressed against the window. Even one sign, one gentle word or tender look, maybe every thought process inside me would weave into a ball of wool and I would roll, bouncing, back down this hill or any hill. People think it's easy. People really do think it's no trouble at all. I've met that type of person, I keep meeting that type of person who thinks it's easy.

Cresting the hill, Amanda could see the light from Albion down the little road to the left, firelight and candlelight and another kind of light that has no name.

Michael had lately found that sleeping with his friends' girlfriends was in a weird way less complicated, emotionally, than with unattached women. Transaction reduced to its elemental component, pure drunken lust, he thought. No possibility of further entanglement, no need to make up excuses not to call or find ways to avoid her in public, in a small place like here. The trick is to keep moving, he thought. The alternative is a slow death by relationship, masses of conflicting emotions overlapping and tugging in different directions, each carrying a piece of what Michael regarded as his true self. The whole complex of disparate elements comprised a constantly wheeling ball of identity, and the loss of even the smallest piece would result in the eventual breakdown of the unkempt structure. Which in any case was just a construct of will. You will yourself into being, and you will yourself into feeling.

Love is a thing you either control or don't mess with, like everything else.

He took a drag from a menthol cigarette and stood against a wall hung with tattered silk, faded from its original red to a dull brick color that reminded Michael of the bricks outside the studio downtown where his band had recently recorded some new songs. In his right hand he held a coffee mug filled with a very good red wine.

If I forget the angle at which her cigarette hung from her mouth while she reached in the refrigerator for a beer, does that erase the fact of the dangling smoke? he wondered. Does that erase the fact of her smile, on which I staked the fat chance of my own life? Memory is pain. Bars on the prison of consciousness. Okay. Memory is light, heat, an empty promise of unending love, empty because it consists of itself only, a lie, a trick of perspective. Memory has no memory, can't imagine its nonexistence. Contains and expresses its own failure, constant reminder of the shape things no longer assume. Every new thing contains the shadow of its own end.

Mary sat cross-legged next to Fiat, beside one of the two easy chairs in front of the enormous fireplace. Amanda Early was sitting in the chair, and their conversation was animated. Every once in a while Mary would dart a glance in Michael's direction. He turned his eyes away to avoid her glances.

Is the world inclusion or is it indivisible monads? thought Michael. Is loneliness solved by love or just hidden or even made worse somehow, the way you can hide a thing and be more aware of its presence than ever? Will you ever kiss me again? Do I want you to? I'm supposed to be happy. I'm happy.

If a person, place, or thing speaks to you, if you recognize its essence or character and consequently become infused with animating passion for the subject, also called inspiration, how do you then remove yourself from the combustion process without the engine failing? Or something like that. Alcohol-speeded metaphors are my strong suit of armor. Read recently that propulsive punning is a symptom of syphilis.

He watched Kurt and Henry deep in conversation, Henry doing by far the most talking. I am a fraud, I don't belong in their company, much less his house. Still there is that prick of ego that suggests, what if? Maybe you are not just as good but better, or maybe you could become better, and then you would not have to leave town to find success like Kurt, and then you would not use Dayton as a militating factor against success, like Henry. His fierce independence cannot hide his jealousy. Inside he wants the recognition he feels his due, that Kurt instead has reaped, honors and laurels and prizes and riches. None of which he seems to want. Nothing on display here, anyway. Look around and you wouldn't know anything about the person who owns this place, who lives here. Having escaped, you'd almost think he's ashamed at returning.

Whether you try to escape from here or whether you acquiesce, you are still fighting the same war if you only don't let the space-fillers get in your way, thought Michael. Not in the sense that you have to go around them physically, in a room like here, but in the sense that there is only so much useful space in the world, space that if you are in it you need to be doing something that helps, something that defines or even strengthens these innate connections that if I were a little drunker I could actually see, like silly strings of consequence—*post hoc ergo propter hoc* spelled out in tiny letters on each brightly colored length—streaming from the tops of everyone's heads, and from their fingers, and their eyes and mouths and omphaloses and crotch-sections. And if you choose to occupy useful space, a choice made through the simple act of recognition of the useful space's existence, we will welcome you, sisters, brothers, and we will show you the secret dry goods locker where we keep the cans of supernatural silly string, and also on Friday nights we have a marathon word-game competition that helps weed out the less serious-minded. A brand of honey-flavored liqueur currently being market-tested in the Dayton metropolitan region will be served, along with indestructible pretzels. From across the room Michael watched as Amanda Early got up out of her chair and walked out of the enormous ballroom toward the bathroom.

Joe Smallman, bitter and lonely, a ghost bowed with sorrows too numerous to bear, threaded through the small group of revelers at Albion, determined that his surly demeanor would attract attention and perhaps concern. No such luck. Why doesn't Kurt bother with heat except the fire? wondered Joe. Freezing in here unless you stick close to the big stone hearth. Hearth of the matter. Trip Ryvvers, professional drunk, held court at the left lip of the fireplace. His audience was small, and only one, the Rose Scholar, appeared to be paying any attention to his rambling accompanied by expansive hand gestures.

"When I'm done with Orville, he will be unrecognizable," Trip was saying, "rearranged like an anagram to form something new, something I hope useful. Love girl with r . . . Incomplete message. Isn't that always the way? Wry, light lover. But that's cheating. How great if Dayton could be anagrammed into anodyne—close, but not quite there. Anyway, I do appreciate the effort on the part of the city's forefathers to cater to my writerly whims."

Is it a trick of light that makes Trip look younger the more he drinks? Thinks he's smarter than us, older, more experienced. Biography of loss. The size of pain is down to the amount of time involved. Time spent a way of measuring Heartbreak A versus Heartbreak B.

"I read today in some fanzine that the word *punk* in punk rock came originally from prison slang," Joe interrupted, swaying on his heels as he did whether drunk or sober, as if at any moment gravity would become too much for his tiny frame to bear. "Like if you were a punk, that meant you were some guy's bitch, in prison."

"A common misapprehension," said Trip, stumbling slightly over the last word. "Perpetuated by monoglot writers. Clearly the true etymology is German. Either *punkt*, meaning point, dot, spot, or place, or *punktierung*, meaning geomancy, divination."

"Nobody likes you," said Joe. "You can stop trying."

His remark garnered amused chuckles from Daryl and Co-Daryl, but the Rose Scholar frowned and tried to direct Trip's attention back to the original topic.

"You think he was really in love with his sister?" she asked.

"It doesn't matter what I think. It matters what you think I think."

"But how do you know what we think you think?"

"I'm just kidding," said Trip, rattling the ice cubes in his nearly empty glass. "Having fun. Same reason I put ice in this exquisite Bordeaux."

He sighed and looked at the Rose Scholar. "What matters is the truth. And don't get all *What is truth?* on me, unless you want Pilate's shade in your room late tonight with a scolding finger poking you in . . . inappropriate ways."

Disgusting the way he talks to girls. Disgusting the way they respond, with curious smiles, drawn by his filthy talk about filthy things. What he knows about Orville Wright, everybody knows. If he knows so much, he should write that book instead of the one he keeps droning on about. Bragging them into bed is the real point. Can't believe anyone falls for. Even *she* fell once, at least, maybe more, you never know with what girls tell you, less than what's real.

Slender epicene leans, in the slate-blue shadow of a tensely breathing maple sapling, against the bricks of a tall building. Always the same place/time, leaning, one leg bent, foot flush against the wall, right angle to the veiny sidewalk, so the blue-jeaned knee juts out and you can see little stripes of pink kneecap through the threadbare part of the jeans. Left arm tucked behind back, right hand pats the front pocket. Keys or coins jingle mutedly. Epicene means boy *and* girl, or both at the same time. Hair is tousled, fine, brown like a dark wood, like cherry almost. Eyes green with spidery streaks of yellow. Small sad beautiful boy/girl waiting for someone, I hope me, I think me, and the heat of the afternoon visibly floats and on it I float, too.

Amanda Early bent down to tie the laces of her burgundy work boots. Her skin was still flushed from scrubbing, and she could feel wet strands of her short dark hair pasted against her nape. Even now when I remember the dream, I remember the floaty feeling. If you know you're dreaming it's called a lucent dream or something. I'm bad with the exact way to say words, but I'm good at describing things.

She straightened and stood before the bathroom mirror. My face, for instance, is, I don't know, is it ovoid or ovular or elliptical, but the word I would use is moonlike or moony. I have pale skin, chalky-white, in addition to the egg shape or upside-down egglike shape of the face. Plus I have a very large head.

Sad lucent epicene: I miss you. I dream about you a lot. This is called *reoccurring*. I've never stroked your fine hair, your smooth skin, or kissed your green eyes. I wake with somehow your smell or the memory of your smell in the folds of my sheets. You have something that makes me happy for the time of the dream, and then when I wake up makes me unbearably sad for its lack in my actual life. The sadness comes from the distance between the possibility and the real facts. But now I understand: You are growing inside me.

Returning from the bathroom, Amanda slumped in her seat and stared at the fire. When you talk to a man and he contradicts whatever you're saying, it's not from his true opinion, it's just the way they establish territory or something. Mary said that and I think she's right. Definitely, with Trip, he has this superiority thing where even if he's wrong and he knows it, and you know it, he finds some way to put a twist on his wrongness that makes him overall right. Somehow, because he's older and a guy, he cannot stand the sound of anyone else's voice expressing an opinion. Like waving a red flag at a bull.

With Michael you get a different problem. Doesn't react to an opinion like a normal male, doesn't react at all. Which can be worse when he's just a wall of no reaction. This creates the effect of listening, but there's no evidence of real listening. Trip, at least you know he understands the words coming out of your mouth because he moves quickly to squash them, like mosquitoes of thought. But Michael will fry before he lets you see a tiny clue about what he might be thinking. If he does say anything in reaction it will be a joke, which is better because then at least you know he heard you.

Amanda turned toward the back of the big room, hearing a commotion. Kurt and Henry were carrying guitars and amplifiers and setting up to play. Never knew Kurt even had music equipment here. Trip walked over to see about joining in but was waved off. Amanda saw Michael Goodlife talking to Fiat, head bent close to her ear. Fiat smiled at something Michael said. Felt good to tell someone my secret, could only be Fiat because you can't trust anyone, not even new best friend Mary Valentine. Always happens you make friends with someone before you leave. Right before you leave. Somehow that eases pain of parting because there's a warm feeling of friendship lingering across distance. Someday after all I'll come back. But it will never be the same.

She surveyed the twenty or so people gathered in Albion's ballroom: drinky, laughy, dopey, silly, angry, smarty, pretty. Likely never see them again. Is that sad? Is that what's meant by bittersweet?

Henry Radio tapped into a microphone plugged into one of the amplifiers. "Hello. We're Blazing Moon Kids, and we'd like to play a few songs to celebrate the record deal recently signed by our good friend Michael Goodlife."

Smattering of applause, some drunken hoots. Amanda looked over at Michael, who had an expression of extreme shyness coupled with arrogance, if that's even possible, she thought, he both wants the attention and hates the attention. Kurt sometimes seems the same way, although since he's had the attention for so long now I think mainly just hates the attention.

Kurt and Henry began playing and singing, Amanda didn't recognize what. Their two voices sounded good together, raspy or ragged or some word like that. The song sounded familiar but old-fashioned, like something from the '70s. Where's know-it-all Trip when you need him.

Amanda watched everyone listening with either real or feigned interest. These are all good people, one way or another. I won't miss them. I'll find more good people, or not even any people, because I can make my own people now. A power no Druid priest could command or bestow. I will see the stones and the sites.

I will see them because I have wanted to see them for so long, the desire to see them has an automatic quality, like breathing.

The song ended and Kurt motioned to Michael to come join him and Henry. "You know 'Little Black Egg'?" asked Henry. "The Nightcrawlers?"

Michael shrugged in gesture of no idea.

Henry pretended outrage. "Kid signs a major goddamn record deal, never heard of The Nightcrawlers? Big hit in '66. Well, not a big hit. Come on, we'll show you. It's cake, man. Nothing to it."

Michael strapped on a guitar and huddled with Kurt and Henry, who shifted their hands up and down the necks of their guitars and hummed a quiet melody. Michael nodded that he understood the gist of the song and the three boys started playing. It made a lovely sound, Amanda thought, three guitars gently plucked and strumming. Soundtrack to my exit.

Henry started singing: "*I don't care what they say, I'm gonna keep it anyway.*"

Will anyone notice my leaving? She stood up and made her way toward the door. All eyes fastened on the musicians.

"*I won't let them stretch their necks to see my little black egg with its little black specks.*"

She slipped out the door. Eye contact with Fiat Lux as she quickly shut the door behind her. Slight smile and nod.

Amanda Early stepped into the cold and cloudy night. A scrim of snow remained along the edge of the sloping lawn and the steps leading to the street. Strong scent of coming rain in the air. Fading now, in the distance, she heard the song following her down.

"*I found it in a tree just the other day, and now it's all mine I won't let them take it away.*"

Michael Goodlife struggled to control his self-consciousness, face hot with mingled pride and shame, as he moved through the changes to the song. Try not to think about. Playing with Kurt and Henry. Try. AEDA AEDA AEDA AEDA. Don't look up or you will melt.

"*Here comes Mary, here comes Lee, I know what they want to see.*"

F♯mEF♯E F♯mEDE. Will I ever do anything this thrilling again? No, because a thrill repeated loses its. EF♯D. Walking lead-in. AEDA.

"*Oh father, what can I do? Little black egg's gonna tell on you.*"

She's watching. I can feel her eyes on me without even looking. In the car. Glad to get that off. Lighter now. Did I ever? Oh God, I did. I do. I still do. That's what all this is about. AED AED AED.

Mary Valentine watched Kurt and Henry and Michael play the song, watched without listening, eyes fastened on Michael, on his long lovely fingers. Tears brimmed her eyes. I thought I heard my name. What's done is done.

"*I won't let them stretch their necks to see my little black egg with the little white specks.*"

She dabbed her eyes with the robin's-egg-blue scarf. I don't care who sees, she thought. I don't care who thinks I'm being dramatic. I don't care. I'm going now. I'm going.

"My little black egg."
"My little black egg."
"My little black egg."

Notebook Seventeen

I will admit, because I am in an admitting mood—and likely ought to be admitted, at this point—that there was a quality to the last night at Albion, both special and strange. Events seemed to unfold in a tule fog (Scirpus *californicus*), or tularemic haze (Francisella *tularensis*), in the shade of a tulip tree (Liriodendron *tulipifera*), under a bridge too far, sorry. The angles of coincidence converging at Albion—like the wires on the utility pole outside my apartment on Hickory, on a rare cloudless day, black lines framing trapezoids of azure—helped produce this effect: Henry Radio, a rare and welcome guest; Michael Goodlife, a rare guest, celebrant; Mary Valentine, a frequent guest but never before in my memory synchronous with Michael; Amanda Early, a frequent guest, bursting with secrets that suffused her lunar face with a rosy glow; Joe Smallman, troubled, distracted, worried, enthralled; Trip Ryvvers, drunk and prolix; Kurt, our host, unusually animated, almost merry.

Fiat Lux, bittersweet.

Sometimes you understand more than you think. Sometimes you have feelings of melancholy at the exact moment everything looks swimming. By any measure, this night was one of the happiest and most carefree in the short sad history of Albion. By any measure, I knew that this night would be the Last Night. I didn't *know*, of course, but I had a foreboding. Many people have forebodings when things seem to be going too well, when everything's just absolutely too perfect: These people are nuts. More charitably, these people are superstitious, and I am not superstitious. When enough bad stuff happens to you, you become conditioned to expect bad stuff, and bad stuff no longer surprises you. That's exactly when bad stuff stops happening, because surprise is its chief asset. So I would have no reason, granting the logic of my premise, to expect this night to be the Last Night, or to expect any other unpleasant news or incident, because that would not take me by surprise. In other words, my foreboding was unassisted, and unprompted, and uncorrupted by the usual incunabula.

This dread and darkness of the mind cannot be dispelled by the sunbeams, the shining shafts of day, but only by an understanding of the outward form and inner workings of nature. Furthermore, you must not suppose that the holy dwelling places of the gods are anywhere within the limits of the world. Flimsy nature of the gods, he goes on to say, and who's to disagree?

Here you see Henry and Michael and Trip gathered around Kurt. There you see Mary and Amanda emerging from the bathroom with tear-stained faces, smiling and laughing. Here, Michael and Mary in cordial conversation. There, Joe Smallman glowering, love-struck, unnoticed. Here, Kurt imparts to Michael hard-won advice on navigating the shoals of industry. There, Henry and Trip do the same, as Michael nods and sips his whiskey drink. Here, Mary says to the boys for ten dollars she will make out with me for three minutes.

Here, Amanda imparts a secret to me. Here, I explain to Joe Smallman that we are not in high school, and if he has something on his mind he should just say. Here, Kurt goes into another room and brings out some guitars. Here, we laugh and listen as Henry and Kurt and Michael play old songs, and sing, a thing I have never seen them do before, and Mary cries bright tears, and slips away unnoticed. Here, Trip imparts a secret to me. Here, Joe Smallman, courage failed, says goodnight and leaves. Here, Michael imparts a secret to me. Here, we sit and recline around the fire, drinking, smoking. Here, Kurt brings out an old pipe he says he found in a disused desk drawer, filled with what he thinks might be a residue of opium, and lights the pipe, and passes it around.

These all are gods, and partake of flimsy nature of gods. Some no longer exist, some exist still, some never existed at all. I have trouble remembering the next few hours, or more precisely ordering my memories, because I took a few puffs from the pipe, and my senses went all wobbly. My senses are wobbly now, too—but it's an unpleasant wobble, a sort of Lofoten Maelstrom (67 deg. 48 min. N, 12 deg. 50 min. E) of the body/mind. Nothing like the gentle eddies of my opium high, though if I hadn't been drunk I probably wouldn't have smoked the pipe, as my stand regarding opiates (anti-) is I think well-documented. But you never know what a girl will do when in her cups, and I took several deep draws of hot smoke into my lungs, without questioning what mixture might be in the bowl, because I like to smoke, I like to draw hot smoke into my lungs.

The windows and walls of the house open out, collapse into the unreal horizon. Rivulets of light stream into the room, exploding in slow motion. Even my bones have turned liquid. I grip the edges of the carpet and fly off, over the city. I spy: Bergson's *Matière et Mémoire*, one copy, facedown near a lamppost on Wyoming; three drawings in colored chalk, nature of representations unknown, sidewalk along Wayne; several stinking beggars the breath of my compassion causes to choke mightily and spit greasy gobs onto the shoes of passersby, Patterson just outside the Montgomery County Fairgrounds; the Pelasgian Hercules, father of Actaeon the stag-cult king, walking into the Moonlight Diner near the Cinerama movie house; buckets of unattended mineral paint in an alley behind Burgers and Cold Beer, West 3rd; Mother Zero, twisting her way down Ludlow toward 1st Street; a 12" x 15" print of Turner's *Beach & Inn at Saltash Cornwall* nailed to a tree next to a dumpster behind the Canal Street Tavern; the very image of Oscar Wilde, slumped shirtless in a chair at entrance to same, drool puddling in his lap; a book on numerology, hollowed out and stuffed with vials of crack in a plastic bag, under the right rear tire of an old, broken-down Utero near the entrance to the interstate on Stewart; an aboriginal hand-stencil on the outside of a Ukrainian church, Germantown; a broken and pitted double terminal head of Joe Jones, King of Southern Ohio Recreational

Vehicles Sales and Leasing, and his wife Blodeuwedd, half-buried in the dirt next to a gingko sapling on the verge of Calvary Cemetery; a rogue elephant trampling through Carillon Park; the sixth and final memo for the next millennium—too late—trampled by the panicked crowd, pages flying all over the place, one of which I grab at great personal risk as I fly overhead, but turns out to be, instead, the sheet music for an obscure sonata by a composer I wouldn't know from Adam/Eve; a huge silvery sheet hung like a sail from the top of an apartment building on St. Paul Avenue; several dozen clothespins sprinkled with gold glitter, two of which are affixed to a small icon of the Madonna on a gallery wall, Dayton Art Institute; a yellow coincidence, hovering on my window sill, Hickory.

When I returned—to my senses, to consciousness, to Albion—everyone had left. The fire had died to embers, and when I lifted my head from the moldy silk pillow on the floor by the hearth, I saw Kurt sitting in his usual chair, slump-shouldered and striated by the dying firelight.

"You snore like a horse," Kurt observed dryly.

"Thanks. How long?"

"Couldn't say. Long enough."

"Everyone gone?"

"Just you and me, kid. You and me and the ghost of Christmas past."

"I . . . What was in that pipe?"

Kurt didn't respond. He closed his eyes for a few moments.

"You know that thing," he said after a while, "when it's dark and you close your eyes tight and then open them and you see all these sparkling silver dots? Like somehow the light was stored in the sockets or the iris or the tips of your nerves?"

"I get that when I sit up too fast sometimes," I said.

"Then you close your eyes again, and an artificial light appears before your eyelids? Then through the red transparency of light I can see a close-up view of blood cells floating."

"Are you sure that's blood cells? I always wondered if it was germs or, I don't know, plankton? I don't know the science."

Kurt nodded, opened his eyes. "Things have been different around here lately."

"Different? I hadn't noticed," I lied.

"Yes you have. Everyone has. I've been gone a lot. And even when I'm here, most of the time I'm barely here."

I couldn't resist. "Where do you go?"

He shifted in his chair, leaned forward, staring into the fire. "Different places. If you mean physically, mostly on the West Side."

"The West Side? You mean here, in Dayton? But you're gone for days, and when you come back it's like you've been on an expedition or something, you're all haggard, and—"

"I'm a junkie, Fiat," Kurt interrupted, flatly. "I go to drug houses and take drugs. Specifically heroin. I go on binges and sometimes I'm out of it for a while, and when I come back down I don't know where I am or what happened. That's the best part. For however long, getting out of my head. Not being me. Even for a minute, it's worth everything. I think you know what I mean."

* * *

O Lord, I have called to Thee, hear me. I have spread out my hands toward Thy holy dwelling place. Construct my soul and do not cast it away. Put away from me the sins of my youth. Only the living thank Thee, all they whose feet totter.

Do you know about the singing forest? In the concentration camps the Nazis erected a series of poles with hooks protruding. They would hang the Jews from the hooks and twist their bodies, too, and the howling and the screaming, horrible to relate, was inhuman and chilling and incomprehensible. And these unheard sounds mingled with the unheard screams of the burning children in fire-bombed Dresden and the unheard screams of the vaporized victims at Hiroshima and Nagasaki. Most of this set in motion by one man, by a person or rather figure of world-historical import who was above natural law and thus moved the world-historical spirit by Hegelian directive in some direction, backwards most would say.

I want to make sure something like this never happens again, but more importantly, I want to end all human suffering forever. And I think I know how to do this, but I'm scared, and I'm not sure that it will work. I wish I was as certain of the end of all troubles as of the authenticity of the imagination. I am certain of nothing but of the holiness of the Heart's affections and the truth of Imagination.

Kurt's confession punched a hole in my heart: to think I hadn't noticed or seen the signs. In retrospect I saw all the signs, as anyone would, who had even minimal experience with junkies, as I did. My only excuse is that Kurt was rich, and I am not used to drug addicts with money. You will note that none of us, who are extraordinarily attuned to the usual symptoms, had guessed that Kurt's recent aberrant behavior was drug-related. None of us have much skill dealing with the moneyed class, and so—even though, given the bundle of clichés concordant with rock stardom, or what we thought we knew about rock stardom (having no familiarity with that, either), you'd expect us to leap to the obvious conclusion, but nothing else about Kurt seemed clichéd, would be my excuse—as far as I know, and I think I *would* know if some careless whisper of heroin use attached itself to Kurt, at least in the confines of our crowd, but I pride myself on noticing what no one else notices, and I had not noticed this, I had missed it completely.

Kurt tried to ease my self-recrimination by saying he'd gone to extreme lengths to keep his secret, using dealers on the West Side that didn't know him, that no one from our circle would know, who turned out to be, as far as dealers go, swell people, who took care of him and let him crash in spare rooms until such time as he was ready to return. Of course they liked him, I thought but did not say, he paid in cash, probably overpaid, and was gentle and harmless and tiny.

He explained to me that he had started using as a palliative for his intractable stomach problem; but that after a while the habit grew to monstrous proportions, and he had gone through several stretches confined to fabulously expensive rehab centers, and had managed to stay clean for reasonable periods of time, up to and including the first few months of his arrival at Albion.

He'd moved back to Dayton in part as an attempt to change his environment and unmake the easy availability of drugs: wrong choice. Here you can have anything you want, if you know where to look, and a determined junkie always knows where to look, eventually. And so he began using again, sometime after Christmas, which explained the change in tenor we had all sensed, but perhaps most keenly myself.

O for a life of sensations rather than thoughts.

Work boots shift, or what's becoming more.

He pckedi one of the razors, cloplastic double blades tted with, arrranged hapat random hazardly. Have to, consideredbe careful, though, or soon the big thrift storereful, though, or soon the, which already buzzes with mispl which already buzzes with tension, will sexual collect and concentrate's energiesjucedi and alcoholic emotion and erupt in a dangerous way. As likely a lightning rod as any.beer-fueledaggressionfury-hostility. Native is a kind of considerregarded his true slefregarded his true self ballwheelingbreakdown structurally—regarded his true self. T of identity, and tunkempt contructs chinin even in daylight, and the few thrift store lamps did little to front warehouseelec-tronics place, is third shift, or what's become. But you didn't need much to get by inou didn't need much to get by here. Brighten the gloom, so it was lamps.

Short walked smiling into the bar which threatened even. For instance: but I guess it doesn't compare to the thrill of having, saring aheadt, absorbed in parallel worldsblankly. There weret of course you get used to anything after a while, including l), including the the sweet thrillkick of love, including loneliness, extreme habitual disappointment, loss of innocence, and the constant and comforting presence of death and same. Alsoyourself from the combustion process without the engine failing? But they tell you it's wrong, wrong, stick to the. Or something like that.

All sweatyreallysweating glasses. Humid, toostuff. Laughter is a slipped sibilant from slaughter. Odivinationpaid him much attention. Whaat this broken f my ambition. Thaman, this shell, could represent his dreams.

See: condescension, arrogance, life on the mountaintop, airless, sterile, and lonely. See further: snowfall, a small cabin with fireplace, burning, the curl of smoke pearl-gray against the whiter sky, a history book, the end of time.

Hate disease of intuition. *Resolution No. 6: If happiness is the goal of living, then we are doomed, because we are not selfish enough by nature.*

Reflected in storefronts dim as church windows. That convenient farrago of nonsense, the Sibylline Books. Jackal-headed Annubis, Thoth, Horus, Nephthys, Set. Hut. Hike. A nice conditorium. Shattered, fuguelike, obnubilate. Anu—goddess of the dark blue night sky and the dark blue sky. Girls of Britain stained themselves blue all over with woad (Isatis *tinctoria*), paler than Japanese-blue and redder and duller than Peking-blue; in Ireland, at least, this was a female mystery that no male was allowed to witness. Chiliast. Still in my memory's good ear rings the note. A victim of the vine. Salesman of intangibles. All blue is beautiful: a shy dryness, reasons of clarity and space. Broke his hand of yesterday. *Sachlich*. A night breeze lifts the saffron flush of the moon through a thicket of ash leaves. A blurry of bats, an escaping train. The conchoids of Nicomedes, a planar curve of the fourth order, concinnous. The ungracious duchess has pelted me with a set of as pitiful misadventures as ever small Hero sustained. My Heart Laid Bare. *Sapiens dominabitur orbis*.

Apologies. The change has started, sooner than I thought.

As the gray light of early dawn seeped through his tall windows, Kurt looked at me with a curious expression.

"Would you do me a favor?" he said.

Notebook Eighteen

Record 5 (2:18)
Beauty and Proportion
Parenthesis
Hunting Accidents

The relevant elements of our story—like kind and dutiful children who plan a surprise party for their parents' fiftieth anniversary, but, worried that the shock will prove too much, each independently drop heavy hints beforehand so that by the time of the party no one's surprised, but everyone has fun anyway—have been preassembled. In other words, you know what comes next, because we worry about you.

We dreamed about Gail. At least we think we did. We have a distinct memory of dreaming about her this morning, sometime after we finally fell asleep around 8 or 9 a.m. The substance of the dream remains elusive, because we've never been good at remembering our dreams, because they're usually too boring to note: Most of our oneiric life's spent mulling and rehashing the previous day's events, so that lately we've been dreaming about smoking cigarettes and drinking bad wine and typing, endlessly. In another recent dream we'd gotten carpal tunnel syndrome so severe that we couldn't feel our fingers on our right hand. We woke to find that we'd been sleeping on our arm. In any case, we remember Gail crying, and us crying, and her asking if we'd started drinking again. Then she asked us to forgive her, and we kept saying, "For what? For what?" but she wouldn't stop sobbing.

When we woke, our phone rang, and we unwisely answered, perhaps influenced by our disturbing dream. The caller was our editor at Enormous Publishing House, and the news was not good. He had no further information regarding Gail's whereabouts, nor did he seem to care. He was fed up with our constant delaying tactics and was canceling our contract, part of a general house-cleaning, nothing personal. Our desperate attempts to assure him that the book was all but finished, although certainly not the book he had commissioned, but a book not entirely unlike the one he had been expecting, fell on deaf ears. We were free to keep the advance we had already been paid, but we would not receive the other half, the portion due upon delivery, as there was to be no delivery. We had waited too long. The tides of rock had turned, in the ways detailed earlier, and the commercial prospects for a book sketching our life in an era of rock all but forgotten were uncertain at best.

In book publishing this happens all the time, the editor told us, by way of softening the blow. But the blow was not soft; the blow was severe, and drove us back into the welcoming arms of demon rum. By rum we mean of course whiskey, and sometimes wine. We went on a possibly historic bender, during which time we may have tried to jump out the window of our ground-floor apartment in a suicide farce that amused no one, as no one was present. We also managed to have ourself thrown out of nearly every bar on Brown Street—so we were told later by Henry Radio, who one night picked us off the sidewalk and into his brother's car, who drove to Henry's house, where he piled us onto his leather couch, from which we awoke and peeled ourself with an uncomfortable sticking sound from the humid flesh of our back and bare legs as we sat up. The abstract pattern of raised swirls on the plastic were represented on our skin by corresponding incarnadine impressions, similar to those crenations produced (and often admired for long minutes at bedtime) around our waist by the elastic band of our boxers. We also proposed marriage to several girls, some of whom we knew, and at least one guy.

Nothing rhymes anymore. Have you noticed? Our environment, or what you could call our atmosphere, has become an extended exercise in free verse, prosy and dull and susceptible to bureaucrats, and while there's occasional correspondence, accidental assonance, poignant, momentary collusions of rhythm and color, there's no longer—from our perspective, at least—an obvious pattern, an ABAB or what-have-you. Maybe rhyme has simply used itself up, become unfashionable, but we don't think so. We think rhyme has gone into hiding, obscuring itself in an act of willful self-preservation behind sprawling untended hedges of meaning. In other words, we think rhyme still exists,

288 ※ Artificial Light

and may one day reappear. When that day comes we intend to be surprised.

A broken man has one advantage over an unbroken man: He knows he is broken. That knowledge is a thing, a real thing, an object you can keep in your wallet, like money, but better than money because the knowledge of brokenness has no currency. It can't be spent. Not the brokenness itself, but the knowledge of brokenness allows you to pass freely through the artificial borders between time and place. Though these borders are real, you can, by knowing, shortcut the rules. Once transversed, the borders inevitably reveal their jewels. I won't fail, said the blind man, to remember (in detail) your face.

Upon recovering from our binge, we decided, ridiculously, that our life had snuck away from us while we were drunk, which made us quit drinking for exactly three days, until we realized that we could not handle the pain—of Kurt's death, of Michael's, of the end of our literary career—without alcohol. Though we knew Kurt was dead, we wrote him letters, after drinking all night, and although we didn't retain copies of these letters we remember them as paradigms of the letter-writing art, effusive and eloquent where appropriate, direct and heartfelt where necessary. All lies, too, which aspire to a kind of truth that truth can't match.

After that comes the erection of an internal authority, and renunciation of instinct owing to fear of it—owing to fear of conscience. In this second situation bad intentions are equated with bad actions, and hence comes a sense of guilt and a need for punishment. The aggressiveness of conscience keeps up the aggressive-ness of the authority. And here at last an idea comes in which belongs entirely to psychoanalysis, and which is foreign to ordinary people's way of thinking. This is of a sort which enables us to understand why the subject matter was bound to seem so confused and obscure to us. For it tells us that conscience (or more correctly, the anxiety which later becomes conscience) is indeed the cause of instinctual renunciation to begin with, but that later the relationship is reversed. Every renunciation of instinct now becomes a dynamic source of conscience, and every fresh renunciation increases the latter's severity and intolerance.

The panic attacks that started on our first European tour did not disappear, or even lessen, once we got back to America. If anything they grew worse. What we had figured a purely Continental affliction, as we had never experienced it in the States (where the bulk of our touring took place), probably the result of cultural dislocation, turned out to be something more pervasive, and worrisome. We were crippled with anxiety while riding in the tour van, at soundcheck, while rehearsing in our Dayton practice space, in the recording studio, and eventually while sitting at home quietly reading or even lying in bed.

Nothing seemed to help. On tour, at least, every few days the feeling would dissipate of its own accord, heedless of our own state of dissipation, and we did over time notice a correlation between the intensity of our own discomfort and the size of the stage (the larger the better), the proximity and ease of access to the dressing rooms (the closer and easier the better), and the relative "importance" of the show (while we didn't generally think along these lines, shows in minor provincial towns tended to provoke less anxiety than shows in major capitals).

We experimented with different methods of dealing with what we considered essentially a claustrophobic reaction: getting more drunk, getting less drunk, not drinking at all (terrible idea), but nothing seemed to work. We did not at that time consider our condition psychologically oriented, because its symptoms were so clearly physical, and we did not have health insurance, or much money, so we were not inclined to visit a doctor and discover what any fool reading this already knows: that we suffered from a general anxiety disorder, and that medications existed that would palliate but not entirely relieve this disorder, and that some of those medications we had already been taking anyway in a recreational sense. We happily purchased illegal prescriptions from friends who had smuggled them over the border from Mexico, where we are told you can walk into any pharmacy and buy anything, in any quantity.

After several months of enduring and to some extent managing our claustrophobia, we decided to seek psychiatric help, proceeding from the theory that we might receive more plentiful and powerful drugs. The theory proved true, but had an unexpected side effect: The psychiatrist explained that our very real anxiety, or panic, extruded from a source inside our head and not necessarily dependent on environment or the self-abuse to which we had subjected ourself on a regular basis both before and after the attacks began. That source had nothing to do with being cooped up on a rock stage and everything to do with being cooped up in a rock band, he gently suggested. In other words, that even though we were under the impression that Whiskey Ships was the sole stable fact of our quicksand life, that the ability and opportunity to participate in rock music our lone salve against the slings and arrows, the psychiatrist, whose name was Dr. Wright—show us a sign!—suggested that rock was killing us, and not softly.

Naturally we disagreed with Wright's diagnosis, vigorously, actively, and futilely. Because Wright was right. The very thing that we loved the most was literally killing us, and our much smarter unconscious mind was patiently explaining that to our pigheaded consciousness, by way of crippling its ability to function in any useful way. It may well be true, as the hoary adage holds, that you kill what you love; but we can say for certain that what you love will kill you. That this should be so continues to puzzle and amaze us, but we are as sure of its truth as we are sure of any truth, and we are sure of very few truths.

His face grew suddenly solemn. "But you should not be so quick to dismiss stories. Truth, being unapproachable directly, cannot be apprehended in its pure state. If you saw it and understood what you were seeing, you would go insane, or, as the Old Testament sages colorfully put it, 'surely die.' Most likely, when confronted with what you call the unadorned truth, you would neither understand nor value what you have seen. There is more truth, for instance, in the slender brown hands of our—incidentally very lovely—waitress than we will ever grasp. Stories present fragments of truth in more digestible portions, like crushed pills pressed into chocolate cake."

We were left with no choice but to—reluctantly and with great effort—cease and desist our rock activities. We had made our decision in potential: but it's one thing to form potential and quite another to turn form into content: for this to happen requires an inciting incident. That inciting incident took place at a rock show we played to help celebrate the tenth anniversary of a rock magazine, whose name was *Popular*, which had self-fulfilled its own prophecy on the strength of the very alternative revolution that had lent ballast and heft and momentum and several engineering-related terms to the continued viability of Whiskey Ships, as well as many other similarly worthy but little-known groups.

There hung a huge cardboard replica of the Tenth Anniversary cover, with Kurt C—'s smiling face, positioned from the balcony directly in front of the band, so that we were in effect playing for Kurt, and we refused to play for Kurt. So we had to close our eyes the whole time, or stare at our shoes, or look at the kids in the front which is always a bad idea because they're so young and good-looking and full of energy and enthusiasm it makes us ill. After that show we realized not only the truth of Dr. Wright's diagnosis but the immediacy of the danger to ourself if we continued playing in the band. We had to quit, and soon. Even so, we found it difficult to announce our resignation in a vanful of bandmates, and resolved to take the first opportunity upon returning to Dayton the next day. Or the day after that. Or at any rate within the first couple of weeks.

The coincidence of our decision to quit Whiskey Ships and the arrival of a documentary crew in Dayton whose purpose was to film the story of Whiskey Ships—more accurately, the story of Henry Radio, our wise and powerful and unfailingly quotable leader—was not a happy one. But we had delayed matters too long already, and were preparing for a long tour. We were convinced we would not survive the tour, and we further realized that Henry needed time to find and rehearse a new guitar player. The crew's presence, at first intrusive—to the extent that we were occasionally awoken by a knock on the door and a camera in our hungover face—after a few days by the magic of familiarity became invisible, which we gather is the working method of documentary film crews, and so by the time we mustered the courage to let Henry know our decision, we had become so accustomed to the film crew sitting in the backseat of our beaten-up old Utero that we forgot that everything we said was being recorded. (By luck, or perhaps some other word, the segment containing our resignation was left out of the final product, entitled *Hunting Accidents: A Brief History of Whiskey Ships*, a brisk seller among our fanbase.)

[Trip Ryvvers and Henry Radio driving through the streets of Dayton, both drinking from cans of beer. The car stereo blasts Whiskey Ships music. Trip pulls up at a red light. The light turns green. He doesn't move.]

HENRY RADIO
[re the traffic light] Ain't gonna get no greener.

[Trip comes out of his reverie, continues driving. The song comes to an end.]

TRIP
Cool.

HENRY RADIO
We should put it on the B-side to "Tin Can Girl." That's just the demo.

TRIP
Maybe we shouldn't rerecord it. I don't know how you're gonna fit that vocal around the whole band . . .

HENRY RADIO
My guitar playing's pretty messed up.

TRIP
But it's the good kind of messed up.

HENRY RADIO
Maybe . . . Hey, pull over, okay? I gotta piss.

TRIP
What, here?

HENRY RADIO
Right over there, by the curb.

[*Trip pulls the car over. Henry opens the car door but remains seated. He swings his legs out over the pavement. We hear him unzip his pants.*]

HENRY RADIO
The secret to pissing like this? You have to relax your asshole.

TRIP
Relaxation of the asshole. Right.

HENRY RADIO
That should be my solo album! *The Relaxation of the Asshole!*

[*Trip laughs appreciatively. We hear the sound of Henry peeing on the pavement.*]

HENRY RADIO
The cover could be a picture of me sitting on the couch holding a beer. *Relaxation of the Asshole.*

TRIP
Henry, I have to quit the band. I'm sorry, but I have to.

[*Henry zips up, swings his legs back in the car, closes the door.*]

HENRY RADIO
I know. You're not into it anymore.

TRIP
It's nothing to do with you, or the music. Whiskey

Ships is my favorite band.

HENRY RADIO
Don't worry about it. One thing about my songs, it doesn't take a genius to play 'em. We'll find somebody.

[Trip starts driving again.]

TRIP
I always thought music was the most important thing in life. I don't know, maybe I'm just getting old.

HENRY RADIO
There's getting old, and there's growing up. If I ever get too old to do leg kicks and jump around on stage like an idiot, I'll move on to the porch-rock phase. Sitting in a rocking chair on my porch singing songs. But I ain't ever growing up, man. In here . . . *[He points to his chest]* . . . I'm thirteen years old. That's all I'll ever be. When I die, stick a bone up my ass and let the dogs drag me away.

[He punches a button on Trip's car stereo. Music blares.]

HENRY RADIO
[over the music] I belong to the Church of Rock & Roll & Beer. That's my faith.

We're sorry, we don't think we can keep doing this. Whatever motor drove us this far, even after Kurt's suicide and Michael's death and Gail's disappearance, and the cancellation of our book contract, has run out of gas. Time to finish up.

There's a misprint in our edition of *Madame Bovary*, on page 113 (translation by Alan Russell). The misprint reads *"life a leaf"* instead of *"like a leaf."* Outside our apartment, right now, a summer storm is bundling through the night sky like a woman late for her date with anyone but us. The wind in the ash tree by our bedroom window makes the reticulate shadows of the leaves on the streetlit carpet, on the mussed sheets of our empty bed, quiver with regret. The rain that beat for a few minutes with martial severity on our tin porch has retreated, victorious. The wind and the rain together have pasted ash leaves on the cobblestoned street, and the tin porch, and even our grime-streaked windows, leaves torn from the tree before their season for dying, still green.

Henry Radio's right: The circumscribed borders of this town—the mythological land of Dayton, Ohio—are enough, should be enough, for anyone. Everything outside here is a dream of flight, and we've gone to great lengths to prove to ourself that the dream of flight is always better than the thing itself.

This close to the horizon we feel hollow and pure, renewed, ready for anything. Even if, as we suspect, there's nothing. Maybe we'll return to Orville. Maybe we'll abandon him the way everything we've ever loved has abandoned us, which is our fault because we let them down in the first place. We let everyone down, we let ourself down, we let you down. We did, too, we let you down, didn't we? Sorry. And now you'll leave us, you'll take your things, pack them in that little cloth bag you always carry around, containing who knows what, the mysteries of the universe probably, and clear out. You won't even say goodbye, because to say something destroys the thing you say, which is the whole reason for this book in the first place, even though no one will ever read these words, even though we write simply for ourself, which is never enough, never enough, never enough.

We never wanted the world in the first place, you know. We only wanted to play a part, and for a while we did. For a while that part stood for the whole—a glorious, if brief, synechdochic moment. All these years later, we're drunk on cheap wine, looking out our screen door at the water sluicing from our eaves into the privet hedge guarding our porch. The rain's mostly stopped, but there's a lot of gathered water, still, pooling in the street and in bright puddles at the foot of the ash tree and streaming down the storm drain across Hickory. Tangerine streetlight dusts the bricks of our apartment's outside, and we walk out onto the tin porch in our bare feet to touch the bricks with our palm. Despite the cooling rain, the bricks feel warm, still exhaling the sun's heat all these dark hours later. Moths beat time against a buzzing streetlight, stippling the light's halo with black flecks. A musk of ozone and azalea (two bushes under our living room windows, under the clouds punctuated with stars) perfumes the air—there's a drugged quality to the silence, underlined by stridulating crickets and an early-riser mockingbird, who runs through his repertoire of birdcalls, which sound in sum like a conversation we're not invited to join.

Against terror, against malice, against ignorance,

against the composite horrors of war and peace wheeling in cycles that gash the earth—spinning, itself, in a void as empty as the gesture of a preacher invoking Heaven, or a conductor marking time, or a writer proof-reading galleys, and as beautifully potent as the sum of these things, freed of their temporal chains—we can muster only love. Love's a thing we can let go but will not let us go. Love's life's lone reward.

Notebook Nineteen

8.

• Do you remember, Orville, Orv, Mr. Wright, you prig, the hallogallo when Lindbergh came to town? Oh, you were embarrassed then. What moved you to invite him? Admiration, I suppose. You were young, still, and easily impressed. Less than a month after his cross-Atlantic flight, you invited him to stop over in Dayton. He flew into Wright Field in the *Spirit of St. Louis*, the same plane in which he'd braved the transcontinental flight, alone, and you met him with General Gilmore, ready to take him on a parade route through downtown. Thousands had gathered in anticipation of seeing a true hero, a man of real daring. But Lindbergh explained that he had promised his moneymen that he would make no public appearances until he returned home, so we had no choice but to drive straight here, to Albion, bypassing the parade route. I was mortified that I had put him in such an awkward position, but Lindbergh, as was his nature, responded graciously that I had no way of knowing, and thanked me (as was his nature).

• He was a supernally handsome man; you could not take your eyes off him. I do not know whether I was struck more by his looks or his achievements, but in either case I was struck, even to the point of awe, and found myself in difficulty with regards to casual conversation, as was often the case, especially in those days, in the presence of young women. But, it seems to me, for different reasons. When I found myself alone with a young woman I was more often than not overcome with a fear that she would find me companionable, and used every means to dissuade her of such an impression; whereas with Lindbergh my fear was that he would not find me companionable, that he would not, in the most vulgar sense, *like* me. To cover my fear I began to babble the most fearsomely dull technical talk, and though he responded, as ever, with equipoise, I thought I could detect a note of weariness in Lindbergh, as though he would rather speak about anything but the mechanics of flight. But that may have been a trick of my imagination.

• Though twenty-eight years ago, the memory of that night remains fresh. We had an excellent dinner, organized by Miss Beck. Somehow word had spread through town that Lindbergh had come to Albion, so that before dark a crowd of perhaps more than a thousand Dayton residents had gathered on the lawn. At first just the front lawn, then the side lawns, and finally the back, where people had to climb through the woods and brush and up the hillside. At length a few bold souls even ventured onto our front porch, so that we had to retreat to the second floor. Still the mob would not give up clamoring for a glimpse of their man. I began to fear for the safety of the house—and so prevailed on the good grace of Lindbergh to appease his public by means of a brief appearance on the balcony. As I stood beside him in the twilight and savored the warmth of the town's affection for him, I not only tasted that unqualified admiration and goodwill that was denied Will and me for so long but fell myself under the magnetic charm of the man's presence. Here was a man of courage and far greater resources of character than I could ever dream to possess. He waved to the crowd, which responded with a hearty roar, and as he turned to go back in, his left hand brushed against mine and I felt a thrill of excitement that I can only ascribe to the electricity of Lindbergh himself, the electricity that must course along the skin of all great men. I lingered at the balcony a moment after he went inside, and watched the throng slowly disperse, sated by this glimpse of all that is potential in mankind made manifest. I have never wanted public acclaim, never aspired to public honors; so my feeling at that moment cannot be called jealousy. It was more like love.

9.

- Will's first letter to Chanute began, "For some years I have been afflicted with the belief that flight is possible to man." He was a more eloquent writer than I, in any case, but his choice of words in that preamble was as prescient as anything ever written concerning the long and toilsome history of flight. Solving the problem of manned flight was, certainly, an affliction—an affliction its aftereffects, an affliction the lifelong burden of responsibility and the empty hours following success. So easy it seemed once found, which, yet unfound, most would have thought impossible. And most unwilling to believe had been found: The first real notice of our achievements appeared in a journal called *Gleanings in Bee Culture*, written by a Medina apiarist named Amos Root. We had to persuade poor Amos not to publish his article until we had assured ourselves that we had ironed out most of the kinks in our regular excursions over Huffman Prairie. Amos had to hold his tongue, or rather his pen, for over three months, from late September 1904 to the beginning of the next year. Naturally no one paid any attention to Mr. Root's announcement (he had a somewhat discursive prose style, as I recall), and the story of our trials in getting anyone at all to take seriously our invention, not least the United States government, has been told and told so often that I am too bored by it to provide even a synopsis. But it seems to me that this is always the case: that the man most willing to believe in the works of Man is the one who has followed most keenly the works of Nature, that is to say of God. How could it be otherwise: We learned much of what we needed to know to solve the problem of wing curvature by observing a flock of buzzards gliding on currents of air—the story of the cardboard box that Will idly bent in his hands and inspired our wing-warping technique is true, but can any accident put to use be considered accidental? No. We were guided, Will and I, by a succession of intimations from a source that can only have come from outside us: in the first place, by the bold experiments of those who had gone before us, like Lilienthal; in the second, by assiduous study of those creatures to whom God had already granted the gift of flight; and in the third, by application of such rare thunderbolts as punctuated our long, wearisome days and nights of fruitless labor.

- All that is so long ago now. Battles lost, battles won, the field of flight strewn with wrecked ideals and bitter feuding. I will have no more of this. I have convinced my doctor, a wise and understanding man, to give me an extra month's supply of morphine for my sciatica under the pretext of traveling to Georgian Bay. I think he knows I have no plans to travel to Georgian Bay. I have made all other preparations: My will was updated some time ago, and I have this very night drafted a letter consigning the original Flyer to the Smithsonian, ending its long exile in London. My health has declined greatly in the last few months, and though the strictures of my religion—of all religions, most likely—forbid taking one's own life, I must trust that my Savior's grace in this matter will forestall the consequences of my decision, though even were I convinced that the result would be eternal damnation, I would still proceed with my plan. Eternity stands outside time, and time is the thing that I daily curse, that afflicts me, to use Will's word, and that I can no longer abide. Therefore I hated life; because the work that is wrought under the sun—whose power we have now harnessed to a terrible end, because it is only a facsimile of that true power, just as manned flight is only a facsimile of the graceful maneuvers of natural creatures; and artifice, the basis of any human action, can do no better, can only mimic, can never create—is grievous unto me; for all is vanity and vexation of the spirit. Tonight, for me at least, that vexation ends, even if my spirit does not. God help whoever comes to reside here at Albion after me, for I fear I have imposed my own affliction upon its very foundation, and through its roots, and veins, and in its blasphemous heart. Or perhaps I have it wrong; it's possible that a spirit resides in these walls that has over-manned me, and waits for someone with a more appropriate or receptive makeup. These thoughts swept me back again into the gulf where I was being stifled. But I did not sink as far as that hell of error where no one confesses to you his own guilt, choosing to believe that you suffer evil rather than that man. So much wasted effort. We spend our lives striving to become little creators—what else is an inventor? a solver of puzzles he himself has designed—rather than to understand the nature of our own soul. I cannot tell you how I know the things that I know. I can only say that none of it has any use. So full of artless jealousy is guilt, it spills itself in fearing to be spilt. Ah, Will. Forgive me, brother. What I do now, I do for us both. There is no other way.

10.

• In 1921, the writer Rafael Sabatini published a wildly successful swashbuckling novel, *Scaramouche*, later adapted with equal success as a film. *Scaramouche* was a romance of the French Revolution, whose main character, named Andre-Louis Moreau, is inspired to join the Revolution in part because of the example of a young seminarist, Philippe de Vilmorin, described by Sabatini as "young, ardent, enthusiastic, and inspired by Utopian ideals." It seems quite clear that Andre-Louis is in love with Vilmorin, and when the latter falls in an unjustly provoked duel, in Chapter 3, the fate of the impressionable Moreau is set. Sabatini was born April 29, 1875, in what is now a suburb of

308 ✳ Artificial Light

Ancona, in Italy. His parents were well-known opera singers, and traveled extensively around the world. The renowned Irish tenor, John McCormack, studied under Sabatini's father. Upon reaching the age of majority, his family sent Rafael to Liverpool, where his youthful travels had prepared him well for a career as a translator to the many shipping companies that then had offices in the largest port city in Great Britain. As a boy Sabatini had read Dumas, Jules Verne, Walter Scott, and chose for his own endeavors to write in English. His productivity was admirable. He wrote a book every year even after the accidental death of his son Binkie, from an unhappy first marriage, by an automobile accident that Sabatini happened on only minutes afterwards. The wealth provided by his books enabled Sabatini to buy a home near Hay-on-Wye, a town that since has acquired fame for its preponderance of antiquarian bookstores. The home he called Clock Mill. He has lived there almost twenty years. Another son, by his second wife, trained to become an aviator for the RAF. He'd just received his certification as a pilot, when on a celebratory flight over Clock Mill he tipped his wings in salute, lost control of the plane, and crashed in a nearby field in sight of his horrified parents. For many years afterwards, Sabatini's second wife Christine had nightmares about the event, until on a trip to Switzerland she came upon a yellow mountain flower, unidentified in any recorded source. She took some samples back to Clock Mill and planted them, in the shape of a plane, in the garden. The nightmares retreated.

Notebook Twenty

In the last minute before I killed Kurt, he told me something. It happened this way: After helping him tie off with an old brown leather belt, and watching him inject a syringe full of high-grade heroin into his right forearm, he lay down on the floor by the bookshelves in the corner of the room farthest from the windows. We had propped up some pillows to rest his head, and to allow for the proper angle for me to shoot him. He handed me the gun, a Sig Sauer P226 pistol with one 9mm bullet in its chamber—he explained to me, slowly, the way a person explains things when the rush of heroin hits his bloodstream—and it remained for me only to cock the hammer, once, for single-action fire, and place the muzzle of the gun at a slight angle against his left temple. He explained how I was to hold the gun, how to prepare for the kick of the shot, what to do with the casing, which would be automatically expelled by the silver-ellipsoid extractor, how to wipe the finger-prints, place the gun in his cold dead hand, disappear. Then he wanted to say something more, and gestured for me to lean close as he was no longer capable of speaking above a hoarse whisper.

Tears slicked my face. Kurt reached up to dry them with the frayed cuff of his shirt, smiling. "I suppose you want to know why?" he whispered.

I felt immediately stupid, because it had never occurred to me to ask why. I assumed, again stupidly, that the reason had something to do with the pressures Kurt had faced from the outside world as a result of his sudden success, or what I understood to be his sudden success. Or the natural, and naturally intolerable, depression he had faced his whole life, as he told us, even before the fame and the fortune, made worse by his hapless attempts at self-medication, especially heroin, and thence heroin addiction, which in my own second-hand experience seems enough itself to make someone want to shuffle off. I had not asked because it would have been—and I know this is stupid, because I felt stupid then and I still feel stupid—somehow impolite. A person has his reasons. He asked me a favor, and I agreed.

But I was wrong in my assumptions. Because when Kurt told me the real reason, I was stunned. I was stunned and I am still stunned, which is why all these words have been pouring out of me in the days since his death. He told me a secret, Kurt did. A real secret. Maybe the only Real Secret. And as his last dying wish (apart from asking me to kill him, which as I said was more of a favor than a wish), he made me promise not to tell the secret.

I have not kept that promise. That's the part that breaks my heart. A man asks you, his last dying wish, to keep a secret, you keep that goddamn secret. You keep it if it kills you.

But I couldn't, because the secret did not kill me but it changed me. In that instant, the moment those words entered my brain like a 9mm bullet fired from a Sig Sauer P226 pistol at close range, I became Fiat Lux. I broke the shell of myself and entered into the realm of potential made manifest. Fiat Lux is not my real name. You will have guessed that.

So my reasons for breaking my promise to Kurt are straightforward: The girl who made that promise no longer exists, at least in the commonly understood sense of the word, and so I can't break a promise that I, myself, Fiat Lux, did not actually make. You will probably judge this an absurd rationalization, even a lie, but if you knew the secret you would perhaps understand.

And you *will* know the secret. I have buried it in these pages, and buried it well, I think, but everything buried comes to light, if not immediately then so much the better. In this way, I tell myself, I've remained true to the spirit if not the letter of my promise, notwithstanding my cheesy promise loophole. In order effectively to bury Kurt's secret herein, I've had to do some fairly difficult things: because I know nothing about the past. Because I know nothing about music. Because I know nothing about the future. Because I know nothing about two doomed characters who recognize their love for each other too late. (And lest you think that I have given too much away by telling you what I've done, a warning: You have not guessed the secret. If you think you have, then you certainly have not. The only way to know if you have guessed the secret—and here I really am giving too much away—would be to ask me. When you have understood correctly, you will understand how.)

After he told me, I took a moment to regroup. The world inside me was still reeling, trying to gather enough force to escape, to complete the change that Kurt's secret had set in motion. I looked at the gun in my hand, and suddenly didn't understand why I had a gun in my hand. I didn't even understand it as a gun: I didn't know what the thing was, or what I was supposed to do.

So I asked. "What is this?"

"Jawbone of an ass," replied Kurt. "Smite me."

My mother's death continues to dog me. When you watch someone die, in stages, over a long period of time, you lose to some extent the ability to fear the event itself. A prolonged stint of bedside attending, bedsore bandaging, and bedpan changing will produce, eventually, an immunity to the final effects of death's long-awaited appearance. Admittedly, violent, sudden death was something unknown to me in personal experience, although my father died in this way; but I was not there, I didn't see what happened, and the brutal truth of his passing was kept from me for some years out of an understandable delicacy with regard to its possible effect on a young girl. But I did not see the difference between killing Kurt and watching my mother die: I saw instead the similarities. In both cases, I saw a human being in the grip of great suffering, at the end of a process of dying whose result could only be the cessation of pain. If I'd had a gun, or some other effective means of dispatch, and the sense, or had my mother asked me, I would—in retrospect, mind you, the thought never occurred to me at the time—without hesitation have hastened her end.

I placed the gun at the instructed angle, pressing lightly against Kurt's temple. For some reason, I gently pushed a few stray strands of his greasy blond hair from the side of his head, tucked them behind his ear, as if the presence of these frail fronds might deflect the path of the bullet. We still say descent of night or nightfall. Thus in Homer: *"Bright light of sun sank into the ocean, dragging down dark night."* Thus in Cato: *"se nox praecipitat."* In the *Book of the Dead*, the red of sunset is the blood of Ra as he hastens to his suicide. To the poetic vision of early seers, the crimson West seemed ensanguined by some great massacre that had been perpetrated there. Hommel and Hilprecht *(Die Insel der Seligen)* have identified the gateway through which Gilgamesh (the bright Day-God) had to make his way to the West: the "Twin Peaks" of Central Arabia, the mountain of Sunset, now called Jebel Shammar. Two peaks, Aga and Salama, stand apart confronting each other, and form a natural portal. Egyptian representation of the sky as a great dome resting on two pillars, Shu and Tefnut. Tum-Ra, the evening sun, sets in darkness; he seizes these pillars and overthrows the sky. Aborigines of Australia believe the sky to be supported on props which keep it from falling. (This is an almost perfectly universal idea.) *"It is these pillars the blinded giant (the dim-grown sun of evening) withdraws when he brings night down upon the world in the final catastrophe which involves his own death."* (Smythe-Palmer). Samson, bound between the twin pillars of the temple at Gaza—enraged, blinded (in actual fact blind only in one eye, although this is not

316 ✳ Artificial Light

recorded in the Bible but can be demonstrated through myth-redaction—the sun in one eye, the moon in the other)—shakes the pillars until the roof collapses, killing himself and far more Philistines, in death, than he had ever killed in life. Likewise the Sun God, (Shamesh, Shu, Gilgamesh, etc.), blinded and enfeebled by the encroaching dusk, pulls down the twin towers of the firmament at day's end, and sky collapses into night.

Matador manhandles minotaur. By the window—sycamore, sycamore, rock. Praise be to God for addled things, for piebald sodden brains dappled with alcoholic insight. Oh, and the smooth circuitous way she lies. Incunabula of moot resistance. You cant untangle threads of mein herr, nor plum the death of sea's own sad light.

Broken day, sepia tint. Last falling down myth: sacrament of marriage. Linnaeus caroling through Lapland—reindeers' balls, hags' pudenda. Sun sags to bed, world-weary, unfortunate. Moves on the face of the waters. Paraclete.

Make lines of light where no face has ever peered, seen, sunk, drooled, wept, wiping tears with hand maid of light, lettered in green ink, shining, like raggened blankets of green rushes, burny, reflex of scratch of optics of glasses.

His last girlfriend, in the meaning you mean in the meaning: even, mourn, day flouring, on her face and over the dour, everywhour. Travel swell.

O shore.

O lift us all, hymn.

Philomel. Singer in the eye. Ten vocabularies

scumbled inner hello, stippled wit black inc. Octagonal runs to seed or runny plum. Inappropriate name, muser. Inaccurately dressed. Missed her. Moralist anger, more and less, strung along the hinge of reason, blossoms bright in rage. Time sit. Truth ache. Come put her, thousand calculations, face launched, rite in the center.

High and holy hill. On it grows them guts and morning glory.

King Ibn, thin. Littoral translation.

Winter harrows the land, harrowing winds dump hurricane sugar on highlands like croppings of snow. O the beauty and the bees. Nutting ear.

Again, aging. Trump.

Ace.

Aces.

Access.

Ate.

In the Latin, lads, its ove for egg, in Eytie dove for where, in Angleterre Dover for endall beall. Lovers leap. Lovers leap, lads, and you shall leap.

You shall leap.

Through trope and metaphor, the Revelator, immortal scribe of Spirit and of a true idealism, furnishes the mirror in which mortals may see their own image—if the mirror has a deliberate flaw, is it God's patience or subtlety of evil? Take art, dear sufferer, for this reality of being will surely appear sometime. Not yet elevatored to deific apprehension through spiritual transfiguration. This city of God has no need of sun or satellite, for Love is the light of it, and divine Mind is its own interpreter. All must walk in its light.

I pulled the trigger. Hwæt! . . . Beowulf wæs breme (blæd wide sprang). Amore abundas, Antipho. *Aber den Einsamen hüll in deine Goldwolken!* For all to sicker, as cold engendreth hail, a liquorish tongue must have a liquorish tail. *Illud iam voce extremo peto*: Daybreak dry me. Hell of later. Zero sum. *Per me si va ne la città dolente, per me si va ne l'etterno dolore, per me si va tra la perduta gente.* The pale of settlement. Things that burn (list). Ancient Rites of the Condoling Council. At the wood's edge: *Niyawenhkowa kady nonwa onenh skennenjy thade-sarhadiyakonh.* The Doctrine of Eternal Life, as though *ha Unas an sem-nek as met-th sem-nek anxet hems her xent Ausar.* The Niche for Lights (*Mishkat al-Anwar*). *Peut-être l'immo-bilité des choses autour de nous leur est-elle imposée par notre certitude que sont elles et non pas d'autres, par l'immobilité de notre pensée en face d'elles. Bismi Allahi alrrahmani alrraheemi.* First line of Chromosome One of the human genome: GAT-CAATGAGGTGGACACCAGAGGCGGGGACTTGTAAA-TA ACACTGGGCTGTAGGAGTGA. Bodhichitta. Engine of combustion: life. Correspondence. Repetition. Duplication. The light that draws the flower draws you, too.

Notebook Twenty-one

The rain, blackly bursting from the predawn sky, gathered force and came in slanting gusts through the windows of his station wagon; Michael Goodlife had no choice but to roll them up. No matter: He was almost home. The left arm of his midnight-blue jacket was drenched. He wrung the material of the jacket with his right hand, and rivulets of cold water ran down the underside of his arm to the floor, gathering in the margins of the floorboard and disappearing down a tennis-ball-sized hole near the clutch that had been patched with duct tape but nevertheless admitted to the interior of the car a quantity of carbon monoxide, which, it was later determined, was what killed him. The inside of the windshield acquired a thin patina of condensation, in which Michael rubbed a dark hemisphere with his dry right sleeve. His headlights groped gingerly the seal-slick street, and the steady thrum of his wipers provoked from his pleasantly drink-fogged brain an answering hum, the threads of a half-remembered song Michael could not immediately place.

He puttered grayly in his old car down Main,

through the uninhabited regions of downtown, past empty and disused storefronts, abandoned churches, the shell of a long-gone gas station. The steps of the courthouse at 3rd Street, usually peopled even at that early hour with homeless drunks, crack enthusiasts, and whores, were sullenly vacant, glassy-eyed and strangely swollen with rain, as Michael slowed to a stop at a purposeless traffic light. No other cars disturbed the watery night. The light winked green, reflected diffusely on the glossy steel of his wet hood, and he accelerated toward the narrow bridge over the Miami River, braking only as he reached its verge as a precaution against the cops who were fond of hiding in the penumbra of the ornate stone portal to catch careless drivers.

Tonight he was lucky: no cops. His car susurrated over the bridge, and he noticed with a small thrill of delight that the traffic lights on the other side wore a nimbus of green as far as he could see, all the way up North Main Street. All the way home. "Permanent green light," Michael mused, and here time abruptly split. His car seemed all at once to lose power, and glided to a halt just outside McCabe's.

Michael popped the hood and got out of the car. His limbs felt oddly light, and for a moment he had the sensation of floating rather than walking as he moved to the front of the car. He shook his head, its dark tangle of curls dimly limned in the reddish gleam emanating from somewhere inside McCabe's. The rain had stopped, as suddenly as it started. Michael looked up curiously at the sky, where strong winds had already torn a ragged hole in the web of storm clouds, and he could see a small clot of glimmering stars. Something in the aspect of those stars seemed to hold his attention; he craned his head to one side as if listening, and his features were bunched in an effort of concentration. At length his brow settled, and he gave at the same time a quick smile and a nod of recognition.

Mary closed the door behind her and sighed. Was it a sigh of satisfaction or relief, or maybe just a sigh of being tired. She kicked off her left shoe, used the heel of her foot to pry off the right. Advancing toward the bathroom, she stepped out of her skirt, and, reaching the bathroom door, flicked the light switch and in one smooth movement slipped her shirt over her head.

That I could run a bath. That I should run a bath. Mary unhooked her bra and threw it on the tiles of the floor next to the sink. She turned the taps and cupped her hands under the flow of water. Lowering her face to her hands, she noticed with some surprise that her cheeks were already glossy with tears.

Crying again, and for what reason on earth? she thought. Makes no sense. The feeling swells inside like a tumor when I picture his face, when I watch his hands enfolding a beer bottle wet with dew, the way he talked to Kurt at Albion, so sweet, so entirely unguarded. Because he showed a capacity for kindness I have not seen in so long, and thought gone forever. Toward me anyhow. Something inside gives way—or the spigot wrenches on, is that right?—then the waterworks, within me and without me. For those brief moments of our conversation I turned to liquid. I am deliquescent.

She braced her arms on either side of the sink and

looked in the mirror. A bright girl. Bright pink and scrubbed and hair that almost glows. He came behind me now, I'd let him, I'd say yes to anything—which was never the point. Only too late do you learn the right time and the right time.

She stood and turned, reaching for the matted and musky olive-green towel on the rack behind. Still wet from evening bath, she thought, burying her face in its cotton furrows.

Mary Valentine turned off the bathroom light and walked with care the ten feet between the door and her mattress, an obstacle course in the dark and drunk. Having achieved the distance without mishap, she sank to her knees and crawled on top of the sheets.

Lying on her back and staring into the formless pitch that at some invisible spot was bounded by the ceiling. If nothing else the weight of unresolved emotion had lifted, or shifted, perceptibly. Mary spread her arms wide on the thin mattress. Her body seemed to recede, allowing some important part to rise, or float, even to fly, slowly and she thought naturally, perfectly in accord with nature, toward the invisibly visible ceiling, which after all did not exist, because there were no more ceilings, no more boundaries, strings, attachments, ties, chains, strands, webs, nothing to hold her here anymore. The last knowt cut. Mary giggled, then her giggles turned to sobs, and her tears like drops of black rain fell from a great height onto the sheets of her bed.

She turned on her side and stared at the dark square of window on the near wall. He will nevermore come into my bed, come crawling on his fours and slip under the sheet, brush my face with his lips. A hundred times since then I have disported with young men in pleasant grooves, but never in this bed, never under this sheet. Why? I'll tell you why, Mary Valentine, because when you leave the darkness behind, what's left is not necessarily light.

Several blocks down the road, at the North Main Street house the two shared, Joe Smallman, Michael's roommate, lay on his bed drinking the last of a large glass of vodka and Tang, a cocktail Michael had dubbed the "John Glenn" in honor of their home state's favorite astronaut. Joe was brooding over Amanda Early, as he usually did at this hour, in the brief lacuna before surrendering to sleep. He sighed resignedly, and doubled again the lower part of his pillow under his head, despite which it again stubbornly slipped out and flattened against the bed. If she had wanted to keep the baby I would have married her, he thought. Or not married, but still. Even if only that one time, though, on the porch, as the sun set, I will have that always, I will hold on to that moment until I die. But she wants to get rid of the kid, makes sense, too young for the responsibility. Even so I would stick with her. Even so I would, yes, say the word, love her. But whenever she's around I affect a listless nonchalance. An instinctive defense posture. There is something wrong with me that no drug can cure.

Nearby he heard sirens, a common occurrence in his violence-prone neighborhood. Joe chuckled softly at the thought of some beer-bloated briar being hauled downtown to sleep it off in the county lockup. He stroked lightly the bristly ends of his thin mustache with thumb and forefinger. Later, the police would tell him that Michael had passed out as a result of carbon monoxide poisoning, lost control of the car, spun completely around, and smashed into a utility pole. He was still alive after the crash but comatose from the gas, and died soon thereafter without regaining conscious-ness. It fell to Joe to break the news to Michael's family and friends.

Joe slipped slowly into a vague and restless sleep. He had not been asleep long, and had just begun dreaming, something about Amanda taking a trip by train—who takes train trips anymore?—and him at the station seeing her off, when the phone in the hall outside his bedroom began to ring.

He stood on a platform and watched her pull away—in oneiric time, impossibly slow, but giving somehow the impression of movement nonetheless. The rhythmic ring of the phone insinuated itself into his dream, taking on the sound of the train's leisurely chug. Amanda leaned out of an open compartment window in a way that only happens in movies, or dreams, waving and blowing kisses to him that he would pretend to catch with a clownish clapping motion and smuggle into his pocket. Fat tears rolled down his cheeks, propelled by a sure sense that she was leaving for good, that he would never see her again. "Don't go!" he pleaded, or tried to plead. His mouth opened but no sound came out. "Come back!"

Strange are the structures unconscious fate imposes on our formless desires. One man, drugged insensible by an invisible, scentless gas, will imagine he sees a group of stars in a chance clearing in the clouds and hears with perfect clarity the astral music of his own death song; another, held close in the arms of sleep, will translate the incidental intrusions of the waking world into the language of his secret fears.

The ringing phone became more insistent, but Joe was not yet fully awake. The cadence of the phone now gave voice in his dream to departing Amanda Early, who kept repeating calmly and evenly, her brown eyes with ochre flecks fixed at a spot well above his head, "I love you, goodbye. I love you, goodbye."

Appendix A: Sources Consulted

Barthes, Roland, *Camera Lucida*, Editions du Seuil, Paris, 1980

Benjamin, Walter, *Das Passagen-Werk*, Frankfurt Suhrkamp, 1982

Bergson, Henri, *Time and Free Will*, Authorised Translation by Pogson, F. L., M.A., George Allen & Unwin Ltd., London, 1910

Browne, Thomas, *Religio Medici*, Roberts Brothers, Boston, 1889

Cope, Julian, *The Modern Antiquarian*, Thorsons, London, 1998

Cordier, Henri, *Ser Marco Polo: Notes and Addenda to Sir Henry Yule's Edition*, John Murray, London, 1920

Lieber, Lillian R. and Lieber, Hugh Gray, *The Einstein Theory of Relativity*, Rinehart & Company, New York, 1945

O'Hanlon, Sean, *Miserogeny*, Odeon Press, New York, 1948

Palmer, Abram Smythe, *The Samson-Saga and Its Place in Comparative Religion*, I. Pitman, London 1913

Pollard, Robert and Sayers, Stephanie, "People Are Leaving," *Waved Out*, Matador, New York, 1997

Ryvvers, Trip, *Exit Flagging*, Unpublished Manuscript, 1995

Shorbuck, Stanley, *I Shit You Not: A Rational Guide to Irrational Music*, Vintage Classics of Rock Criticism, New York, 1989

Vollman, William T., *Rising Up and Rising Down*, McSweeney's Books, San Francisco, 2003

Wright, Orville, *Unpublished Journals*, 1889–1948

Zamyatin, Evgeny, *We*, Gregory Zilboorg, Translator, E. P. Dutton, New York, 1924

Appendix B

Translation of a fragment from Das Bienenzüchter sucht nach Ruth, *by Wilhelm Kneissl*

. . . ridiculous theories about dancing bees and color vision. Might hoodwink the academy and the Vienna graybeards and Saunders at Princeton (idiot), but I am not misled. His methods are flawed, his conclusions unsupported by a shred of reliable evidence—and yet the plaudits, the laurels, are his and his alone! That his dance language might be accepted (however temporarily) galls me. Sooner someone destroy my own hives, my tapes, my notes, than see his pseudo-science adopted as doctrine.

The scientific community is often impugned by the public it serves for making of skepticism a religion, but in this case a little attention to creed might have been in order. His eloquence and passion for honors has conquered the better judgment of reasonable men, unprepared for the onslaught of Von Slipp's fierce *[the word Kneissl uses is* grell, *which is more commonly a quality of light, harsh, dazzling. ed.]* ambition. The ridiculous photographs of himself he provides the scientific journals to accompany his papers (what vanity!). His profile, his aspect: every inch the profound and respected biologist. Pah! I've never seen these pictures myself, but I've had them well described to me. Meanwhile, my own work in the same area molders in neglectful shade, and I can scarcely afford even the rent on this two-room shack in the shadow of the Matterhorn. O Fame! O Fortuna!

"How vainly men themselves amaze," the poet writes *[Quotation in English—from Marvell. ed.].* I have a sufficiency of truth unto myself. Watching this buffoon crowned with honors and riches—as if he were not already an aristocrat!—grows tiresome, and I am tired, too, of writing letters of protest to the appropriate organs.

"*Dear Gentlemen of the Academy, it is my sad duty to bring to your attention the following errors . . .*" "*Dear Editor, perhaps it would interest your readers to know that you have printed an article containing lies . . .*" "*Dear Professor, I warn you for the last time to stop all this nonsense before the Cause of Science is irreparably harmed . . .*" Never so much the courtesy of a response. I must look a proper fool [*Gimpel, ed.*], a country simpleton [*Einfaltspinsel, ed.*], a stupidhead [*Dummkopf, ed.*]. I, who: struggled from the day I was born; had to educate myself; was not provided with the privilege accorded a high-born like Von Slipp—I am the one to be scorned? I should be worshipped for my efforts. I have earned my way by the careful husbandry of what small talent God granted me. Unlike some, I was not able to avoid the rigors of military service, nor the unspeakable horror of two wars, by hiding in a research institute.

As a result—even now I am ashamed to admit—I am blind as Von Slipp is rich. The hindrance my disability has presented in my work bothers me less than the burden to my daughter, who has in addition to her own troubles the better part of mine to carry on her frail shoulders. She is only sixteen. Because of me the ordinary delights of a young girl are foregone. Because of me she spends her time attending to an old man's needs instead of attracting a young man's attentions. She is beautiful, and sharp-minded, and graceful in every way, and were she not stuck nursing a cripple in the middle of nowhere, suitors would pile up like the drifts of snow under our eaves every fortnight.

We do our best, though. We live. Anna's mother, Hilde, left us when Anna was a baby, not even one year old. Hilde (née Grolsch) had married a reasonably able-bodied university graduate who, before the second war, had a reasonable career as a librarian at the University of Vienna, a fine institution, the oldest university in the German-speaking world, founded in 1365. I worked there happily for twenty years, in the Art and

Architecture department, under Dr. Feldman, a wonderful man who went meekly, uncomprehending, to the camps and never returned. After the war, everything was different, Vienna no less than my sightless self. I made inquiries at my former office but no one had use for a blind librarian, and I was unwilling to take the position I was offered—a pathetic sinecure, offered out of pity for a broken war veteran, and hardly enough to support a wife and infant daughter. But I do not blame the university: What else could they do? Likewise, I do not blame my wife for leaving: What else could she do? I had returned an invalid, bitter and proud but useless, who had moreover saddled her with a child and no means to feed or clothe her. Anna was conceived during a two-day leave from the Eastern Front in fall of 1944, three months before the grenade blast that robbed me of my eyes.

I was hopeless with guns. In the literal heat of battle—which is always hot whatever the weather, because the body heats radically in its suit of fear—huddled at the bottom of a foxhole next to the severed parts of several colleagues, it was much more than I could do to stop my hands shaking long enough to bolt my rifle, which moreover was clotted with mud and ice and grease. Even had I mastered myself sufficiently to climb to the top of my hole and try to shoot, nothing but vague images, shadows, running through the artillery smog, would present themselves as targets. I will tell you now that I shot only once in my military career, and that in so doing I murdered the woolen hat of my sergeant which he had lost leaping into a nearby defilade. By the time the war was over, in May, and I had returned home, guided by a fourteen-year-old Wehrmacht recruit, my wife had remaining less than one month of confinement before giving birth, in late May, to the daughter I have never seen but whose existence has been my only joy. Before the end of the year Hilde was gone, moved back to her mother's in

Salzburg and remarried within two years' time to a bricklayer, who naturally prospered in the postwar reconstruction.

Had begun keeping bees before being called away to the war, and when I returned and could not find any real work, the bees were our salvation. Soon learned the layout of my backyard's rows of hives, and could navigate without help their orderly ranks. When she was old enough, little Anna helped carry the dripping combs to the little shack, where we scraped them into pans and then filtered the raw honey into mason jars. I hired a housekeeper when I could afford one, but for the most part we made do for ourselves. I learned to judge locations from intensities of sound. I learned the pattern of echoes from familiar objects, and developed such familiarity with their unseen outlines that I imagined, in my inky cave, that I could see the shadows on the wall, so to speak. At night I had vividly colored dreams—my night life was bright, well-sighted, visionary in the truest sense. I often woke up crying.

What is the language of bees? I know, and you know, Anna, my only daughter, my love. We know. The bees speak to you, and you alone understand their honeyed tongue. We discovered your gift by accident, years ago—you could not have been more than nine—when you chased a little blue butterfly in the clover between the rows of my hives while I checked the humming honeycombs. Accidentally you knocked into the leg supporting one of the hives and the whole construction toppled over, perilously close to where you frolicked. I could not see this happen, of course; but my memory of the event, stitched together from the evidence of my remaining senses and your own account, has stayed with me as if I had. I shouted an alarm: but you turned and faced the gathering swarm, and spoke several inhuman syllables in a sweet, singing tone that had an immediate calming effect on the bees, who regrouped and returned to their damaged hive—which I rushed to set right upon receiving assurance that you were unharmed.

"Papa, the bees are sad," you said to me.

"I know, sweetheart, but we will make them happy again soon. Their house is broken but we will fix it for them. I'm only glad they did not choose to sting you."

"Oh, but I told them I was sorry."

"That was surely the right thing to do. But the bees don't speak our language, so they may not have understood you."

"That's why I used their language, Papa. At first they were angry about the damage to their hive, but when I explained that it was an accident and that I was only trying to catch the little butterfly, they laughed and warned me to be more careful."

Naturally I ascribed Anna's story to the invention of a precocious child. Naturally I treated her with the benign con-descension of all good parents everywhere. I asked her how she had learned the bees' language, when no one else had even thought the bees might speak. She replied, sensibly, that she did not know, but that she understood everything the bees said and they seemed to understand her as well. I asked her to demon-strate. She did, to my satisfaction (this process took place over several weeks and months, but I am conflating for effect). When she spoke bee-language, Anna's voice took on a pure high tone that her regular speaking voice would not seem capable of producing. Indeed she told me later, when she was older, that the tones were produced largely in her nasal cavities, and that if I could see her when she spoke bee-language I would laugh, because she had to throw her head back and flare her nostrils to get the right sounds.

Convinced that she was neither inventing nor imagining her ability to converse with bees in their own tongue, I resolved to document her gift when I had accumulated sufficient evidence to present to the unsuspecting world the irrefutable secrets of the *apis*. Who knew what wisdom lay locked in the many-chambered hive?

Then came Von Slipp, with his dancing bees, who direct their colleagues to fruitful pollen sites and back by means of a complex system of wagging and wiggling. He has published articles and books detailing the experiments he has conducted to prove his ideas. Anna has read me these books and articles, and described to me these ludicrous diagrams. She has related to me the derision of the bees themselves when told about Von Slipp's crackpot notions. "Figwort-head" he is called in their language, which is bee-slang for fat-faced and stupid, Anna tells me. But the immediate acceptance by the scientific community of Von Slipp's ideas doomed my own efforts to present the true bee-language with any degree of credulity. I had not his credentials, his connections, his eloquence. I was the crackpot, not he. I dictated letters, I dictated articles, and now I dictate this journal, although no longer to my daughter Anna, sweet amanuensis, *qui a disparue [thus in French in the MS. ed.].*

Now I tell my tales to the recording machine, as I once recorded the secrets they vouchsafed to you, on spinning reels of magnetic tape, and while you slept in the other room analyzed the patterns buried in the bees' true words. Because the bees do not speak in plain language, but in cryptic phrases that appear nonsensical to those untrained in the apian way. I think that here my blindness gave me an advantage: The loss of one sense sharpens the others, it's said—and truly so. In the phrases Anna spoke into my tape-recording device I heard memes of sense, whole threads of meaning, which were left to me to unspool and rewind according to the dictates of reason.

Where I have failed, I alone am to blame. Where succeeded, God *[manuscript breaks off]*

Other selections in Dennis Cooper's **Little House on the Bowery** *series*

GODLIKE a novel by Richard Hell
141 pages, a trade paperback original, $13.95

Godlike, Hell's second novel, is a stunning achievement, and quite likely his most important work in any medium to date. Combining the grit, wit, and invention of *Go Now* with the charged lyricism and emotional implosiveness of his groundbreaking music, *Godlike* is brilliant in form as well as dazzling in its heartwrenching tale of one whose values in life are the values of poetry. Set largely in the early '70s, but structured as a middle-aged poet's 1997 notebooks and drafts for a memoir-novel, the book recounts the story of a young man's affair with a remarkable teenage poet. *Godlike* is a novel of compelling originality and transcendent beauty.

WIDE EYED stories by Trinie Dalton
170 pages, a trade paperback original, $13.95

"With linked anecdotes substituting for plot, Dalton's 20 quick, vibrant, wild tales read more like fantastical diary entries than short stories . . . The latest in Dennis Cooper's Little House on the Bowery series, the work is ripe with sensuality and playfulness . . . Dalton's unique blend of dream and bracingly honest observation makes this a delightfully weird and disarming read."
—*Publishers Weekly* (Starred Review)